Also by Rob Ashman

The Mechanic Trilogy

Those That Remain (Book 1)

In Your Name (Book 2)

Pay The Penance (Book 3)

DI Roz Kray series

Faceless

Praise For Rob Ashman

"Five stars from me, would have been six if Amazon and Goodreads went up that high!!" **Donna Maguire - Donnas Book Blog**

"Faceless is fast paced, it's twisted and it packs one hell of a punch into every page!" **Sharon Bairden - Chapter In My Life**

"I'll definitely be reading more from this author in the future. Loved it." **Philomena Callan - Cheekypee Reads And Reviews**

"The story is very fast paced with lots happening and lots of twists and turns that kept me on the edge of my seat, sometimes quite literally!" **Joanna Park - Over The Rainbow Book Blog**

"Faceless is a fantastic, jaw-dropping journey as I was introduced to DI Roz Kray." **Yvonne Bastian - Me And My Books**

"It is jam packed with tension and OMG moments in fact there is nothing not to like and is the best book I have read this year so far...." **Shell Baker - Chelle's Book Reviews**

"This is a seriously addictive read. There were so many shocking twists and revelations..." **Lorna Cassidy - On The Shelf Reviews**

"Dark, nauseating, intense, destructive, yet incredibly written..." **Kaisha Holloway - The Writing Garnet**

"If you want a seriously twisted and deranged serial killer thriller, then look not further!" **Jessica Robins - Jessicamap Reviews**

"His writing is so slick that you cannot help but be drawn into this fascinating novel." **Kate Eveleigh - Portable Magic**

"...it's a read that will keep you guessing from page to page..." **Jo Turner - Life Of Crime**

"A brilliant start to a brand new upcoming series that is bound to blow us all away!" **Gemma Myers - Between The Pages Book Club**

"My jaw is on the floor, but I loved every single second of this fabulously sadistic read." **Katie Jones - Katie's Book Cave**

"Faceless is a gritty, compelling and thrilling serial killer thriller that kept me utterly engrossed..." **Eva Merckx - Novel Deelights**

"The story itself is exciting and addictive in the way a good thriller should be." **Susan Corcoran - Booksaremycwtches**

"A super unique and thrilling story line that had me feel uncomfortable even in a room full of people." **Susan Hampson - Books From Dusk Till Dawn**

"Faceless is a rollercoaster of a ride with twists and turns at every corner." **Caroline Vincent - Bits About Books**

"I love Ashman's books and recommend anyone that loves a good, bloody, and gory thriller to check them out." **Jessica Bronder - JBronder Book Reviews**

For Don, who told me about the trick with the lollypop stick. He was such a storyteller I have no idea if it's true. If not, he would be laughing to see it in print.

Preface

'As you watch your life drain away, I want you to remember one thing … I never wanted any of this.

'I was the man with a wife and kids, who lived in a house, went to work every morning and enjoyed the occasional holiday. But that was never enough. You made that clear.

'You lined up for your pound of flesh and, one by one, tore apart the building blocks of my life. You each took a piece, shredded the goodness from it, and handed it back. Then laughed in my face as I crumbled to dust.

'Life is all about change, and things are about to get worse. Much worse.

'You know who you are …

'You all know who you are …

'But what you don't know is …

'It's time to make the piggies squeal.'

Chapter 1

'Bloody hell, this is a s–' He dances at the end of my arm as I jab the metal pins into his stomach, sending his central nervous system into meltdown. His face resembles a landed carp, mouth gaping open as his muscles go into spasm. He topples back into the hallway landing face up on the parquet floor.

His body jolts and convulses at my feet. I step across the welcome mat and into the house, closing the door behind me. I unzip my bag, rummage around and bring out a handful of thick black cable ties. I roll him onto his front, securing his wrists tight behind his back and bind his feet together at the ankles. He continues to jerk and spasm as I straddle him. I reach forward and ram a tea-towel into his mouth, shoving it past his teeth with my thumb until his cheeks bulge. I tie it in place with a length of cord knotted behind his head. I step off him, pull a white coverall from the bag and slip it on, zipping the front right up to my neck. The hood covers my head and the drawstrings pull the material tight around my face. Next, I don a pair of overshoes and gloves.

The hallway is large, and straight ahead, through an archway, I can see the ornate staircase. It leads to the first floor, then splits left and right, a series of bedrooms run along the landing.

I take my bag, walk through the arch, up the stairs and circle back on myself until I'm stood directly above the foot of the stairs. I remove a chain block and a coil of thick rope and feed the rope through the balustrade. I tie it off and lower the chain block down to the first step.

I head downstairs, into the hallway where the man is twisting and turning on his front. I kneel beside him, and he cranes his neck to look at me, screaming through the gag. I take my new toy and hold it up for him to see. It crackles, and he goes berserk trying to roll over. I ram the pins into his back, and he once again does the million-volt dance.

I grab him by his feet and drag his twitching body through the arch and along the carpet, dumping him at the bottom of the stairs. I bind a heavy leather strap from my bag around his ankles and snap the carabiner in place. The links chink through the pulley block as I yank on the chain, raising him feet first into the air. The metallic sound resonates off the walls as I continue to raise him up; his hips come clear of the floor. His bodyweight takes over, and he swings, hitting his head on the bottom step. I hoist him over it and press the stop-lock. He sways back and forth, suspended upside down from the first-floor balustrade.

He is coming around, rotating slowly in mid-air. I take the knives from the bag and set to work. He jerks when he sees the blades; now, a different sound bounces off the walls —muffled screams and choking. I brush past him and climb three steps, grasping the hem of his trouser leg.

He freezes.

The point of the scalpel pierces the denim, and I slice downwards, severing the material until it gapes open to reveal his underwear. I do the same with the other leg. The material falls to his crotch, I reach for the hunting knife. The heavy blade makes short work of the waist band, and in two cuts, his jeans and boxer shorts hit the carpet.

I grab his shirt collar, cutting through the cotton at the back. This time, he bucks and spins, swinging wildly on the hoist. It makes no odds and the shirt is soon hanging in two pieces. I cut into the cuff, and in one slash the sleeve comes away. I do the same with the other. He yelps when the razor-sharp blade scores his skin.

I walk back down the stairs to replace the knives in the bag. He is staring at me bug eyed, suspended by his ankles, completely naked, apart from his socks. Well, a man has to have some dignity.

I make my way into the kitchen and root around in the cupboards for the biggest pots I can find. I fill them with water and load up the six-ring hob. The gas burners have a satisfying hiss as they crank up the heat. They're much better than the camping stove I was forced to use last time.

I leave the cooker and return to the bottom of the stairs. The man is making a right commotion, his cock and balls are flapping around as he jack-knifes his body, yelling at the top of his voice – as much as that is possible with a mouth crammed full of towelling.

He's going to hurt himself, if he's not careful.

I reach into the bag and pull out a three-inch square black box with a rotary dial on the top and wires dangling from terminals on two sides. I remove a plug from the wall socket and replace it with my own. The man stops making a fuss and watches me. The red LED on the box tells me we have lift-off and I sit cross-legged in front of him. His eyes are the size of snooker balls popping out of his face. I attach a sticky pad to his left temple and another to his right. He flails his head around but it's no use.

He screams and resumes his jack-knife acrobatics. I flick the toggle switch and the green LED comes on. My fingers ease the dial off the zero back-stop and the screaming intensifies.

The dial goes all the way up to ten. By the time I reach three, he will be much calmer.

Chapter 2

Acting DCI Roz Kray nosed her car into the driveway of sixteen Farnham Close and came to an abrupt halt. Two police cars and a crime scene investigation van were blocking her path. The doors to the van were open and a white boiler suited person was leaning into the back. Kray jumped from her car and flashed her warrant card at the sergeant holding a clipboard and pulled on a similar cover-all and over shoes. She drew the zip all the way up to the top, hoping it would help keep out the cold.

She hated October; it heralded the onset of dark nights and cold mornings at a time when the roads were teaming with tourists. The arrival of over one million lights spread across six miles of coastline was enough to ram Blackpool until it was bursting at the seams. A tradition that had come a long way from when it had consisted of eight carbon arc lamps and, when it was billed as the greatest show on earth, they convinced the world it was artificial sunshine.

She also hated it because the eighteenth day of the month marked the anniversary when Rampton stuck a knife into her husband's neck and took his life. Today's date was the seventeenth. October was shit month.

Standing in the doorway of the house was Mitch, her favourite coroner's office doctor. He was approaching fifty with a bald head and a straining waistline, he was old-school and well respected. His style was business-like and to the point, bordering on rude. But that was just the way Kray liked it. He always wore the facial expression of somebody who had just stepped in dog shit, but this morning, even from this distance, the look on his face said – *this is bad.*

Kray felt the gravel crunch beneath her feet as she walked up to the imposing double-fronted property. She ran the numbers in her head.

This sized house, in this type of neighbourhood, gotta be pushing a million pounds plus.

'Morning, Roz,' Mitch said in his usual I-got-a-sore-throat voice.

'Mitch,' Kray replied.

'I hear you got Acting DCI, congratulations.'

'Yeah, though I'm not sure congratulations is the word I would use.'

'Have you spoken to Jackson?'

'No.'

DCI Jackson had been her fuckwit of a boss before he signed himself onto the sick with stress, claiming the behaviour of ACC Mary Quade as the reason for his breakdown. In Kray's view, the two were made for each other – he was bloody useless, and she was a corporate sadist with epaulets. It was a match made in heaven.

'How have you been since you got back to work?' Mitch asked.

'Oh, you know, plodding on, putting things behind me. Anyway, since Jacko's wheels fell off I haven't had two minutes to myself, let alone time to dwell on things. And from the look on your face, you're not about to make that any easier.'

'I'm afraid not.'

He beckoned her over the threshold into a cavernous hallway with long tapestry curtains framing the windows and pictures on the wall.

'What have we got?' Kray asked taking in the opulence.

'Take a look.' Mitch waved his pudgy hand. Behind him, through the archway, she could see a naked body, suspended upside down by his ankles, hanging at the base of the stairs. She pulled on a pair of blue medical gloves. Mitch continued, 'His name is John Archibald Graham, fifty-four years of age, lived here for ten months or so.'

She stood under the arch. The ornate chandelier hanging from the ceiling above sprayed pockets of bright light across the walls giving the place a dance hall feel. The kitchen, lounge and office led off from the space like the spokes of a wheel. Ten feet in front of her, the grey carpet gave way to a dark brown colour. Stretching out along the floor was a patchwork of twelve-inch square, aluminium checker plates with corrugated tops. The stench of oxidising metal filled her senses. Kray made her way towards the body, stepping carefully on the plates.

She came to the break in the carpet where the colour changed. 'Is that …?'

'Blood, yes, it is. By the size of our vic, I would estimate about thirteen pints.'

'Any prints in the carpet?'

'Only the size fives of the housekeeping lady who found him at eight-thirty this morning when she turned up to do a little light dusting. She's sat in the front room on her fourth cup of tea, still in shock.'

'Not surprised. This is way above her pay grade to clear up.'

Roz reached the bottom of the stairs and stared at the dead man. His arms were secured behind his back with black cable ties and the edges of what looked like a tea towel were poking from the corners of his mouth. His eyes stared straight ahead, crazed red with ruptured blood vessels.

His face was the colour of uncooked pastry, but the rest of his body was red raw. Kray sniffed the air.

'Not only blood,' she called out to Mitch.

'No, I think there is urine soaked into the carpet as well.'

Kray flicked on a pencil torch and the piercing beam sliced into the translucent face. She moved the cone of light over his chest, stomach and genitals. Patches of skin were missing while in other areas, large blisters covered the flesh.

'What the hell is this?' Kray asked.

'Some sort of burning, not sure with what but it was hot enough to cause the skin to peel away.'

'Fuck,' Kray said under her breath as she trailed the cone of white light around the body.

'And this?' she asked shining the torch onto what looked like confetti on the stairs.

'I think it's his skin,' replied Mitch. 'There are two circular burn marks on each temple, and the jugular vein on the right-hand side has been severed.'

Kray shifted her position to see the single stab wound to the victim's neck and two circular blemishes stood out black against the colourless skin.

'By the look of the blood spatter against the balustrade, he was stabbed when he was still alive,' Kray said.

'Yes, it looks like arterial flow.'

'Do you have a cause of death?'

'Exsanguination. Whatever happened to him beforehand didn't kill him. He was alive when his jugular was severed. His heart was still beating and pumped his blood onto the floor.'

Kray looked around at the extent of the discoloured carpet. 'I reckon it took more than nine pints and a full bladder to make this mess.' She dabbed her index finger into pile and held it to her nose. 'What's the deal with him being stripped naked, apart from his socks?' Kray tipped her head towards the ceiling.

'Don't know. Until we get him down and conduct a thorough examination, there are a lot of unanswered questions.'

'The carpet on the stairs is wet but not from blood. Any ideas?'

'Not yet. We've taken a sample away for analysis.'

'Got a time of death?'

'Best estimate at this stage is between eight pm and midnight yesterday. The first officer on the scene reported there was no sign of a forced entry.'

'Does the maid have her own key, or does he leave one out for her?'

'Wow there, Acting DCI Kray, I think you'll find that's your job,' Mitch called over his shoulder as he walked out into the hallway.

'Thanks for that. This is going to take a bit to unravel.' Kray stood up and was about to retrace her steps when something caught her eye on the bannister. She clicked on her pen light and shone the beam onto the wooden handrail to her right. 'Did you see this?' She called after Mitch.

'See what?'

'Looks like blood on the bannister.' The torch beam illuminated the dark red smear.

'No, I missed that. Is it a hand or shoe print?'

'Now who's job are we talking about?' Kray stared at the blood. After what felt like an age, Mitch broke the silence. 'What is it?'

'Why would there be blood this high up?' Kray muttered under her breath.

'What? What did you say?'

'Oh, nothing, I was just talking to myself.'

Kray negotiated her way out along the checker plates, through the archway and stood on the front step breathing in fresh air. Her mobile was pressed against the side of her head.

'Hey, Duncan, can you get a team down to sixteen Farnham Close ASAP.' She paused allowing space for the usual questions. 'When you're here, you can see for yourself. It's not pretty.'

She hung up and marched back to the car to await reinforcements.

The scar on her right shoulder tingled.

What the hell is blood doing up there?

Chapter 3

There was so much blood. I knew John was a big man but come on! He bled out so much, I thought I might drown. When I pulled the knife out of his neck a torrent hit the woodwork, which, I have to admit, was a relief because I thought I'd over-done it.

I had sat on the floor in front of him, turned the dial onto setting No.1, and he went berserk. Bucking wildly at the end of the chain. I slipped the pointer onto setting No.2, and he jack-knifed at the waist, nearly catching me in the face with his head. I was forced to duck out the way as he twisted and turned like a fish on a line. It was a good job he lived in a detached house, because the tea towel stuffed into his mouth was doing a shit job.

I shifted the pointer to No.4, and his body went as stiff as a board. I watched as the whites of his bulging eyes burst into crazy paving, the tiny blood vessels rupturing with the pressure in his head. Then something unexpected happened. I glanced up to see an erect penis jutting out above me. It was pulsing up and down.

That's a bit rude.

After fifteen seconds, I rotated the dial to the off position and disconnected it from the wall. I returned to the kitchen to see if the gas rings had done their job. One by one, I carried the pots through and placed them on the stairs. His erection had thankfully shrivelled into a fleshy blob.

I squeezed through the gap between him and the banister to sit on the stairs. I pulled my knife from its sheath on my belt and plunged it into his neck.

He didn't flinch.

That's when I thought, *Fuck it, he's dead.* But I needn't have worried, when I yanked the blade free, his heart pumped a rhythmic stream of blood onto the stairs, the initial spurt hitting the balustrade.

My lovely reminiscence is shattered by the waitress banging my breakfast down onto the table along with a glass of tap water.

'Order number seventeen.' She smiles.

Seventeen other people have had breakfast here this morning?

I smile back.

Seventeen other people? But it's a shit hole.

I remove the small Tupperware container from my coat pocket, flip the lid and line them up on the table – the round one, the white one and the yellow capsule. To be taken once a day with food. I pick them up in turn and pop them into my mouth swilling them down with the water. A daily ritual which I am still not used to.

I peel back the top of the croissant and give it a squirt of tomato ketchup. A bacon and egg croissant – French and English breakfast cuisine collide in a holiday resort on the west coast of Britain, how very continental. I squash down the pastry top and take a bite. Despite its appearance, it actually tastes quite good.

I stare out the window across the Promenade and out to sea. I know there is an array of wind turbines off the coast but the murk and mist cloaks them from my view. It's October, and you don't come to Blackpool for the weather in October. The illuminations are in full swing and the town is bouncing. The hotels are crammed full of families and the trams are bursting with people going 'Ooo' and 'Ahrrr'. Children walk about with their necks permanently craned back looking to the sky, while the Pleasure Beech and piers are a buzzing hive of noisy activity at night. Well, when I say night, it gets dark at three pm.

I sip my second espresso of the day. I reckon I could drink ten of these and not get any higher than I feel right now. Though, there is one thing that is spoiling an otherwise perfect morning. The mouth of the road was cordoned off with yellow tape and guarded by a uniformed officer, sporting a pissed-off face and a high-viz jacket. I had fancied treating myself to a drive-by but it was not to be. The police were already on the scene and the street was in lockdown.

Hence winding up here, enjoying a mad fusion of continental cuisine for breakfast while gazing out of the window onto…well…fuck all, really. I check my watch. I need to get a move on.

I swallow the last of the bacon, drink the dregs from the cup and pay my bill. The young woman gives me the same smile as she had done earlier and wishes me a good day – if only she knew. I elbow open the door, stepping out into the cold wind. I don't mind it, I find it exhilarating, but then, I am on such a high, I would find catching my bollocks in a drawer an exhilarating experience, to be honest. My car is across the street, and in ten strides, I am sitting behind the wheel with the hot air blowers warming my legs. I pull away into the empty road and head off.

The town soon melts away into the countryside as I drive over the chaos of the M6 heading for Inglewhite. I've never been there, even though I have travelled this route many times, because a mile and a half before the village, I take a sharp left onto a narrow lane. Soon, the road becomes a single track which winds its way between the hedgerows and dry-stone walls. The route becomes narrower and narrower with overhanging foliage grabbing at my car from both sides. Sections of tarmac have lifted away making the wheels bounce and scrape against the hardcore below.

After half a mile, I edge through a set of five-bar gates onto a derelict farm. I have no idea what type of business this farmer was conducting, but all I can say is, he can't have been very good at it. The place has laid empty for years.

I park at the back of a large barn and snatch my bag from the footwell of the passenger seat. To the side of the building is the farmhouse, or more accurately, a collection of half walls and tumbled down roofs where the farmhouse used to be. I walk to the back of the barn to an underground storage facility that used to be house wood and coal.

I unzip the holdall and retrieve the white coverall suit, overshoes and gloves. I drop them into the old rusting brazier bolted against the wall and squirt a generous amount of lighter fluid on top. The match ignites on the third strike and the sweet smell of sulphur fills my senses.

There is a "whoofing" sound as the fluid-soaked material bursts into flames. I stare into the fire dancing in the bin and can see John's eyeballs bursting in their sockets, the electrical current frying his brain. The clothes burn bright against the gloom - his skin is peeling away while his lifeless body hangs limp and white.

Pretty soon, the flames subside. I poke at the smouldering embers with a stick to mix them with the burned remnants at the bottom. I check my watch.

I got a few more things to take care of and I don't want to be late.

Chapter 4

Kray bounded up the stairs to her office. For a woman who smoked enough cigarettes to kill three people and only ate enough to keep a six-year-old alive, she was surprisingly spritely.

Detective Duncan Tavener had taken over the reins at the house which had allowed her to get back to the station to make a dent in the avalanche of paperwork that had descended on her. She reached her desk and her shoulders dropped. Stuck to her phone was a post-it note. *'ACC Quade wants to see you as soon as you get in.'*

Kray tore the note off the phone screwed it up and tossed it into the waste paper bin. She looked at the neat piles of correspondence stacked on the round conference table. *How the hell did Jacko get through all of this and do his job? … Oh, but hang on, he didn't do his bloody job, did he?*

Kray did as she was told and sloped off to the third floor where the top brass lived, stopping first to arrange the pens in an orderly fashion at the right-hand side of her desk. She did the same with the pencils, on the left-hand side.

That's better.

The third floor smelled of wax furniture polish and air freshener. Kray nodded to the gaggle of PAs busying themselves booking meetings and lunch appointments and made a bee-line for the end office. She knocked on the open door and walked in. ACC Mary Quade was the only person on the ACPO floor who made her desk look small. She looked up and smiled as if Santa had just walked in.

'Roz, good to see you. Come in and take a seat.'

Kray gritted her teeth. She was so preoccupied with keeping her feelings in check, she missed the collection of pens and pencils sitting in the same pot.

'I got a message you wanted to see me, ma'am,' she said when her teeth had finally unclenched themselves.

'Yes, messy business, I hear, at Farnham Close.'

'It is. I have a team out at the house and we will know more when they do the post-mortem and get the forensics back.'

'Good work. I wanted to say…'

Kray zoned out, she knew what Quade wanted to say - it was the same bloody thing she always wanted to say. Kray spun her wedding ring round and round. It wasn't long ago that Quade had wanted to drum her out of the force, and now, since Kray had returned to work, she was behaving like a long-lost friend.

Kray zoned back in.

'…so, you see, I wanted you to know that you have my full support. You must think of me as your…' Quade was banging on.

Friend, trusted colleague, confidant? I don't fuckin' think so.

Kray had zoned out again.

When the full details surrounding the Jason Strickland case had emerged, Quade had gone into damage limitation mode. The officers from internal inquires and IPPC were all over them like a dose of the clap. Kray was on sick leave following the injuries she had sustained at the hands of Strickland, but she fully participated in their inquiry. After all she needed to know they were getting her side of the story.

Kray had found herself the main focus of attention for the initial part of the investigation, but then given her actions, that was hardly a surprise. Her vague recollections, coupled with her plea of self-defence, had carried the day.

It was not hard to convince them; after all, she had killed a man who had the faces of two dead women in his freezer, a dead man in his basement and kept a venomous snake in a fish tank.

Kray didn't need to pull off an Oscar-winning performance, the decision to believe her side of the story kind of made itself.

Quade had done a remarkable job of shifting the entire blame onto DCI Jackson. Despite the fact that she had been the one calling the shots, Jackson hadn't stood a chance. After all, it would not have gone down well for such a senior officer to be found guilty of professional incompetence. Especially one who ticked so many boxes on the diversity scale. No, carrying the can was Jackson's job, and Quade had made sure the investigation buried him. Hence, Jacko was now on the sick, no doubt talking to his Federation Rep on a daily basis, and Kray had been made up to Acting DCI.

To add to her woes, as head of CID, Kray now had the delights of DI Colin Brownlow to manage. He was knee-deep in a missing person's case and making heavy work of it. Kray knew sooner or later she would have to step in, but for now, let him get on with it. Under normal circumstances their relationship before could best be described as distant distain. Now Kray had the acting role it was open hostility, from Brownlow's side anyway. He thought he should have been given the job due to his seniority and length of service. The top brass felt "being good at your job" was a far better recruitment criterion and had given it to Kray.

Funny how things turn out.

Kray zoned back in.

'…so, if there is anything you need, Roz, you come to me. You are a credit to the force and a brilliant detective. I'm proud of you and so is the chief.'

That's funny, you weren't saying that when you fucking suspended me.

'Of course, ma'am,' Kray responded. 'It's good to know you have my back on this one.'

'Good. Anything you need, Roz, you know where I am.' Quade heaved her ample frame from her chair to signal the meeting was over.

Kray nodded and left the office.

Know where you are? You block out the sun, how the fuck could I miss you?

Back at her desk, Kray had signed off the overtime rota and authorised a batch of expenses. Her unread emails stood at three hundred and eighty and she had switched off the inbox alert because it was driving her nuts. She leaned back in her chair, stretching her arms towards the ceiling, her mind drifted back to the house with the body suspended in the stairway.

Buried beneath her expensive make-up, the one-and-a-half-inch ridge that ran along her left cheekbone began to tingle. The dark red line made by Rampton's Stanley knife was itching – telling her something wasn't right. The more she wandered through the house, the more it yelled at her.

She gathered up her keys, snatched her phone from the desk and pressed two buttons.

'Hello…hello, Duncan, are you there? Can you hear me?' There was a pause on the line and the sound of someone talking under water. Kray bustled out of her office and down the stairs. 'That's better, yes, I can. Have they taken down the body?' she said, hurrying from the building and across the car park. 'Good. Don't let them do it until I get there.'

She threw herself into her car and powered into the flow of traffic. The scars that criss-crossed her body weren't tingling, they were on fire.

Kray swung the car into number sixteen and hit the brakes, skidding to a stop in the empty driveway. She jumped from the car, pulled on her forensic gear and ran to the front door only to meet Tavener coming the other way.

Tavener was a high flier, exhaustively keen and highly competent. He had a face that wouldn't look out of place in any boy band, all clean lines and a ready smile, but he had the build of a second row forward. His soft Glaswegian accent completed the package. Kray didn't believe in having favourites, but if she ever changed her mind, she knew he'd top the list.

'I'm sorry, Roz. I went outside to take your call and when I got back–' He blurted out.

'What? What are you talking about?'

'The body, Roz. When I got back–'

Kray barged past him into the vaulted hallway. She looked through the archway to the bottom of the stairs. It was empty – no detectives, no crime scene investigators and no body.

'Fuck!' Kray said as she spun on her heels. 'I thought I made myself clear.'

'The signal in this house is shit. I had to go outside to take your call. When I got back in, they had already taken the victim down.'

'Bollocks!' Kray slapped her hands against her sides and turned away. For all his six feet three stature, Tavener looked like a naughty year-seven schoolboy. Kray regained her composure. 'Okay, okay, I'm sorry. I shouldn't have blown up like that.'

'By the time I got back, it was too late, Roz.'

Kray took a deep breath. 'You can help me walk through what happened.' They stepped across the aluminium plates to the bottom of the staircase. 'You go first. What do you think are the sequence of events?' Kray asked.

'Okay. The killer disables the victim strips him and hangs him upside down. Then, he tortures him by burning his skin and electrocuting him.' Tavener pointed to the disconnected power source for the telephone. 'I reckon the killer used that socket.'

'Good, carry on.'

'Then, when the killer has had enough, he or she slashes the victim's neck and lets them bleed to death.'

'If you were the killer, where would you be when you were electrocuting the victim?'

'I suppose I would be here.' Tavener positioned himself at the foot of the stairs.

'That's what I think, because if you are going to go to that much trouble, you would want to see the effects. What about the burning?'

'I don't know, same thing, I guess. The killer would be facing the victim.'

'What next?'

'I stick him in the neck, and he bleeds out.'

'The victim is stabbed on his right-hand side which means…' Kray left the sentence unfinished for Tavener to fill in the gap.

'The victim is inverted, so that would make the killer right-handed.'

'That's what I thought originally.'

'How do you mean?'

'Think this through. I sever the carotid artery and jugular vein of a fifteen-stone man who is hanging upside down. If I don't move fast I'm going to be ankle deep in blood in no time. But there are no shoe prints, other than the ones left by the cleaner.'

'He must have legged it.'

'But how do you explain the blood smear on the banister half way up the stairs?'

Tavener shook his head. 'The killer must have grabbed it. Maybe when he was on his way out?'

Kray moved around the stairs and reached her left hand into the air; it fell a good two and a half feet short of the blood. The cogs whirred in Tavener's head.

'But you are hardly normal–'

'Shut it.' Kray said not wanting to hear about her woeful lack of height. 'Even by the standards of a six-foot-three-inch Scotsman, you would have to raise your hand high in the air to make that mark. And who the hell runs away from a body, gushing thirteen pints of blood onto the floor, with their hands in the air?'

'Fucking most people, I would have thought,' he said. Kray fixed him with her best glare. 'I get what you're saying, Roz.'

Tavener looked at Kray with a "come on, then – tell me" look on his face.

'I think after the killer tortured the victim, he or she made their way up the stairs.' Kray shuffled past Tavener and sat on the fifth step. 'The killer was behind the victim when he slashed his neck. Which would make our killer left-handed.'

'He could have spun the vic around, slashed his neck and spun him back.'

'But the blood spatter does not support that. The killer stuck him with the knife and the blood hit woodwork.' Kray pointed to the dark red stain on the balustrade. 'Once the guy is dead, the killer climbs up onto the banister and drops down to the other side avoiding the pool of blood. But he fails to notice he has blood on his hand.'

'Why would the killer do that? It makes no sense.'

'You're right, it doesn't. It only makes sense if the killer was standing here for a reason.'

'Maybe he needed to go upstairs.' Tavener's phone beeped in his pocket. He pulled it out and shouted into the handset. 'Yes, wait…wait until I get outside.' He cupped the phone in his hands, 'I need to take this, Roz,' and skipped along the floor plates disappearing into the hallway.

The place fell silent. The house was still.

Kray closed her eyes.

The scar running diagonally across her body began to itch again. She grasped onto the handrail, and she could see the inverted body, hanging in front of her, large areas of skin peeling away from the flesh.

She reached out with her free hand to touch the figure suspended from the landing above.

The killer climbed the stairs to do something with the body.

The puckered red line that started to the left of her navel, traversed her stomach and bisected her right breast burned beneath her clothing. Every pinprick where the surgeon's needle sewed her skin back together was red hot.

You did something to the body – what did you do?

Kray's hand felt cold as it passed through the space where the victim's legs had been.

What did you do?

Kray could see the killer stood on the stairs. He had something in his hand.

What the hell is it?

'Sorry about that, Roz.' Tavener returned, breaking the moment. 'That was the guys back at the station. They have set up an incident room and are ready for the first briefing.'

Kray's knuckles were white beneath the blue latex glove. She steadied herself, gripping the banister.

'Roz, are you okay? The guys at the station are waiting.'

Kray opened her eyes and snapped back to reality. 'I'll be out in a minute.'

Tavener beetled off to start the car.

She closed her eyes once more – but it was gone.

Kray headed down the hallway to the waiting car. With every step she took, she uttered the word, 'Fuck.'

Chapter 5

It's Tuesday. I quite like Tuesdays.

I drive through the gates and pull into my usual spot next to the entrance. It's grey and cold outside, and the clock on the dashboard says ten-forty am. I like to arrive early. The wind cuts through my shirt and chills my skin as I step from the car. I'm working a split shift today, which is fine. Some of the guys hate working them because it screws your day up. But I don't mind.

I push through the side door into the clinically white corridor and head towards the changing room. The place resonates with the sound of cheap locker doors opening and closing, the usual dawn chorus that greets you at the start of shift.

I nod my good mornings while holding my wallet against the clocking on machine, the sensor recognises me and emits a beep. I strip off my jeans and shoes, pick my prized possession wrapped in tissue from my pocket and drop it into the container. I should feel elated but I have a headache, dulling my senses. The white work trousers and wellington boots feel warm as I pull them on. I slip my head through the neck of a red plastic apron and tie it tightly about my waist. The gloves are still where I left them, folded in the front pocket.

The rest of my personal belongings are placed into the locker and I close the door with a metallic clunk. I make my way down a second brightly-lit corridor, looking forward to the day.

I shove open a heavy white door and splosh my way through the sanitizing foot bath into the main hall. The cacophony of noise assaults my ears while the stink of meat and steam hits me in the back of the throat. The squeal of a band-saw tears through the air every thirty seconds like a metronome. I wander down

21

the cordoned off walkway to *High Care*, a bizarre name for such a place.

I pass through two more sets of doors and arrive at the rear of the building. I can hear a delivery as it backs up to the unloading bay. The heavy doors of the wagon bang open against their hinges.

I reach my workplace and enter a small room. It is eight feet square with stainless steel walls and a grey resin floor that slopes away to a drain in the corner. I twist the isolator switch a quarter turn clockwise and the red LED lamp bursts into life on the control panel. I run through the safety checks.

I can hear my first customers being driven from the lorry and corralled into pens. They know something is up. They can sense it's not going to be a good day.

The sound is getting louder and I open up the door at the back of the room to see ten of them advancing towards me. Hustling and bustling their way down the increasingly narrow walkway. A big one is leading the charge. There is a whoosh of compressed air and a metal gate closes behind them.

I allow them to settle, then usher the big one into my room and close the door. She spins around, expecting to see the others following in hot pursuit, rotating on the spot when she realises she is on her own.

I reach up and remove the tongs from the hooks on the wall. They resemble a massive barbeque tool with a heavy metal cable running from one of the handles. She is looking up at me, her eyes flash with confusion. I lean forward, tapping her on the shoulder, and she swivels around in the confined space facing away from me.

I clamp the tongs either side of her head, just behind her ears, push the button and hold on tight. She arches her back and goes rigid, with her front legs thrust out in front while her back legs collapse. I squeeze the electrodes into her flesh for three seconds. The electrical surge forces her brain into an epileptic seizure; 200 volts and 1.25 amps coursing through her grey matter does the job nicely. Sometimes, when their skin is dry, puffs of smoke and steam rise into the air as the metal contacts burn into them.

I release her from the tongs and she keels over against the wall. She is now in the tonic state, if I remember my training correctly. I replace the tongs and pull at her back legs to manoeuvre her into position, slipping the chain around her ankle and pressing the button.

The conveyor hoists her up and her free back leg kicks in circles. She is now in the clonic stage, and the clock is ticking – we only have a minute. She disappears through a shrouded gap in the wall.

I open the door to find the next one looking up at me. Her face says, 'Is my friend in there?' I step to one side and she trots into the room. I close the door and lift the tongs from the hook. She turns away from me.

I must admit, I quite like Tuesdays.

Chapter 6

The briefing went as planned. The room was filled with a mixture of uniform and CID. Quade had made good on her promise of providing enough resource to do the job. Kray stood at the front and systematically stepped through what they knew and discussed the best lines of inquiry.

Tavener dished out the tasking for the day and the room emptied faster than you could say, 'ACC Quade is on her way'. Background checks, social media, phone records, known associates, door to door, forensics, CCTV were all on the agenda. Kray sat in her office, trying to make a dent in her burgeoning admin.

The figure of ACC Quade loomed in the doorway. 'I missed the briefing,' she chorused not waiting to be invited in.

That's because you weren't invited.

'I know, ma'am. It would have been good for you to have the opportunity to talk to the guys. Maybe next time.'

'Yeah, next time. Are you happy with your team?'

'Yes, we have a lot of ground to cover, so we need all the help we can get.'

'As I said, Roz, if you need anything, my door is always open.'

I preferred it when you hated my guts.

'Thank you, ma'am, that's good to know.'

Quade closed the door and pulled up a chair. Kray sighed and her head dropped.

'I wanted you to know, Roz, I am not one to bear grudges,' she said, parking herself onto what now looked like a kiddie's chair. 'I mean, with what went on between us is in the past.'

That's very good of you to say so, but you weren't the one who was fucking suspended.

'Neither am I, ma'am. It was a stressful time for all of us.'

'It was, and of course, we must not lose sight of the fact that DCI Jackson was the SIO. So, unfortunately, the buck stops with him.'

You mean, you threw Jackson under the bus to save your own skin.

'We were all under considerable stress at the time, including DCI Jackson.'

'This case is the—'

Kray's phone buzzed on the desk.

'Excuse me, ma'am.' Kray picked it up quickly. 'Okay … yes … I'd better take a look … that's good work, I can be there in fifteen.' She put the phone in her pocket and stood up. 'That was Tavener. He wants me to take a look at something he's found at the house.'

'Never a dull moment.' Quade rocked herself forward and stood up. 'I do like our little chats.' She opened the door and waddled out.

I'd rather have my head fried in a wok.

'I will keep you updated, ma'am.'

Kray found Tavener sitting in the lounge of house number sixteen, flipping through his notebook.

'Hey, I thought you were knee deep in paperwork,' he said, looking up.

'I was until I got a visit from a certain ACC.'

'Good to see you and Mrs Blobby getting on so well.' Kray flashed him a look and Tavener held up his hands in a sign of surrender. 'I know, I should be more respectful.'

'You should be on a verbal warning.' Kray paused, enjoying the Blobby comparison. 'She was holding me hostage in my office when I got a call from my mum. I pretended it was you and ran for it. So, if she asks…'

'I won't drop you in it. How is your mum, by the way?'

'Bloody confused now.' Kray took a seat opposite him. 'Anything of interest?'

'It's too early. Everyone is out and about and I've just finished speaking to the neighbours. Turns out John Graham was a likeable chap. He was widowed about six months ago when his wife died suddenly of cancer shortly after they moved here. He sold his metal bashing business and went into semi-retirement. The neighbours didn't think he had a full-time job, more that he dipped in and out of work when he felt like it. No one had seen anything out of the ordinary and no significant other since his wife died.'

'Well, somebody didn't like him.'

Tavener bent forward and started undoing his shoe. 'Excuse me, Roz.' He fumbled with the laces and yanked the shoe off his foot.

'What are you doing?' she asked.

'I need new shoes. The in-sole keeps creasing in this one. It's doing my head in.'

Kray watched as Tavener forced his hand into his size elevens to straighten out the sole. She looked down to see he was wearing grey socks. She stared at his feet.

Her mind raced through the images of the man hanging upside-down only ten feet away from where they were sitting. She could see his burned flesh, his bloody eyes, his skin peeling from his body, she could see his socks…

'Fuck!' Kray jumped up from the sofa.

Twenty minutes later, Kray was heaving her shoulder against the heavy door to the mortuary. Tavener lent a helping hand over her shoulder and followed her in. She showed her warrant card to the woman sat at a corner desk wearing a white lab coat and trousers.

'I'm Acting DCI Kray, this is DC Tavener. You have the body of John Graham. He was brought in earlier today. I want to see him, please.'

The young woman clicked away with her mouse and consulted a spreadsheet. As Kray waited, the smell of formaldehyde mixed with a hint of rotting chicken filled her senses. She remembered it vividly from the last time. The memory made her shudder.

'Yes,' said the woman in the white scrubs, 'would you like to follow me?' She ushered them down a corridor. 'He has not been prepped yet, so he is in the same condition as when he arrived.'

'That's fine, thank you.'

She swiped a key card against a black box on the wall and the door clicked open. They put on protective gear and filed into a room. The place was cold and resonated with the dull hum of industrial refrigeration units. Fluorescent lights bathed the walls and floor in crystal white light. She tugged at one of the handles. The compartment slid open about a foot.

'This is him, I'll leave you to it.'

She left Kray and Tavener staring at the partly-exposed body.

Tavener moved forward and grabbed the handle. The large refrigerated drawer containing John Graham slid towards them. His face was porcelain white while his body was steaked with flashes of red where the skin had peeled away. There was torn flesh around his wrists where the cable ties had gouged deep into his flesh.

Kray donned a pair of blue gloves from her pocket.

'Will you tell me what this is all about?' Tavener was fed up of asking the same damned question.

'When I saw the victim's body at the house he was suspended by a leather strap buckled around each of his ankles.'

'Okay.'

'The strap went over one of the socks but not the other.'

'I don't get it.'

She reached down and lifted the victim's left foot clear of the bed, gripping the toe of the sock between her thumb and first finger of the other hand. She pulled, and the sock slid off his foot.

'What? What is it, Roz?' Tavener was losing patience with his boss. Kray shook her head.

She lifted the other foot and removed the sock in the same way.

Both of them stared at the foot.

'What the hell is that?' asked Tavener.

'I know what it is. The right question to ask is "why?"'

Chapter 7

I'm back down to earth with a bump. Despite my headache, the rush of endorphins I experienced this morning had me on a permanent high for most of the day. But as my shift came to an end, I could feel myself plummeting. By the time I got to the car to drive home, it had become a full-on crash.

I couldn't face going back to my three-room bedsit over the top of the Chinese takeaway to watch TV and eat food from a plastic tray. Instead, I drove into town and pulled into the Rowdy Rascal carpark. I could hear the music from the bar as I cracked open the door. The place was jumping with holiday makers and day trippers enjoying a cheap meal before hitting the town. I ordered a burger and coke – an absolute steal at £5.99, with a free refill on the coke. I no longer drink alcohol because it plays havoc with my medication.

I squeeze my way through the gaps between the chairs to find a corner table facing the TV. Sky Sports is showing a football game involving two foreign teams I have never heard of. I had hoped the noise would fill my head and stop my thoughts from racing. It was a great plan, but it doesn't work. I stare down into the bubbles bursting across the surface of my drink. Dark thoughts saturate my mind.

I never wanted any of this shit. I simply wanted to go to work, earn money and take care of my wife and kids – with the occasional holiday abroad, somewhere hot. That's all I ever wished for in life. But the bastards wouldn't let me do that. They tore down the building blocks of my life, one at a time, until I was left with nothing. Nothing to live in, nothing to live on and nothing to live for.

The fabric of my very being dissolved into mush over the space of eighteen months, and it was like watching it happen in slow motion to someone else. Piece by piece, my world fell apart, and no one cared. Not even the kids. My wife saw to that.

My name is Kevin for Christ sake, Kevin Palmer. When they talk about me in years to come, I'm sure they will say, 'Do you remember Kevin Palmer and what he did?' ... 'Kevin? You sure his name was Kevin?' will be the response. Nobody has ever been remembered in history with the name Kevin.

My decline started innocently enough.

'Do you mind if I ask your wife to dance?' he said.

'You'll have to ask her,' I joked in return.

I stare past the TV into the distance, reliving every second. It haunts me whenever my mind is in a dark place. It is like my mental screensaver. When the storm clouds gather and I spiral down into that black void that was my life, it kicks in – playing the scene over and over. My thoughts wander back to how it all started.

We were guests at a New Year's Eve dinner dance with the local Chamber of Commerce. A big customer of ours, Brixton Construction, was hosting one of the tables and we got an invite. I remember coming home and handing the envelope over to my wife Sadie and saying, 'I reckon that's going to cost me a new dress.'

She opened it up and squealed. 'That's fantastic! And I'll need new shoes to match. Who else is going?'

'I don't know,' I said, laughing. 'John has an invite as well and I've met the bloke who runs Brixton a couple of times, but other that, I don't know.'

We owned and ran a small fabrication and welding business out on an industrial estate not far from where we lived. The business was doing okay. It kept a roof over our heads and two cars on the drive, but nothing special. In the early days, I had a vision for growth, we could take on more staff and deliver larger jobs.

Our reputation was good – after all, we delivered gold-plated service for cast-iron money. No wonder people liked us. We employed ten tradesmen but kept losing them to the competition who paid higher wages.

However, the business had a fatal flaw and his name was John. He was my business partner and had a catastrophic lack of ambition. He was terrified we would overcommit ourselves and go bust. When the financial crash hit in 2007 he saw this as confirmation that his cautious approach had been right. I tried to tell him it was down to the fuckwits at the bank not being able to run a piss up in a brewery, but he wouldn't listen. In the end, I gave up arguing. So, we pottered along, playing the role of a third-tier supplier, picking up the smaller add-on contracts while the others lapped up the cream. Hence the excitement at being invited out to dinner.

The event held in a huge room decked out with a winter wonderland theme. Crystal white tables dusted with artificial snow and Santa's sleigh hanging from the ceiling sent my wife into a whirlwind of delight. The men wore black tie while the women came in their decorative finery. The collective clothing bill alone was probably double our company's turnover.

We were shown to our table where our host was pouring bubbles into tall champagne flutes. Three other couples had already arrived, we introduced ourselves and took our seats. My wife's eyes were as wide as saucers as she took in the electric ambience of the room.

She leaned over and squeezed my arm. 'See, this is why I keep going on about expanding the business. This is what I mean when I tell you to be more dynamic. This is amazing. We belong amongst people like this.'

I smiled back. The same smile I always gave when Sadie was giving me a hard time about *expanding the business* and *being dynamic*. Which she seemed to do more and more as time went on.

'Why can't we move house? Why can't we buy this? Sharon is off to Florida again, Sharon has enrolled her kids into private school' were fast becoming her favourite topics of conversation. A conversation I found difficult to join in.

We sipped our champagne and looked happy. Our host was a larger than life character with gelled back hair, broad shoulders and a twinkling smile. The woman on his arm looked like an agency girl, short on conversation but long on bedroom technique. She smiled at the others around the table, not bothering to engage in conversation, probably thinking she was doing more than enough to earn her cash.

I have to say my wife looked stunning. The dress hugged her trim figure and the corseted bodice gave her a deep cleavage, the like of which I'd not noticed before. As we chinked our glasses together I felt a very lucky man, indeed.

'More fizz!' Our host pulled another bottle from the ice bucket and held it in the air. My wife squeaked her excitement.

The food did not quite live up to expectation, probably a function of the mass catering, but that didn't bother Sadie. If they had served her up a Pot-Noodle, she would have been fine. The more she knocked back the drink, the more the bottles kept coming. The more they kept coming, the more she accepted the challenge.

Our host and Sadie hit it off immediately. His flamboyance and charm bedazzled her, while his credit card kept her interest on red alert – much to the annoyance of the hired help sitting next to him.

The conversation around the table was loud and raucous. I was having a good time but nowhere near as good as Sadie. She was the loudest of them all. If I had a pound every time she leaned into me and said, 'See, this is what I'm talking about', I could have bought my own winter wonderland.

After the meal, the dancing started. A live band was knocking out classic Christmas hits and Sadie dragged me up onto the dancefloor with an 'I luuurrrve this one!' The others around the table clapped. When Sadie passed by our host, they high fived each other.

By the time we got back to the table, the young, glamorous woman with the face like a slapped arse had vanished. Our host had an empty seat next to him.

'Is she okay?' Sadie blurted out across the table.

'Fucked if I know!' he answered. They both dissolved into gales of laughter. 'Want a top up?' He pulled another bottle from the bucket and staggered around the table.

Sadie held out her glass. He tipped the bottle and poured fizz over her hand. More gales of laughter ensued.

'I luuurrve this song,' she shrieked as the band played the intro to another festive classic.

Our host abandoned his attempts to dispense champagne and leaned across to me. 'Do you mind if I ask your wife to dance?'

'You'll have to ask her.'

'May I have the pleasure?' he said, holding his hand out to Sadie.

'You may, kind sir.'

He stepped back and she rose from her seat. As she glided by his arm slid around her waist on their way to the dance floor. She came back half an hour later.

The crowning glory for the evening was the count down at midnight. By this time, everyone was well oiled, including me. The compere went through his routine.

'Are you ready?' he yelled into the microphone. 'Three, two, one. Happy New Year!'

The first sound of Big Ben chimed out across the vast hall and a hail of party popper steamers exploded into the air. People gathered in circles, linking arms and sang, "Auld Lang Syne". My arm was wound around Sadie and we shuffled back and forth to the music singing our heads off, banging into those around us. Balloons and tickertape rained down from the ceiling, coating the revellers below. The last bars of the song rang out and I kissed my wife. I could taste the alcohol as she squashed her body against mine. It hadn't felt this good in a long time.

Someone slapped me on the shoulder and I spun around. John was there with his hand outstretched. We gave each other the mandatory man-hug, and I moved on to embrace Miriam, his wife. I could see Sadie with her hands resting on the shoulders of our host, he had one hand on her waist and the other on her hip. They went in for a peck on the cheek and missed, connecting instead with a full blow mouth to mouth kiss.

I never got invited to another Chamber of Commerce dinner dance. Sadie did though and the first crack in my life opened up.

'Your burger, sir.' The young woman with a wide smile and gaping top slid the plate across the table. 'Will you be wanting anything else?'

I shook my head. 'No, thank you, this is fine.'

It was then I realised I was starving and hadn't eaten anything since my croissant breakfast that morning. No wonder I was crashing like a bastard.

I stuffed my face into the burger. The soft meat, crisp salad and jalapeño chillies made my taste buds dance and it immediately made me feel better. My plans were working out fine, I was on track and eating a delicious burger, watching the footie. What the hell did I have to feel down about? My spirits lifted, and I reached across to the table next to me, grabbing a local newspaper. Across the top the banner headline read: *Local Businessman Found Dead at Home*.

I take another chunk out of my burger and swirl a chip around in the mayonnaise. See, there was no need to feel down. No need at all.

Chapter 8

Kray threw her keys onto the hall stand as the front door clattered shut behind her. She dumped her bag in the hallway, kicked her shoes into the corner and skidded her way up the laminate flooring to the lounge. She reached down, flicked on a lamp and headed straight for the fridge.

The cold white light illuminated her face as she stared into the empty void. A half-eaten bar of chocolate, an egg and two bottles of white wine stared back at her.

'I need to go shopping,' she muttered under her breath. 'The wine's getting low.'

Kray pulled a bottle from the top shelf with one hand and the chocolate with the other. She walked through the lounge, back into the hallway, glancing up to see the heavy dead bolt fitted to the door. Every muscle in her body was telling her to yank it across.

She had fitted it after she realised Strickland had broken into her house. Since the attack, waves of paranoia washed over her on a daily basis.

'He's fucking dead,' she told herself over and over, but it was no good. Try as she might, no matter how many times she repeated the phrase to herself, Kray was plagued by fear and mistrust. Her mind played tricks on her with noises and coincidences.

A cat knocking something over in the garden or a strange car parked in her road was all it took to have her reaching for the baseball bat. She had convinced herself that she was getting better, when the truth of the matter was, she was getting worse.

In work, things were so hectic she didn't have time to be scared but when she got home, that's when the demons in her head came out to play.

Kray looked at the bolt – it was like a daily test. A test to see if she could keep her rising panic in check or give in to her urge to bolt the door.

Who's in control here, me or my fear?

After what seemed like an age, she put the bottle and chocolate onto the floor, reached up and slammed the bolt across with a thud. She plodded up the stairs, promising herself that next time she would leave it unlocked.

Hot water cascaded into the bath making the foam rise. The room smelled of lavender and linen, or at least that's what it said on the bottle. She discarded her clothes onto the bed and padded through into the bathroom. Bottle in one hand, chocolate in the other.

'Bollocks,' she said, realising she had forgotten a glass. Then, she saw one sitting on the wooden plank that spanned across the bath. A forgotten item from when she last took a bath. Kray swilled it under the tap – it would be fine.

She caught sight of herself in the mirror. Her foundation had faded, and the lines in her face were harsh under the halogen lights, dark rings circled her eyes. The scar across her cheek was visible. She stared at her reflection, wincing at the dark red lines that crisscrossed her body and the inch-long stab marks peppering her shoulders.

Kray traced her fingers across the puckered skin; it felt alien to the touch, as though she was feeling the pain of someone else. She closed her eyes and could see the flashing blade as it arced through the air, slashing her skin. She could feel the searing agony of the blade ripping her open. She saw her husband, lying on his back with Rampton's knife sticking out of his throat. The blood-soaked stranger kneeling beside him, his balled-up T-shirt pressed hard into his neck trying to stem the flow.

Kray dropped the glass into the sink. It chinked against the porcelain. She gasped.

Her head dropped and she gathered herself together. The glass lay on its side still intact. She tore her gaze away, avoiding the mirror and set the glass down onto the wooden board. The bath was full and the foam stood above the waterline by ten inches. More than enough to hide her scars from view.

She slipped beneath the water and poured herself some wine, glugged at it and then topped the glass back up, desperate for the familiar numbing effect to come quickly.

'That fucking bolt,' she said to herself.

Chapter 9

It's Wednesday. I quite like Wednesdays.

I pull my car into the usual space and step out into the bracing wind. The sun is not yet up, and the sky is inky black with grey patches scudding across it. Pin pricks of rain sweep from nowhere to sting my face. I hurry to the side entrance and into the warm. Walking down the corridor to the changing rooms, I'm welcomed by the cacophony of locker doors slamming.

The clocking-in box emits a beep as I hold my wallet up to the sensor – five forty-five am. I like to be early.

I change out of my day clothes and into my work gear. The preparation hall is particularly noisy today and the band-saw screams as it encounters hard bone. The stench of hot steam and meat once more fills the air and sweat breaks out across my brow.

Is it me or is it hot in here today? Maybe it's the medication playing havoc with my body.

I wander through the foot bath, sloshing my wellingtons against the blue sanitised water and step out along the cordoned off walkway to High Care. After pacing through two more sets of doors, I'm at my work station. I nod a good morning to the supervisor, Vinny Burke, who grunts back. He is a miserable bastard and ironically thick as pig shit.

I open the door and enter the ten by twelve feet room. It is much the same as the other one but with a three feet wide stainless-steel grid that runs the length of the room, set into the floor. We practice job rotation which is supposed to promote workplace flexibility and prevent boredom. All I know is, I get to do different stuff. Which is good.

I check my apron is securely tied and pull the chain mail glove on my right hand. I can hear snorting and grunting coming from the room next door. They are bang on time today. Then all is quiet, except for the sound of scuffling hooves on a resin floor. The chain conveyor above my head starts up. Any second now, I will have my first customer of the day.

The thick rubber partition at the one end of the room parts open and she comes trundling in, hanging upside down from the conveyor by her back hoof. Her free leg kicking rhythmically in circles. I cannot afford to hang about; the clock is ticking.

I turn her around so she is facing away from me and steady her. I lean forward, taking a good look at my target. It is always good to get a clean one right off the bat. I plunge the knife into the pink flesh and feel the momentary resistance of her thick skin. Then, the blade sinks in and I push it forward and out.

The initial plume of blood arcs through the air and into the drain. I spin her around. The next gush of blood pumps out. She probably weighs in at around sixteen stone, heavier than me. I often wonder if my blood would pump down the drain as fast as hers.

The avalanche of claret continues until it begins to drain down and stop. By this time she is nearing the exit built into the opposite wall, being pulled along by the overhead chain. I help her on her way with a shove, and she disappears into the next room, just as the partition gives way, another customer comes to see me. Hanging upside down with her back-leg dancing.

I twist her around and pick my spot. A plume of blood gushes into the drain.

I must admit, I quite like Wednesdays.

Chapter 10

The morning had come around way too fast for Kray. She drove to work with the window wound down in an attempt to blow away the cobwebs. The combination of a bottle of Pino, ten squares of chocolate and a shit night's sleep had taken its toll.

She parked in the nearest available spot and bounded up the stairs, trying to shake the tiredness from her aching limbs and headed straight for the coffee machine. She reached her office with an Americano in each hand and downed them like they were shots. Gathering up her stuff, she rushed to the incident room.

Kray loved conducting morning prayers. It was the one opportunity in the day where she could get things straight, check on progress and demonstrate leadership. This morning though was different. This morning was not good, due to the incident room looking like it had just hosted a kid's birthday party.

Kray stood out front and surveyed the eager faces staring back. One face that was not eager was Tavener's. He had worked with Kray on the previous case and knew how she felt about running a tight ship, and that meant keeping the room in an orderly fashion.

Kray surveyed the debris. There was paper everywhere. The incident boards looked like they had thrown information at them, and the workstations were cluttered with files. Not to mention there were pens and pencils occupying the same side of the desk – her OCD levels were off the scale.

'We made a discovery yesterday, two in fact,' Kray announced to the room. 'But before I share them with you I am going to treat myself to another coffee.' Tavener sunk down into his seat, he knew what was coming having heard this speech before. Kray continued,

'I know you are all chomping at the bit to hear the news so we can catch the sadistic bastard that did this, but that will have to wait. Because the other discovery of the day is we will not be capable of catching a bloody cold working in a shit heap like this!'

Kray strutted about the room waving her arms. 'This is the way things get missed.' She pushed a mound of paper across the desk. 'This is how information gets lost.' She pointed to the post-its stuck to the wall. 'And this…' She stood in front of the incident boards. '…looks like the work of a five-year-old.' She marched back to the front picking up a handful of pens as she went and depositing them onto a desk that didn't have pencils.

'I am going to piss off and cool down while you make this place look like a professional incident room. Now, I know this is our first proper day on the case and we may as well get off on the right foot. My style is always to promote discussion and encourage challenge – ask Duncan, he will tell you.' Tavener flinched when she mentioned his name. 'So, in the spirit of starting as we mean to go on, does anyone have anything to fucking say?'

The room was so quiet you could hear one of the post-its falling off the wall and hitting the carpet. Kray scanned the room. Seven faces looked back at her with their mouths slightly open. She turned on her heels and walked out.

Tavener breathed a sigh of relief – it could have been a lot worse. All eyes were on him. 'Do as she says.'

The room was filled with the sound of chairs being scraped against the floor in a mad rush to get to work. Files and paper were relocated and desk surfaces cleared of rubbish. The bins filled up with unwanted material and the printers were kept busy, creating proper documents to replace the scribbled notes. Photographs were straightened and white boards cleaned of their previous content.

Every now and again, somebody would shout out, 'This okay?' The comment was aimed at Tavener, who would nod his approval. He didn't much relish his new-found position as head of QA – it meant anything out of sorts would be down to him.

As the last sheaf of unwanted paper went into the confidential waste bin, the door flew open and in walked Kray, positively buzzing from her double espresso and three bites of a cinnamon swirl. She had conceded when she was sitting in the canteen that the ferocity of her outburst could be down to her missing breakfast – again.

She stood at the front as the last of the team took their seats.

'That's better. I don't expect to have to do that again, understood?' The faces nodded. 'Let's make a start.' She walked over to the incident board. 'I do not intend to go over all the information most of which you already know. Suffice as to say, John Archibald Graham, fifty-four years of age, was found murdered at his house at eight-fifteen yesterday morning by the cleaner. His cause of death was exsanguination. It would appear from the initial findings from the post-mortem that being tortured did not kill him.

'He was electrocuted with electrodes placed on each temple.' She pointed to a high-resolution photograph showing the circular burn marks. 'And his jugular vein and carotid artery were severed on the right side of his neck.

'Now to the stuff you don't know.' She opened up a file. 'The carpet was covered in three things – the victim's blood, urine and water. It would appear that the killer dowsed the body in water. The flesh was then scrubbed with a tool that left ridges in the dermis.' She passed around four photographs taken from the file each one a close up of the shredded flesh. 'At this stage, we are not sure of the precise order in which these actions took place, we are awaiting further results to come out of the Forensics Lab which might shed further light on it. I'm expecting a call from them anytime now.'

'Now comes the weird part. The killer left a blood smear high up on the banister. It is unlikely he made that mark while standing on the floor. It's more likely that he was standing on the stairs at the time.

'The killer poured the water over the victim's body while stood in this position. We are safe to make this assumption because if he was standing in front of the victim, we would find shoe marks in the blood. Which, of course, we don't have. Secondly, the killer stood on the stairs so he could do this…'

Kray passed around another photograph showing the victim's right foot.

'We missed it when we were at the house because the vic was wearing socks. One sock was trapped underneath the leather strap binding his ankle, the other sock was over the top of the strap. The killer did this then climbed over the banister dropping down to the floor on the other side avoiding the blood. He must have had blood residue on his hand from when he severed the victim's neck and not noticed. When he climbed over the stairs, he left a trace.'

The photograph made its way around the room and was handed to Tavener. He stood up and pinned it to the incident board. It showed the victim's right foot resting on the mortuary slab. The second toe was missing.

Chapter 11

The smell of rotten meat almost made Kray gag. The odour was not strong, but it triggered a response deep in her psyche that catapulted her back to a time when she was stood over the feted corpse of a young woman. Her flesh dissolving into soup. Her body being devoured by fly larvae.

She stopped in her tracks, feeling that, at any moment, her morning coffee was about to make an appearance. Swallowing hard, Kray shook her head.

I was here yesterday, for fuck sake, and I was fine.

Kray bent forward at the waist as if to catch her breath.

'You okay?' The soft voice behind her caught her off guard.

'Oh, err, yes. Sorry, I had a twinge of indigestion,' she lied.

She tilted her head to gaze up at the voice. Then, drew herself up to the full extent of her impressive five feet four inches.

'I get that after eating curry,' said the tall man, wearing a fitted waistcoat and matching suit trousers. 'Doesn't stop me eating it though. Whenever I've drank enough beer and fall out of the pub, my body craves it. How does that happen?'

Kray stared up at him, he looked like he had just stepped off the set of a doctors and nurses TV soap opera. His blond hair was swept across his forehead while his eyes sparkled below the fringe. There was something familiar about him.

'I don't know, that never happens to me.'

'You don't eat curry?'

'No, I never know when I've drank enough beer.'

He laughed. 'No, seriously, are you okay?'

'Yes, I'm fine now, thank you.' The nausea had subsided. Kray walked away, embarrassed that she had made a show of herself in front of him. After six strides, her phone buzzed in her pocket.

'Hey, Duncan,' she answered and watched as a pert arse covered in fitted trousers walked past her. The man glanced back.

Shit! Did he catch me looking? What the hell is wrong with you, woman?

'Sorry, Duncan, can you start that again.' Kray was more than a little distracted.

'I said, Quade is looking for you. I wanted to give you a heads up.'

'Okay, thanks for that. I've had a missed call from her but she didn't leave a message.' The neat looking backside made its way down the corridor and disappeared around the corner.

'Maybe give her a call?' he said.

'I missed her call because I didn't answer the bloody thing. I'm busy right now.'

'I think she wants to see you when you get back.'

'Yeah, okay. Thanks for letting me know.' Kray hung up. It was good to have Tavener watching out for her.

Kray pushed her way through a set of double doors pulling a hairnet over her head as she went. She leaned her back against the wall to put on overshoes and overalls. The next door was labelled Mortuary. Inside was clean and fresh, the forced air-con making sure the occupants didn't go home at the end of the day smelling of preservative fluid and dead people. A man was hunched over a computer with his back to her.

'Excuse me I'm looking for Dr Christopher Millican.'

'That's me.' The man turned, sweeping his blond fringe across his forehead. His eyes twinkled. 'We meet again, and please call me Chris.' He came over with his hand out stretched.

Kray could feel her face burning pink. 'Hi, I'm Acting DCI Roz Kray. You must be the new Home Office pathologist.' She shook his hand. It was soft and warm.

'Interim, for now. They have yet to appoint a permanent replacement for Aldridge after he parted company in such a hurry.'

Parted company? Kray thought. *That's one way of putting it. Sacking the bastard for stealing Suprane to supply to a serial killer and murdering his drug dealer is the way I'd put it.*

'Yes, it was a rapid departure,' said Kray. She could feel her face returning to normal.

'Thanks for coming, I sent you an email because I've concluded my findings on the victim, John Graham.'

'What have you got?'

'Two things. The first is the removal of the toe.' He clicked the mouse and a blow-up photograph filled the screen. 'This is an image of the cut site. Can you see how the skin either side is bevelled over towards the bone?'

'And you think what?'

'The toe was removed using a hand tool with two jaws hinged at one end.'

'Like a pair of secateurs?'

'No, a pair of secateurs has one cutting blade and a blunt edge against which the cut is made. This had two cutting edges, each one bevelled.'

'Like…' Kray paused, trying to think of a hand tool to match the description.

'Like these.' Millican produced a set of wire cutters, the type used to cut through electrical cable. 'There are others on the market that do the same thing but this gives you some idea of what you're looking for.'

Kray opened and closed the jaws and watched the blades bite together.

'Also, if you see here,' Millican pointed at the screen, 'this part of the skin is puckered outwards which is consistent with the cutting edges slicing off the toe and forcing the skin to distort at the end.' Kray nodded her head. 'The wound site would suggest this was done when the blood had drained from the body.'

She nodded again. 'Any idea how the victim was incapacitated?'

'No, nothing. I tested for traces of drugs in the blood and they came back negative. There are no defensive wounds to suggest a struggle and no blow to the head.'

'What about a Taser or stun gun?'

'That's a possibility. Both of those usually leaves burn marks on the victim, but with so much skin damage, I couldn't find anything.'

'Okay, what else?'

'That leads me onto the second thing,' he said, straightening up from the screen. 'I think I've worked out the precise sequence of events.'

'Go on.'

'There were signs of capillary damage on both temples, which means that the victim was electrocuted first. There is also a carbon residue from the skin burning underneath the electrodes. Next, the killer severed the carotid artery and jugular vein and the victim quickly bled to death.'

'And the blood stains on the balustrade suggests he was definitely alive at this stage?'

'Correct. It was only after John Graham was drained of blood that the killer turned his attentions to the body. I believe the killer poured boiling water over the victim, which made the skin blister. Then, he used a scouring implement to scrub the body. This removed hair and large areas of skin.'

'What makes you think this wasn't done before he had his neck slashed?'

'Because the wounds are not bloodied. Take a look.' He flicked the mouse again and a different gory image hit the screen. 'See here, the top layer of skin has been lifted away, and you can see the striations in the lower dermis. But they are white, not red. This would indicate that there was no blood present. It was soaking into the carpet by this time.'

'So, let me get this straight. The killer continues to torture a man who is already dead?'

'Yup, that's what the evidence tells me. The water must have been very hot to cause this amount of damage.'

'How come?'

'A person can receive second and third degree burns if they come into contact with water at a temperature of around fifty to sixty degrees Celsius. But at that temperature the severity of the burn depends upon the length of time the skin is in contact with the water. In our case, the killer dowses the victim which would suggest the contact time with the skin is a matter of seconds before it runs off him onto the floor. Therefore, to do this…' Millican pointed at the screen, 'the water must have been pretty close to boiling.'

'So, after he scalded the body, he scrubbed it clean to remove further forensic evidence?'

'I'm not sure that's the reason,' he said.

'If a killer goes to that much trouble they normally use some type of bleach, wouldn't you say?'

'That is certainly a more effective way of destroying forensic evidence. Maybe that was not the killer's intention.'

Kray's gaze flitted between Millican and the image on the screen and back again. His smile was familiar. Kray smiled back. Suddenly, she was flushed with embarrassment and felt the need to say something – anything!

'Our killer tortures his victim first, kills him by draining his blood onto the floor, then pours boiling water over the body and scrubs it clean. But not from the point of view of destroying any forensic evidence,' Kray repeated herself for no apparent reason, forcing her gaze onto the screen.

What the hell am I doing? Get a grip.

'My guess is he's following a ritual, like the steps in a process, and that's where the internet comes into play.' Millican sat at the computer and types into the search bar. 'If you type in the sequence of injuries and scroll past the medical advice, you get this…'

He pushed his chair away from the terminal for Kray to get a better look. She moved in and read the search results. She took the mouse and clicked the fifth one down. Kray pulled away and stared at Millican.

'Pigs?'

Chapter 12

My work is done for the day. That's the benefit of being on early shift, I get to knock off at two o'clock. I'm in my car watching the house. She works from home most days, going into the office only when she has to. I can see her sitting in the bay window tapping away on her laptop. Her black thick-rimmed glasses swamp her face and this week her pixy-cut hair is the colour of sun flowers. I wonder what vitriolic lies she's writing this time.

Whenever I watch police dramas the stakeout is always portrayed as a time for dramatic revelations, a time to eat burgers and drink coffee while making notes and putting life into perspective. Times, people, locations, motives – they make it appear so exciting. The truth of the matter is, it is boring the bollocks off me. But I know it is an important part of what comes next. I need to be prepared and if that means sitting in my car, watching her type away in her bay window, so be it.

My hands feel cold and the tips of my fingers are numb. I wring my hands in my lap to get the circulation going, but it doesn't work. The problem is, when my mind isn't occupied, it becomes filled with the storm clouds of my past. My mind wanders into a dark corner. The screensaver kicks in.

It may have been a miss-timed peck on the cheek that resulted in Sadie kissing Mr Larger-Than-Life on the lips. But when she darted her tongue into his mouth, she tasted the high life and wanted more. More than I could give her, that's for sure.

I chose not to mention the kiss, putting it down to a belly full of fizz and a head full of excitement. How wrong I was. In the weeks that followed, she made it pretty obvious what she wanted, and it sure as hell wasn't me.

Their affair started slow, at first. She would go missing for a couple of hours while popping to the shops and nights out with her girlfriends became more frequent. I stayed in with the kids, but even when I protested by going down the pub, I would come home to find them at a neighbour's house while she was playing around.

She always had a plausible excuse, a good reason for her being out of the house. Then, one day, it was as though an 'I don't give a fuck' switch clicked inside her head, and her affair gained a momentum that was frightening.

I arrived home early from work one day to find his car parked up the road, and his cock parked up my wife. I confronted them. It wasn't difficult; they were both lying naked in bed. My fucking bed. They didn't flinch when I caught them.

'We heard you arrive,' she said when I burst into the room. They both tipped their heads back and laughed. He got out of bed to pull on his boxer shorts, his dick still swinging.

'I guess you two have things to discuss,' he said.

'I don't,' she said, smoothing her hand across the sheets where he had laid minutes before. He dressed and left.

'See you, Kevin,' he said on his way down the stairs.

'See you, Kevin,' she mimicked.

'I'll… I'll…' I ran over to the bed and raised my fist. She laughed.

'What, Kevin, what will you do? Is this you being more dynamic?'

I skulked away and kicked the bedroom door.

'Poor Kevin,' she said, singing the words at me. 'Gonna take it out on the nasty door, are we?'

Then, I remember saying the most stupid thing I've ever said in my life. 'Your mother wouldn't like it.' To which she replied, 'Yeah, well, my mother isn't getting it.'

The next day, I was out on my arse with my clothes and belongings piled into black bin bags. As I stood on in the front porch, I could hear her talking on the phone in the lounge.

'That's fine, babe. Looks like he's just leaving.'

I slammed the front door. The children were watching me from the window. I waved. Can you believe that, with everything going on? I waved at them. They waved back like I was off to London for the day. My humiliation was complete.

The fling with Mr Fuckbunny proved to be just that – a fling. It fizzled out after a few weeks when his head was turned by someone else's wife. I heard on the grapevine that it was over and saw my chance at a reconciliation. But the damage had been done. She no longer wanted to be married to a loser; she was only interested in winners. They proved to be a pair well suited, because no sooner was he up to his bollocks in someone new, she was bucking like a mule on the cock of a chap from the gym.

For the next couple of months I developed a rage so fierce, it ground me to a stand-still. I was unable to function, unable to carry out the most menial of tasks. I didn't feed myself, my clothes were dirty and I stank. I got myself a shitty cockroach ridden bedsit but preferred to spend my time walking the streets, scaring the people I met. I became the person you crossed the road to avoid. I was the man people pointed at and whispered. I was the one who was moved on by the police.

I was angry at everyone. Angry that all I ever wanted was to do was take care of my family, but that was not enough. I took that rage out on the rest of the world.

The alcohol served to dull the wrath. When I entered that fuzzy, blurry sliver of life between being conscious and passing out, the pain stopped. But the relief was short-lived, and when the effects wore off, and the beer ran out, the rage returned in all its ferocious glory. It was the only consistent thing in my life.

Then, I realised one morning, as I watched the sun come up while sat on a park bench, I am not at war with the world – just a tiny fraction of it. My predicament was not the fault of the bus driver that refuses me entry onto the bus, it was not the shop keeper who shoo'd me out of his doorway nor was it the woman dragging her kids to the other side of the street to avoid me. It was not their fault.

I remember the thought went off in my head like a grenade, and from that point onwards, I began to get myself back on track. I got myself a nicer bedsit that smelled of boiled cabbage but at least it had a communal washing machine. I put real food in my belly and clean clothes on my back.

My normal job was a distant memory. John, my business partner, had stopped trying to get hold of me and carried on delivering crappy little contracts as though nothing had happened.

I got another job, cash in hand. It kept me occupied and put money into my pocket. It gave me structure. With my life coming together I had time to give full vent to my darkest thoughts. Fantasies that enabled me to channel the rage onto those who most deserved it. Daydreams and fantasies that gave my anger an outlet and kept it in check. It was a coping strategy that worked.

I was on the way up, then one day, I cracked.

One Sunday afternoon, I was sitting in the café of the Village Hotel. It was a big day. I was waiting to see my children for the first time in over ten weeks. I was taking them to the zoo.

Then, that fucking woman, Vanessa Wilding, walked in minus the kids. She was a solicitor who my wife had employed to broker an agreement between us on visiting rights with the children. I was desperate to see them and would have agreed to anything at the time. Sadie had made it clear she did not want me near them. Ms Wilding convinced me that an arbitrated arrangement was the way forward and that going through the courts would get messy.

'Going through the courts? Who said anything about going through the courts?' I remember blurting out.

'Your wife did, Mr Palmer,' was her flat response.

In the face of that option I thought the introduction of a third party would ease the situation. How wrong I was.

Vanessa Wilding was an unremarkable thirty-year-old woman, with unremarkable hair and an unremarkable face who wore unremarkable clothes. She was, however, remarkable in one particular respect – she hated my guts with a passion that I could taste in the air whenever we met. She was a sadistic bitch who enjoyed nothing more than delivering bad news. Time and time again she had rowed back on previous points of agreement, choosing instead to take my wife's position over mine. It was fast becoming apparent that this woman was merely an extension of my wife's grand plan to obliterate me from their lives all together.

She slid into the booth next to me, placing one hand on top of the other on the table.

'I'm sorry to have to inform you, Mr Palmer, that I've spoken to your wife and she still feels uneasy about you seeing the children today. You've made great strides but she feels it is still too early.'

I had been granted supervised visitation rights by some kind of kangaroo court. The prospect of time with my children was the powering force behind me getting my shit together. This woman's role in life seemed to be to deny me that right.

'But we agreed that I could take them to the Zoo. We agreed that you could come along. We agreed–'

'I have to take a balanced view, Mr Palmer. I have to take the feelings of both parties into consideration and your wife has grave concerns that you're not ready. The children aren't ready.'

'But we agreed…' I said, staring down into my coffee struggling to keep the emotions in check. 'We sat in a room, all of us together, and we agreed.'

'We did, Mr Palmer, but as I said, I have to take into consideration your wife's concerns.'

'My wife's concerns – what about my concerns?'

'What concerns are they?'

'That denying me access to my children will have a detrimental impact on my recovery. I'm doing this for them.' The mug rattled on the table top as my hands began to tremble.

'I appreciate this is a disappointment for you. We can set up another meeting, maybe for two weeks' time.'

'Two weeks!' I spat the words into my drink. 'Two weeks? I'm ready now. We had an agreement and you are reneging on that.'

'Mr Palmer, I know this is hard, but I have to make my decisions based upon both parties, and your wife has made it clear–'

'So, now, you're making the decisions? We *all* agreed a way forward. But now it counts for nothing because you alone are making the decisions? Look, I bought the fucking tickets – I even bought you one!' I fumbled around in my wallet and removed a ticket, tossing it at her.

'Calm down, Mr Palmer. You are not helping yourself.'

'Not helping myself? No, you are the one who is not helping. By choosing to unilaterally go against the agreement we reached, because you, and you alone, now want to make the decisions. That's the part that's not fucking helping.' The mug rattled loudly against the table.

'My role is to take a course of action that is in the best interests of both parties, Mr Palmer. I have to make day to day decisions as I see fit. And your wife–'

'Is a manipulative bitch.' I slid the mug of coffee across the table into her lap. She yelled as the hot liquid burned her crotch and thighs.

Two hours later, I was sat in the custody suite of the local cop-shop, crying like a baby. Earlier, I had been interviewed by a stern looking woman and a tall copper with glasses.

'Fucking assault!' I shouted. The words bounced off the walls of the small room. 'It was an accident, I tell you. I was annoyed – yes. Angry, even…but I did not pour coffee over that woman on purpose.' I was lying through my back teeth and they knew it.

I did a great job of convincing them I was falling apart at the seams, mainly because I was. I pleaded with them that it had been an accident, I had bought her a ticket to join us at the zoo. Were those the actions of a person who wanted to do her harm?

After what seemed like a lifetime the tall guy said, 'Ms Wilding does not want to take the matter further. You will receive a caution. Consider yourself a very lucky man, Mr Palmer. I think we both know what happened in that café, you lost control and let your anger get the better of you. In doing so, you assaulted her. Follow me to the office and we will conclude our discussion in there.'

I remember waiting for a taxi to pick me up and sobbing into my hands. I had really fucked up this time. God only knew when I would see the kids again.

My train of thought is broken by a man driving past, sounding his horn. I snap my head back to the matter in hand. The woman in the thick rimmed glasses and sun-flower hair is no longer in the window.

Shit, where did she go?

The front door opens and the yellow head bobs down the front steps to her waiting car. She's carrying a shopping bag.

Shit!

I was not expecting this, she does her shopping on Saturday. My plan is clear and it says Saturday. I feel a mix of panic and elation rise in my chest.

Today could be the day. I need to get home fast.

Chapter 13

'Pigs?' Tavener's voice boomed through the speakers.

'Yes, that's what I said. Apparently, our killer goes through the same process they use to kill pigs in abattoirs. First, they stun the animal, then they cut its throat so it bleeds out and finish it off by scaling in a huge bath and scrubbing the skin clean,' Kray replied.

'That's some ritual.'

'I checked it out and it's correct.'

'We need to look for someone who works in an abattoir or who has connections with one.'

'Or maybe a psychopath who simply enjoys the way it plays out.' Kray twisted the end of the indicator stick and the windscreen wipers swept away the water. A hedge butted up against the front of her car, the leaves and shoots sprouting from the top danced in the wind.

'Quade is still looking for you.'

'Yeah, well, she's gonna have to wait. I got something to take care of first.'

There was a pause on the end of the line.

'You okay today?' asked Tavener.

'Yes, of course. Just got a lot on, that's all.'

'I know but that's not what I'm asking. Are you okay *today?*'

Kray didn't answer. She stared out the front of the car across the neatly manicured lawns with park benches dotted around. Despite the bite of autumn, patches of vibrant colour burst through the mist and rain. It looked beautiful – she hated the place.

'Yes, I'm okay, thank you for asking.' The professional edge had gone from her voice, leaving behind it a trail of raw emotion. 'I'll be back in the office when I'm done.'

'See you then.' Tavener hung up and the car was quiet.

Kray's knuckles were white as she gripped onto the wheel. *Why the hell did he have to ask? Why did he have to ask about today?* Kray had been avoiding this but could put it off no longer.

She unclenched her fists and reached to the back seat to remove a plastic bag. She opened the door and immediately wished she hadn't. Rain smacked her in the face as she struggled to get her umbrella to do what it was supposed to do.

'Fucking, fuck–' She wrestled with the mechanism while carrying the bag. The black canopy eventually opened up and she ducked beneath it. Water droplets hammered off the taut material filling the space below with a percussive noise. She trudged up the verge, watching the wet grass soak into the hem of her trousers.

She passed along a new row which hadn't been there the last time she'd visited. The sad truth was – more people died in the winter months. At the rate at which this row had filled up this was going to be a particularly bad year.

Kray stopped in front of the black marble stone set on a plinth. She kneeled down and cleared away the dead flowers from the vase, tipping the old water onto the ground. Something caught her eye, glinting in the dirt. She picked it up and held it in front of her squinting eyes. It was a brass pin. Not any old pin, this was the brass pin that she clawed from the lapel of a dying man to free her hands from the cable ties. The brass pin that saved her life. The brass pin that Joe had sent her.

On her last visit, she had left it glinting in the sunlight on top of the headstone. The wind must have blown it off. She cleaned away the soil and placed the pin at the base of the stone.

'Pigs! Would you believe that?' she said, pulling the bouquet of flowers from the bag. 'Fucking pigs!' Her hands fiddled with the cellophane wrapping, struggling to get it loose. Trying to remain under the umbrella. Her hands were shaking.

'Come on!' She snarled under her breath as the transparent material tore apart. She balled it up and pushed it into the carrier bag. Kray arranged the flowers in the urn and opened up the bottle of water, filling up the vase. She smiled as the rain cascaded off her brolly onto the new blooms. *What am I doing?*

'So anyway, how have you been?' It was an absurd question but one she could never seem to stop herself from asking. 'I got back to work and they made me up to Acting DCI. What about that, eh? Quade is doing my fucking head in. After everything that happened, she's now behaving like we're best mates. That woman is weird.'

She busied herself running a tissue over the cold stone, removing the grime. 'I didn't want to come today but then I thought you'd only miss me. So, I thought I ...' Kray couldn't finish the sentence. She rocked forward, grasping onto the stone with both hands. The brolly tumbled from her hand and fell back over her shoulder. Tears streamed down her face and her shoulders shook.

One year ago, on this very day, she had been happy. She was pissed off with her husband but then, what's new? They'd had an argument while driving along the promenade and she had bolted from the car. Joe had shouted at her to get back in, but she was having none of it. Kray had run through the flock of tourists to avoid having *the* conversation. The same conversation they had every time her poor eating spiralled out of control. The same conversation where she knew all along, he was right. She needed to get a grip of her food, or she was going to be ill again. But she didn't want to hear it, didn't want to face it.

Rampton had come out of nowhere, slashing her with a Stanley knife. The first blow sliced her open from her belly across her chest to her shoulder. Then another and another. The short triangular blade punctured her back and shoulders as he slammed it into her flesh.

Then, her attacker was in mid-air, being propelled backwards by Joe. The two men landed with a splat, with Joe on top. Rampton slithered from beneath him, covered in blood. The Stanley knife was embedded in Joe's neck and it all went black.

Kray shuddered and gripped onto the headstone. She could see Joe lying on the ground, she could hear the wail of sirens, she could feel the warmth of her own blood seeping from beneath her as she lay on the pavement. There was a woman running, pushing a toddler in a pushchair. Kray could see the child. The little boy was screaming as his mother shoved him along the promenade away from the crazy man. The boy wasn't wearing socks.

Kray stopped crying. The rain matted her hair to her head and dripped from her lashes.

The image of Joe was gone, the image of the child was gone. Both of them replaced by the man with the translucent face hanging upside down at the bottom of the staircase. His eyes shot through with a crazy paving of ruptured blood vessels. Flaps of skin hung down, his body shredded. Kray's scars burned and tingled. The puckered line across her cheek was red hot. She could see the victim's feet and the gap on the right foot where the toe should be.

Kray flashed her eyes open. The image was gone.

'We've missed one. There's another body.'

Chapter 14

'Roz, slow down.' Tavener was struggling to keep up. 'We've missed one. There is another body out there somewhere.'

'You're not making sense. Roz, you're breaking up.'

Kray put her foot down and the engine revved more than was good for it. Tavener's voice once more reverberated against the inside of her car.

'Can you hear me, Duncan? Get hold of Brownlow. We need to speak with him urgently.'

'Roz what is this about? What body? Where?'

'I will explain everything at the station. Get hold of Brownlow and nail his feet to the floor in my office. He needs to tell us about–' The line went dead. No signal.

'Shit!' Kray glared at her phone.

Fifteen minutes later she pulled into the station car park. Ninety seconds after banging the door shut, she burst into her office to find ACC Quade waiting for her.

'Ah, there you are, Roz, I heard you were on our way back. I've been trying to get hold of you.'

'Yes, ma'am, sorry about that. My network coverage has been crap today. Duncan said you needed to speak with me.' Kray was panting to get her breath back. She looked like she had taken a shower in her clothes.

'Yes, I want to sound you out about something.'

'Can it wait, ma'am? I need to talk to DI Brownlow.'

'Yes, he was in your office when I stuck my head around the door. Him and another chap. They told me you were en-route, so I sent them away.'

You fucking did what?

'Ma'am, it's important that I speak with them.'

'And it's important that you speak with me. The press is hounding us for a comment on the Graham murder case. I want to be sure we have all our ducks in a row. We don't want a repeat of Jackson's performance.'

'No, ma'am, we don't want that.'

'So, I want you to draft a statement today which I can brief to the press.'

'I can do that, but it is imperative that I speak to Brownlow.'

'Have it on my desk by close of play.'

'Yes, ma'am.'

Quade lurched out of the chair and waddled off. Kray pushed buttons on her phone. After two rings, Tavener answered.

'In my office now!'

Kray paced around, annoyed that Quade had side-swiped her with her press statement demand when she had far more pressing things to do.

After several minutes, Tavener and Brownlow beetled into the office and took their seats.

'Shut the door,' Kray said, sitting on the edge of her desk. Tavener stared at Kray with her hair stuck flat to her head, sodden trousers and hands like she'd been digging in the garden.

'You need to invest in an umbrella,' he said.

'Never mind that. Colin, tell me about the missing person.'

Brownlow looked shocked that someone was taking an interest in his case. 'Well, err, there's not much to tell. Nigel Chapman was reported missing when he failed to show up for work. We've been to his house and he's not there. The neighbours haven't seen him either.'

'When, Colin? When was he reported missing?' asked Kray.

'The last known sighting of him was a little over a week ago. Since then he's not used his mobile phone or his credit cards. His car has also gone AWOL– a blue F Type Jag.'

'Has he done anything like this before?' asked Tavener.

'No, he hasn't. By all accounts, he's a bit of a party animal, so I suppose he could be on a bender, but if he is then it's strictly cash only.'

'Do you have any leads?' Kray knew the answer to her question before she asked it.

'No,' said Brownlow.

'Roz, what is this about?' asked Tavener.

Kray collected herself, not sure this was a good idea. It had sounded dead plausible when she rehearsed it in the car, but now it had lost its logic. She started slow. 'Our victim, John Graham, had the second toe on his right foot removed by the killer.'

'I know,' said Tavener, eager for the punchline.

'He was murdered using the same techniques they use to kill pigs in an abattoir.'

'I know that too.'

'I think there is another body out there. A body that we have yet to find.'

'You've lost me,' said Brownlow. 'Run that past me again.'

'This little piggy went to market, this little piggy stayed at home, this little piggy had roast beef ... you know the nursery rhyme? When you play it with a child, you tweak each toe in turn. First the big toe, then the next and so on.' Both men were silent. 'Graham was missing his second toe. I reckon there's another body out there, killed in the same way, but this time, with the big toe missing.'

Brownlow burst out laughing. 'You've lost it, Roz. Is that why you dragged me in here? to tell me a serial killer is out there singing nursery rhymes? You've lost the plot this time.'

Tavener was watching his boss.

'I know it sounds a little off, but—' Kray said regretting she had not listened to her instincts and shut up.

'A little off? Bat-shit crazy is what I call it.' Brownlow stood up to leave. 'I would be careful who you tell that story to, Roz, or you might find yourself back in therapy.'

Kray steeled every muscle in her body to prevent her from punching him in the face.

I bring the car to a juddering halt; my heart is thumping out of my chest. I jump out and jog the two hundred yards to my flat, trying to calm down.

I live above Mr Woo's Chinese Takeaway on Regal Crescent. I don't know how the street got its name, because it is as straight as a Roman road, and there's fuck all regal about it.

My landlord assures me that his real name is Joseph Woo, and he is not stereotyping himself. He is a second-generation, British-born Chinese whose parents came over from Hong Kong in the early eighties to make Blackpool their home.

Joseph worked out that he could earn more money selling egg fried rice to drunk people than he could counting beans as an accountant. So, he quit his job and applied his considerable business acumen to his parents' shop. Within two years, they had moved to larger premises with more passing trade. Sure, it was an issue that most of their passing trade were unable to walk in a straight line, but it was two streets away from the Promenade and the takings went through the roof. After eight months, they had applied for a late opening licence, the bunting outside the premises read: *Mr Woo Now Open 'til Two!* when they were granted the extension.

I knew exactly what I was looking for and when Joseph first showed me the upstairs bedsit, I snapped his hand off. I have three rooms – a lounge with a kitchenette in the corner, a bedroom and a bathroom. I must admit, I had pangs of guilt when I broke the bathroom window. I had not been in the flat long and persuaded Joseph to replace it with a single pane of double-glazing, instead of a window which I could open and close. I told him I was paranoid about being burgled while I was asleep and he was sympathetic to my fears. It means that the place can get a little steamy after I've showered, but that is a small price to pay.

The whole place smells of Chinese cooking and I eat it most days. I like the food, but after a few months, you crave something plain – though I persevere.

I have an excellent relationship with the Woos. There are eight family members in total and they all, in one way or another, work in the shop. I make a point of spending time with them whenever I come home or leave the property. I also chat to their regulars, the punters who either can't cook or don't own a cooker. They are a talkative bunch.

There is one aspect of my bedsit which would switch most people off. There is only one way in and one way out and that takes me through the front of the takeaway. I have a key to the front door and a second key to my flat. Joseph was at pains to tell me that they had plans to knock through and build a separate entrance for the flat which would have its own access off the street. I nod my approval whenever he raises the subject and I persuade him to wait and do it at another time.

I love talking to the regular customers as they wait in the queue for their food. I love chatting to the Woo clan as I head off out to work. I love the social interaction the single access door gives me. One way in, one way out, and a ton of people to talk to – perfect.

I push open the door to the takeaway. Three familiar faces are sitting against the wall waiting for their food.

'Alright there, Kev,' says the man who is always dressed in a duffle coat no matter what the time of the year.

'Hey, how are you?' I ask.

'Hungry but a quick Woo-woo will sort me out.'

I could never understand why he refers to his takeout as a Woo-woo, but he does it every time. The other two raise their hands to say 'Hi'.

'You're home early, Kev,' Joseph says, piling chips onto a plastic tray, wrapping it in paper and placing it into a plastic carrier bag.

'Yes, I was on earlies and I'm knackered.' I try to look exhausted, when in reality, I am fizzing with adrenaline.

'Hi, Kev.' Anabel, Joseph's English wife, appears from the back, her arms piled high with plastic containers. 'You okay?'

'Yes, I'm fine thanks, just tired that's all. I reckon I'm off to bed, get some well-earned sleep.'

'We'll keep the noise down,' Joseph laughs. 'Not!'

'See you later tonight. I'll cook you up something special,' she quipped.

'Number fifty-five?' Joseph calls out and the man in the duffle coat shuffles over to the counter. 'See you later, Kev.'

I ease my way past the counter and head upstairs. I need to make this opportunity count. The police are going to join the dots up sooner or later.

Chapter 15

'Do I make myself clear?' Quade was not a happy ACC. 'I will not tolerate you two having a stand-up argument in an open office when all around are listening in.'

'Technically, ma'am, it was in my office–' Kray said.

'I don't want to hear it. If either of you have a problem managing the reporting lines I suggest you get it sorted out. Because if you don't sort it – I will. And I promise, if I have to get involved again, neither of you will be happy.'

Brownlow stared at his interlocked fingers resting on the desk, saying nothing. He was kicking himself that he had allowed his mouth to run away with him at the very moment that ACC Quade was doing her rounds looking for an update. Having a go at Kray was one thing, getting caught doing it was another.

'Do I need to help you two resolve this?' Quade pushed her point.

'No, ma'am,' they said together.

'Good. Now, go do what you're paid to do.'

Kray and Brownlow skulked out of Quade's office in silence. 'And don't forget I need that press statement on my desk by close of play,' she called after Kray.

'Not forgotten, ma'am,' Kray replied, having forgotten all about it.

They walked out of the ACPO suite without exchanging a word and headed back down the stairs.

'How are we going to do this?' Kray asked.

'Do what?' Brownlow replied as they reached the landing where the CID offices were located. Kray stopped.

'I think there is a link between my investigation and yours,' Kray said, watching Brownlow as he continued to walk down the stairs. 'Colin, where are you going? We need to collaborate on this.'

'No, Roz, I'm not sure we do. If you want to waste your time chasing nursery rhymes, then that's up to you. I have a set of interviews to conduct about a missing person.'

'Do I have to remind you that I am acting head of CID?'

'No, Roz, you don't. But I'm really not that worried, because when you tell Quade the reason why you are diverting valuable resources to interfere with my investigation, you won't be *acting* anything for long.' He disappeared around the corner.

'Brownlow!' Kray called after him. 'Brownlow!' All she heard was the echo of his footsteps shuffling further away.

Kray slammed the heal of her hand into the door and it bounced open into the corridor. She stomped to her office, reached for the phone and punched two keys. *I'll have his head on a fucking spike.*

'I want to see the missing person file for Nigel Chapman please, its urgent. Can you drop it by my office? Thank you.' She hung up and gently seethed.

Kray didn't have to wait long for a rosy-faced man stuck his head around the door, 'you wanted these Roz.' He handed her a buff coloured file with papers protruding from it.

She weighed it in her hand. 'Thank you, I'll let you know when I'm done with them.' The man hovered in the doorway. Kray looked at the thin collection of papers. 'Is this it?' she asked.

'No, ma'am. DI Brownlow has more stuff on his desk. These are the most relevant documents.'

She nodded. 'Okay, thank you.' He turned on his heels and shot off. Kray got up from her desk and made her way down the corridor, pushing open the third door on the left. Brownlow shared his office with four others. The place was empty. Three of the desks were in reasonable order, one was covered with so much paperwork it constituted a fire hazard. It was Brownlow's.

'Give me strength,' she muttered under her breath, sitting at his desk sifting through the mountains of documents and reports. Her OCD was going berserk. 'Where the hell do I start?'

Kray flipped open the file and started reading the summary of background checks for the missing man. Nigel Chapman ran a successful business and lived in a swanky house to the north of town. He was single and enjoyed the high life, owning a property in Marbella and a number of vintage sports cars. He didn't have a steady girlfriend but that did not mean he went short of female company. The names of five women were listed as being "connected" to him in the last six months alone. Kray had no doubt in her mind what sort of *connection* that might have been.

Chapman had been reported missing by a work colleague eight days ago when he failed to turn up for a meeting. His diary was full of appointments and he had failed to show up for any them. Plus, his bank accounts had not been accessed and his mobile phone was dead.

Kray stared at his mugshot clipped to the first page. It was a shot taken from his Facebook page, all smiles and happy. Kray had a dreadful feeling in the pit of her stomach that life was anything but happy for Chapman now. She read through the documents, trying to avoid looking at the mountainous mess in front of her.

Then, a single sentence made her stop. She reached for her phone.

'Duncan, where are you? ... Okay, I will pick you up in twenty minutes ... No, I will explain on the way.' She removed the sheet of paper from the file and left the office. Her scars were on fire.

Tavener was waiting on the pavement outside a house. He had been conducting door-to-door enquires about John Graham when he'd received the call from Kray. He was getting nowhere fast, so bailing out was not a problem. What was a problem though, was when his boss said, 'I will explain on the way', it was generally followed by a high-speed car journey with no explanation whatsoever.

Kray pulled up and he jumped into the passenger seat.

'Hey,' he said.

'How's it going?' Kray asked.

'Nothing as yet but we've only scratched the surface. How did it go with Quade and Brownlow?'

'Don't ask. She rapped our knuckles and he pissed off.'

'Not good, then?'

'Nope, not good.' Kray checked her mirrors and pulled away. Tavener was relieved that he had not been thrown back in his seat nor could he hear the screech of tyres.

'Well? Where are we going?' he asked.

'Red Marsh Industrial estate.'

'Why?'

'Because that's where Nigel Chapman runs his business.'

'And that's of interest to us because…?'

'He owns a contracting firm and one of his suppliers is a small welding and fabrication business which he bought fourteen months ago.' Kray allowed time for the new information to sink in.

'Don't tell me, let me guess. The fabrication business was owned by our guy hanging upside down in his hallway - John Graham.' Tavener said, smiling at his boss.

'That's why you and me get on so well.'

They sped off in search of Brixton Construction.

Chapter 16

I arrive at the lock-up and hurry from the car. Everything is ready but, as they say, time is of the essence. I unlock the up-and-over door and yank hard on the handle. The door yawns open and I step inside.

The white hire van is waiting. Emblazoned down one side is written:

Eric Bronson
Handyman Services
No job too small
07700 900285

I have to say, I've done a cracking job. I decided to use a set of transfer lettering used to make those decorative heart-warming statements which adorn the walls of kitchens and bedrooms. You know the type of thing – *Good food, good wine, good friends.* I went to two shops, one in Leeds and the other in Manchester to purchase what I needed. Annoyingly, I had to buy three sets to make up my sign. But it was worth it.

I change out of my day clothes and put on industrial trousers and a working jacket. A baseball cap, work books and gloves complete the look. I have one last check on the gear in the back and pull the van out of the garage. I swap over into my car, backing it into the vacant space. I close the garage door and head off.

I run through the sequence of events over and over in my head as I drive along, making sure to keep way under the speed limit. I reach her house and draw the van into the curb, stepping out into the darkness. I let out a sigh of relief to see her driveway is empty.

I check my watch. She normally takes an hour and a half. I have twenty minutes to set up.

I take my holdall from the back and stroll up the drive to the back of the house. The back door is old, with six-inch square panels of frosted glass set into the frame. I try to shake the numbness from my hands and rummage around in my bag to retrieve a suction cup which I secure to the glass next to the Yale lock. I score around the perimeter of the pane with my glass cutters, pushing as hard as I dare. The sound of the wheel cutting into the glass sets my teeth on edge.

After going over it several times, I strike the centre of the suction cup and the glass pops inwards, breaking along score lines. I tilt the pane and pull it back through the hole. My other hand eases between the gap and my fingers find the lock and the security chain, freeing them both. The door swings open into the kitchen.

I depress the valve on the suction cup to remove the glass, then, using grey blue-tack, I stick it back into position. The kitchen smells of grilled fish.

The house is long and thin. I'm standing in a galley kitchen which leads through to a dining room. A heavy oak table and four chairs command the centre of the room, and books are crammed into bookcases and stacked on the floor. I walk through the dining room and enter the hallway with the front door directly ahead of me at the far end. To the right-hand side is the staircase leading to the first floor and the lounge is off to the left.

The door is slightly ajar. I nudge it with my foot and it swings open but only as far as the arm of the brown leather sofa located behind it. It opens up onto a large room with two big armchairs in the same style as the settee, a coffee table and a flat screen TV. Set in the bay window is an old oak desk with a laptop on the top and scribbled notes festooned around it.

I stare at the offending article, the laptop that is, and wonder how many other lives she's ruined. How many other people have their reputations in tatters due to the vitriolic bile she spreads using her keyboard. I'm lost in my daydream and almost miss the car turning into the drive.

Shit, she's early!

I duck down, grabbing my bag and force it behind the sofa. I pull the black knitted ski mask over my face and position myself behind the living room door and wait. Previously, my heart was banging against my rib cage like a wild animal trying to escape, but now it is calm and measured. I close my eyes and breathe deeply.

I hear the car door slam and the boot open up. After a while, that too is slammed shut. I hear her heels clip-clopping on the front porch and the key slide into the lock. There is a metallic click and the front door opens. I feel a blast of cold as the outside air rushes into the hallway, the back of her heel kicks the front door shut. This has been a long time coming.

I hear her bustle down the hallway and through the dining room to the kitchen where she puts away her shopping. Her phone rings.

'Yes, I can talk now,' she says in clipped tones. Her voice is high-pitched like a child's. 'Yes, I can get the piece to you before six-thirty, if that works for you. Will that make the cut-off?' She paused for the response. 'Okay, I'll finish it off now and send it through to you.'

The sound of cupboard doors opening and closing echoes down the hall. Then, I hear her shoes land in a heap on the floor and she's in the lounge.

'Bollocks, bollocks, bollocks,' she says to no one. 'Why the fuck we all have to dash about to hit a fictitious deadline is beyond me.'

The sound of her fingernails pecking at the keys fills the room. I edge forward and peer around the door. The first thing that catches my eye is the shock of bright yellow hair cut tight to her scalp. She has her head bowed as her screen fills with words and pictures. I hear her mumbling to herself as she reads the article in her head. Every now and again her hands fly onto the keys, striking out words and replacing them with others. It is getting dark and the room is lit from the glow of the screen and the light in the hall.

Shit, the curtains are open. In my plan, I had imagined her pulling them shut. Now, anyone passing by would be able to see. I feel a momentary rush of panic.

This is no time to fuck about. Do it!

I stride out from behind the door gripping my toy. She barely has time to look up as the silver pins make contact with the bare skin at the side of her neck. She manages to let out a half-yelp before her body goes into spasm and her eyes roll back in her head. I pull her from the chair onto the carpet.

She twists and grabs hold of my collar. The crackle makes her do the million-volt dance again and she collapses in a heap. I move around the side of the desk and pull the curtains shut.

Fuck, that was close.

I roll her onto her front and secure her hands and feet with the black plastic cable ties. I pull a small plastic bag from my pocket and wait for her to come round. She jumps as her brain kicks back into action.

'Wh…what… help!' I stifle the yell by ramming the tea towel into her mouth, she chokes on it. I remove the diving knife from its sheath around my upper arm and hold it close to her face. She freaks out and writhes on the floor. I leap onto her back, holding her down with my mouth next to her ear.

'If you scream, I will take your eye,' I whisper into her ear. 'I am not interested in you, I only want your boss. I need to use you to get to him. Do you understand?' She goes ridged, her brain trying to compute what she's just been told. 'I'm wearing a mask, that should tell you something. I don't want to harm you. I want your boss. Do as I say and you will survive this. Your boss has been a naughty boy and upset some powerful people. I need him off guard. I need you to co-operate – is that clear?'

This time, she nods her head.

'I am going to remove the gag and you will remain silent. If you don't, I will hurt you.' I press the point of the blade into her cheekbone. She winces. I can see tears running down her face. Gently, I pull at the towelling. She coughs as it comes away from her mouth.

'That's more like it. You're not going to scream, are you?'

'No,' she croaks.

'Good girl. I'm not after you. My employer has made that perfectly clear. I'm only interested in your boss and you get to walk away. A little shaken up, but you walk away.'

She nods her head again, careful not to slice her skin against the blade.

'Now, the first thing I want you to do is eat this.'

Chapter 17

Brixton Construction was nothing like Kray had imagined. She had an image in her mind of a builder's yard with galvanised steel sheds and porta cabin offices. She swung the car into the space marked "visitor" and looked at the glass and chrome-fronted office block at the mouth of the industrial estate.

'Bloody hell,' said Tavener, looking up at the four-story building.

'Did I take a wrong turn and we've ended up in Canary Wharf?'

They both got out and walked the short distance to the main entrance. The glass doors whooshed open and a man in a smart uniform nodded his head. A young woman straight off the cover of *Vogue* magazine looked up from her semi-circular desk.

'Welcome to Brixton Construction, how may I help you?'

'I'm Acting DCI Kray and this is my colleague DC Tavener. We are here to speak with David Walsh. I called ahead. He is expecting us.'

Tavener flashed her a smile.

'If you would like to take a seat I'll tell him you're here,' she said, flashing one back.

Kray and Tavener hovered around, taking in the vast central atrium as well as the exotic plants and black leather visitor's chairs.

'Nicer than my house,' Kray said, raising her eyebrows.

'I know,' quipped Tavener, a comment that earned him a scowl.

After a few minutes, the lifts behind reception dinged open and a short man, immaculately dressed in a sharp suit and spectacles came to greet them.

'David Walsh,' he said, offering his hand. 'I'm the Commercial Director here. Please follow me.'

He led them to the lifts and hit the button to the fourth floor. A key requirement when they recruited for the post of Commercial Director must have been an ability to avoid small talk – they travelled in silence.

Exiting on the top floor, they passed another *Vogue*-like woman sat at her desk. 'Hold my calls will you, Jenny?' said Walsh. The woman gave them the whitest smile Kray had ever seen. Tavener was beginning to regret not being on the missing person case.

The three of them entered a modern shiny office, with a huge desk and a smoked glass conference table ringed by six black leather chairs. Walsh ushered for them to take a seat.

'I suppose this is in connection with Nigel's disappearance. We've given your investigation every support we can. We are all very worried. How can I be of help?' Walsh's cufflinks clanked on the glass surface as he leaned forwards.

'Thank you, Mr Walsh, your company and your employees have been extremely co-operative at this difficult time.' He nodded in return. 'We are here in connection with another investigation that is underway at the moment and we wanted to ask you a few questions. Is that okay?'

'Fire away.'

'A while ago, your company bought out one of your suppliers, a business by the name of John Graham Steelworks. Were you here when that sale went through?'

Walsh shifted uncomfortably in his seat. 'Yes, I was. Nigel knew John Graham from way back. They were one of our smaller suppliers but Nigel had a soft spot for them. He bought out the business and we absorbed it into our own. It was a straight forward deal. I understand John died recently. Someone said he was murdered?'

'I cannot discuss the case, Mr Walsh,' said Kray.

'One of our guys read it in the paper. Blackpool is a small place, you know?'

'Tell me more about the deal, Mr Walsh.'

'That's it, nothing more to tell. Nigel bought out John's business; he paid him more than a fair price. That was it.'

'Were there any problems with the transaction? You know, disgruntled employees, people who held a grudge?'

'No, it went through without a hitch. The people who didn't want to transfer were made redundant; those who did want to move were transferred over to us. They had a relatively small workforce. We are a big player in the industry around here and now have a national reach that goes UK wide. Absorbing them didn't cause a ripple.' Walsh spun his cufflink round and round while Kray spun her wedding ring. Something didn't feel right about Mr Walsh.

'Can you show me Nigel's office?'

'Err…yes, sure, if you think it will help.'

They all rose from the table and walked out past the beaming woman behind the desk. Tavener craned his neck to get a better look.

'These are the directors' offices,' Walsh said unnecessarily.

'Business is good, then?' Tavener thought he might as well say something unnecessary in return.

'Yes, very good.'

They came to an empty desk outside the biggest office of all. 'Debbie usually sits here. She is Nigel's PA, but has been too upset to come in since his disappearance.' Walsh pushed open the glass door, which opened up into an office the size of half a football field.

Kray glanced at Tavener and raised an eyebrow. *We could fit the whole of CID in here.*

Glossy photographs of construction projects adorned the walls with their names beneath them in gold lettering.

'The company built all these?' asked Tavener.

'Yes, Nigel is proud of every job we do. "If it's not good enough to hang on my wall then it's not good enough for the customer," is his mantra. Hence the pictures.'

'He never married?' Kray asked.

Walsh looked even more uncomfortable. 'No, he's a confirmed bachelor. He likes it that way.'

'And what about Debbie? Is she one of the ones he likes?' Kray asked, perusing the pictures.

'Um, er, yes. I think they might have had a thing going at one time.' Small patches of sweat were beginning to show on Walsh's expensive tailored shirt. 'Nigel likes the company of women. Nothing wrong with that.'

'No, Mr Walsh, there is nothing wrong with that.' She spun the ring round and round on her finger as she walked along the line of photographs. 'What about this one?'

Kray pointed to a framed picture, bigger than the others, hanging pride of place behind the vast desk.

'Ah, that one is his pet project,' said Walsh, relieved they were off the subject of women.

'It's different to the others, this one isn't finished,' Kray said. The picture showed an aerial shot of a large expanse of land that had been dug up, with shipping containers dotted about.

'That project is all about Nigel wanting to give something back to the local community. When its complete, it's going to be a natural parkland where schools can come and learn about the environment. It will have a small woodland area, a pond and allotment set aside for kids to grow plants and vegetables. He's been at it for years. It isn't anything to do with the business; he's doing it with his own money and using any spare labour we have. Trouble is, the company is working flat out, so we don't have available people. That's why it's only part complete.'

'So, it's been like this for how long?'

'Since before I got here. I keep telling him it's a prime piece of land and he should sell it to a developer, but he won't listen.'

Kray moved closer to the picture, and read the name written below it in gold lettering on a plaque. Her scars burned so hot, they felt like they would singe her clothing.

She almost fell through the floor.

Chapter 18

I'm back at my flat and absolutely buzzing. Having to bring forward my schedule had me in a flat spin, but I coped, and it was amazing. That could not have gone better. The look on her face when I pulled off the ski mask was a picture.

I needed her to be co-operative, I had to give her hope. Wearing the ski mask and the story around me only being interested in her boss was a charade. I had to make her believe she could come out of this alive if she complied. So, when I removed the mask, she shrieked behind the gag and screwed her eyes tight shut. I could just make out the words, 'No, no, no, no.'

I grabbed her by the throat and told her to look at me. 'Do you remember?' I asked. Her brow furrowed. 'Take a good look and think back.' It furrowed again. Then, the penny dropped.

That point of realisation prompted her to jerk violently off the floor. Trying to right herself. Howling behind the towel rammed into her mouth.

'Fucking remember me now, don't you?'

My new toy cracked and she jerked for a different reason.

I left her on the floor and went to the kitchen. She kept a huge bunny boiler pot under the sink. *That will do nicely.*

The rest of the evening went to plan but I had to keep checking my watch. I needed to keep to time.

Lying on my bed staring at the ceiling, Sadie barges into my head. She's always around when I don't want her to be. Spoiling the party. My mind travels back to a time when I was the one full of false hope. I was the one clutching at straws.

I remember that after the incident with the solicitor woman, I simply wanted to talk to my wife. If we could talk, we could clear up this conflict surrounding the kids. It was that fucking Wilding, she was poisoning Sadie's mind against me, making her use the kids as a weapon. If we could chat like adults, without her sticking her oar in, everything would be fine. We just needed to talk.

Sadie was always leaving the patio door unlocked. The kids used it to go and play in the garden and when they came back in they would close the door but not lock it. In all the years we lived in that house, she never thought to check. Not once. That had been my job.

I pushed down on the brass handle, and the door opened towards me. Sadie was out on the morning school run. I thought it would be better if we had the conversation without the children around. I wandered through the dining room into the lounge. I could see through to the kitchen where the morning's breakfast bowls were laying in the sink and toys were scattered across the floor having avoided the morning clear up. The house still smelled the same, a mix of old potpourri and wax furniture polish.

I walked upstairs and stood in the centre of the landing. Jake's room was to the left and Molly's to the right. Our bedroom was straight ahead. I pushed open the door and stared at the double bed set against the wall with the huge picture of a vase of flowers hanging above the headboard. A wedding gift from my mum. She was always shit at presents.

In my mind, I could see the quilt kicked into a heap at the bottom of the bed and the pillows tossed onto the floor. Items of clothing are strewn across the carpet. She is on all fours, wailing like a banshee as he bangs her from behind. She wailed like that in our first year of marriage, but then it all stopped.

I hear a car pull into the drive and hurry downstairs. I fill the kettle and flick the switch. It begins to gurgle and pop. I sit at the kitchen table and wait. Some things never change. My wife could never simply get out of the car and go into house. She would always spend ages getting side-tracked by sweet wrappers, dead heads on flowers, the state of the backseat of the car or rearranging the rubbish in the bin. This morning was no different. So, I sit and wait.

Finally, I hear the key in the lock. The lock that she fucking changed the moment my sorry arse was hauled out of there by the police. After tipping the coffee into that bitch's lap, I had made a bee-line straight home to speak to Sadie, clear up all this nonsense about her feeling uneasy about me seeing the kids. She was not at all happy when I turned up on the doorstep to plead my case. But absolutely freaked out when the police showed up and bundled me into a car.

Anyway, that was a while ago, and I'm sure she's feeling better about the whole situation now.

I hear Sadie drop her bag onto the hallway floor and kick off her shoes. She enters the lounge with her head bowed reading the mail that had been on the mat. She shrieks when she looks up and sees me.

I hold my hands up.

'Sorry, love, I just want to talk. You wouldn't answer my calls, so I thought I'd pop round.'

'What the fuck are you doing here?'

'I want to talk, that's all. Here, I've put the kettle on. Let's have a coffee.'

'How did you get in?'

'How many times did I tell you about locking that patio door after the kids have opened it?'

'You…you…broke in!'

'No, don't be daft. I came in through the patio door – it wasn't locked.' I open the cupboard above the kettle and pull out a couple of mugs. 'I just wanted you and me to talk about the kids. That Wilding woman has it in for me, and she keeps getting in the way. So, I thought, how about we talk things through over a nice cup of coffee.' I busy myself piling two heaped spoons full of ground coffee into the cafetière.

I turn to face her but she's gone.

'Sadie? Sadie, where are you?'

I hear the front door open. I dash to the front room window to see her standing in the middle of the road in her stockinged feet clutching her mobile phone to the side of her head. I run to the front door and call after her.

'C'mon love, don't be like that. I just want to talk. Come inside and have a coffee.'

She's dancing on the spot. When she sees me, she bolts up the road and disappears down a driveway to the left. I can hear her banging on the front door of a house. Loud frantic bangs made with the flat of her hand.

'What? What on earth is the matter, Sadie? Is it...' I hear a woman shriek in a high-pitched voice. The door slams shut. The close is silent again.

I stand in the doorway looking at the semi-circle of houses. I can remember my mind wandering – *Derek needs to trim that hedge or Brenda will go mad at him. She does like to keep her borders with clean lines. And the branches on that tree have grown, they will need chopping sooner or later. That path needs a good jet washing...*

The silence of the close is pierced by the sound of a distant siren. The noise getting louder.

I snap out of my daydream and shake the image of Sadie from my head. I push the button on my phone, eight-fifty pm. Perfect.

I open the door to my flat and walk down the stairs. I'm greeted by a wall of chatter as I enter the takeaway. The Woo family are out in force dealing with the evening rush.

'Hi Kev, had a good sleep?' asked Anabel, wrapping chips up in white paper and handing them over the counter to an eager teenager. The place was full of people wanting to get their hands on a Woo-woo.

'Yes, I feel much better.'

'You hungry?' Joseph yelled from the back, wok in hand.

'Starving mate,' I yelled back. 'I'm fancying duck in orange and some rice.'

'Coming up.'

I take a seat against the wall next to one of the regulars dressed in a hoodie and a bobble hat and wrap my hands in my lap to stop them from shaking. My senses are in overdrive as I sit and soak up the glory. The look on Teresa-fucking-Franklin's face when the first pulse of electricity went through her brain. I thought her eyes were going to burst wide open.

'Popular place tonight, Kev,' says the hoodie sitting next to me, holding onto a small square of paper with the number 152 printed in red. It breaks my train of thought.

'Yes, it is for a Wednesday.'

'That's the trouble. During the illuminations, every night is a Saturday night,' she said.

'One fifty-two.' Anabel calls out over the noise.

'Bon Appetit,' I say to her.

'You're a posh twat, you.' She laughs and heaves herself up by putting a calloused hand on my knee. I follow her up to the counter and stand at the side.

'It got busy early today?' I say to Anabel, chancing my arm.

'It did, hope we didn't disturb you.'

'No, I was up anyway.'

Joseph places two plastic containers onto the pass between the back kitchen and the front counter.

'Kev, yours is ready.' Anabel turns and hands it over. I bring out my wallet and she covers it with her hand.

'Dinner is on me.'

'No, no, I'll pay.'

'Go eat your food. It's a present from me for waking you up.'

I smile and take my food back upstairs and switch on the TV. I find the news channel. Peeling the top off the container fills the room with the most wonderful smell. I stab my fork into a piece of duck and devour it.

There is nothing on the news.

What the hell are the police doing? They've had a week now.

The second one was going to be found fast but the first would take a little detective work. *Come on guys, get your act together. It's not difficult to figure out.*

Chapter 19

Kray brought her car to a halt at the mouth of the site. The weather had taken a turn for the worst in line with her demeanour. The rain was coming down at a forty-five-degree angle and the darkness seemed to swallow them up. In front was a fifteen foot high wire fence with coiled razors on the top. Staring through the smeared windscreen, it looked like they had driven onto the set of a World War Two movie.

Her scars tingled and itched like crazy as she surveyed the scene.

'You have CCTV, right?' Kray said to Walsh riding in the back.

'No, there is very little equipment kept here and the fence keeps out any would-be vandals. There's nothing here but mud,' he replied.

'Fucking brilliant.' Kray said as she got out into the downpour, leaving the car engine running and the headlamps on full beam. Tavener and Walsh followed suit. Kray popped open the boot and retrieved her coat and a torch. 'Let's go.'

Walsh went first, his highly-polished shoes quickly losing their shine in the mud. He fished around in his pocket and brought out a key. A heavy mental chain was interlaced through the steelwork of the gate and a padlock the size of a football held it shut.

He worked the key into the lock, using the light from the car, and gave it a twist. It wouldn't budge. He turned the key again but nothing happened.

'Here, let me.' Tavener eased Walsh out of the way and gripped the lock in one hand and the key in the other, he worked it back and forth, his biceps bulging under his jacket. There was a loud click and the hasp sprung open. 'We're in.'

Tavener unthreaded the bulky chain from around one of the gates, put his shoulder to the steelwork, and the gate swung open. All three of them walked in.

Kray shone her torch onto the ground in the hope of picking up tyre tracks but the place was awash in them. 'How long has it been since there was any work done here?' she asked.

'Don't know. Maybe twelve months.'

'Did he get bored with it?' Tavener asked.

'Maybe, I don't know.' Walsh had mud on the trousers of his seven-hundred-pound suit, not to mention his light grey coloured jacket was fast resembling a dish cloth. The dark shadows of three shipping containers loomed large against the far fence. As they approached, Kray could make out the corrugated steel walls and faded red paintwork of the metal structures.

'What do you keep in those?' Tavener asked.

'I don't know,' Walsh said. 'I've never been here before.'

The dirt track ran out to be replaced by a furrowed expanse of ground. Puddles of water reflected white in the torchlight, the rain making the surfaces dance. They reached the first container. Tavener yanked on the handle and heaved the door towards him. Kray shone her torch into the void. It was empty.

The second container was ten feet away to the left. This one had a padlock securing the handle in place. Tavener looked around and found a metal bar lying propped up against the fence. He picked it up.

'Give me some light over here Roz.'

Kray shone her torch onto the lock. Tavener took aim and brought the bar down hard. It bounced off. He swung it again and with a loud crack the lock jumped open. He fed the hasp back through the handle and pulled it open. The levers disengaged and the door opened up.

All three of them peered inside. There, in the darkness, was the unmistakeable shape of the back of a car. Kray scanned it with her torch.

'A blue F type Jag,' Tavener said.

'Holy shit,' said Walsh.

While Walsh was nailed to the spot, transfixed by the car, Kray and Tavener ran across to the final container. It, too, was locked with a padlock. Tavener broke it open with a single blow and Kray tugged at the mechanism with all her might. The door cracked open and the stench knocked them backwards. Tavener stepped away coughing into his hand while Kray continued to lean all her weight against the door.

The torchlight landed on the decomposing white flesh of a man's naked body suspended upside down from a hook in the ceiling. Parts of his skin were hanging away from his limbs. To the side was a large plastic pot that used to hold paint, now it was brimmed full with a congealed black fluid. The man's hands were tied behind his back and his bloodshot eyes stared straight ahead. The rest of the container was empty.

Walsh appeared at the door and wretched down his front.

'Fucking hell,' said Tavener.

Kray shook a handkerchief from her pocket and clamped it to her nose and mouth. She walked over to the body. He was still wearing his socks. She pointed to them and Tavener reached up and removed the right one. Kray shone the torch beam onto the dead man's foot. The big toe was missing.

'You were right, Roz.'

'Yeah, I fucking wish I wasn't. You call it in and I'll get Walsh back to the car and secure the area.' Kray gripped Walsh by the elbow and walked him across the open ground to the gates. He seemed far less worried about the condition of his suit.

'Was that Nigel Chapman?' she asked.

Walsh nodded and wretched onto the wet ground. Kray handed him her handkerchief.

She put him into the passenger seat and closed the door.

In the headlights, she could see a large sign bolted to the fence. It depicted an artist's impression of what the site was going to look like. The title across the top said: *Project Market Garden*.

The verse played over and over in Kray's head.

This little piggy went to market…

Chapter 20

I can't sleep. I've got to be up early in the morning but the night won't let me rest. I want to say it's because I'm still on a massive high, but I'm not. I have a blinding headache and have popped a couple of tablets but to no effect. The numbness in my fingers has gone only to be replaced with an odd sensation in my legs. I ache all over.

Dark thoughts occupy my mind, crowding out the celebrations. I cannot stop them invading my space. The demons that heralded my decline are all around me, and despite the ecstatic events of the day, all I can think about is how my life crumbled away beneath my feet.

After my catastrophic encounter with Sadie at the house and the resulting trip to the police station, I recall being invigorated with a renewed determination to pull myself together. She didn't want to press charges but getting myself in trouble with the law so quickly after being issued with a caution was not good.

I decided that the best thing I could do to get myself back on my feet was to get more money. And for that I didn't need to get a new job, I simply needed my old job back. So, I put on a work suit, a shirt with a collar and a pair of shoes that weren't done up by Velcro and went off to see my old business buddy John Graham.

I drove to his house and parked on the drive. It was a modest three bed semi that John had lived in since he married Miriam. John obviously had the same risk-averse mentality when it came to houses as he did with the business. I saw the curtain twitch as I drew up and got out. I rang the doorbell, conscious that my suit was hanging off my bones due to the amount of weight I'd lost. I pulled it tight around my waist to mimic a good fit.

Miriam opened the door. I hadn't seen her since that evening at the New Year's Eve party, and the woman who stood before me in her pink slippers did not look well. I wasn't sure how much weight I'd lost but double it, and that was how Miriam looked.

'Kevin, how lovely to see you.' She reached across the threshold and threw her arms around my neck. I wrapped mine across her back, feeling her ribs and backbone prominent beneath her clothing. 'Come in, come in,' she chimed.

I stepped into the hallway and felt the warmth of the house hugging me.

'John is in his study. John! John!' she called, 'Kevin's here!'

There was a scuffling sound upstairs and John's face appeared at the top of the landing.

'Well, I'll be…' John scampered down the stairs and shook my hand. 'Good to see you, mate, we've been so worried. Come in, come in.'

He led me into the lounge, a place I had visited maybe half a dozen times before. It always looked the same as it always had. Miriam patted the sofa next to her. I took a seat.

'How have you been?' she asked. Though I think my general appearance told them precisely how I'd been.

'Oh, you know…' I left it at that.

'We could not believe it when we heard about you and Sadie. I mean, what ever got into her.'

More cocks than a Bernard Mathews' farmyard.

Miriam flashed an awkward smile at John, who raised his eyebrows. There was something in the air that made me feel uneasy.

'I know, I don't understand it either,' I said, holding my hands up. 'I'm living in a bedsit across town.'

'Oh, that's good,' John said, instantly regretted the insensitivity of his remark. The pause that followed was soaked with awkwardness. Miriam kept looking at John, then staring into her lap. It was like I had interrupted something important.

Eventually, Miriam could stand it no longer. 'Let me put the kettle on. I'm sure you boys have lots to catch up on.' She limped off to the kitchen.

'Miriam doesn't look so good,' I said.

'No, she's not,' replied John. 'We are waiting for test results to come back from the hospital but I gotta say, Kev, I'm worried.'

'Yeah, I bet. Fingers crossed, eh?'

'It's great to see you,' John blurted out, needing to avoid another awkward silence.

'This is not just a social visit, John. I want to come back into the business. I want my old job back.'

John sat back in his chair and fixed me with the same face he did when I wanted him to chase bigger contracts. He nodded his head and stroked his chin.

'Not sure it's as straightforward as that, Kev.'

'Why? Why not?'

'Everyone knows what Sadie did and everyone knows what she's doing now. The problem is, she did it with the boss of the biggest contracts supplier around here. If you came back…well, you know.'

'No, John, no I don't know.'

'It's all about corporate risk, John…the good name of the company. I'm not sure they would take kindly to you being back in the saddle.'

'So, this is not about what Sadie did, it's about what I've done. Is that it?'

'People can be funny about that sort of thing. They know you've been sleeping rough and that you're on the bones of your arse. They are not going to place a contract with someone like that.'

'Fuck, John.' I tried to keep my voice down. 'Are you saying there is no longer a position for me in the business?'

John looked at me without an ounce of pity in his watery eyes. 'Yeah, I suppose that's what I'm saying.'

'For Christ's sake, I thought you of all people would be on my side.'

'I am on your side, Kev, but you were the one who pissed off, leaving us in the lurch. You were the one who left me juggling so many contracts I didn't know what day of the week it was. You were the one who would rather chase pigeons in the fucking park with a can of special brew in your hand. Not me. Okay?' He put both hands on his knees to steady himself. It looked like he'd waited a long time to get that little speech off his chest.

I didn't know what to say.

'I am a share holder in the business,' I said quietly, trying to take the tension down a notch.

'Yes, a *minority* share-holder.'

Again, I didn't know what to say.

'You want me out, is that it?'

'I'll give you a fair price for your slice of the business. You could do with an injection of cash, so as I see it this is the best option for both of us.'

'But it's not the best option for me.'

'Well, it's the only fucking one you got.' He rose from his chair and left the room. Moments later, he returned with a sheaf of paper in his hand.

'Here, the severance terms are set out in the documentation.' The top copy looked official, I recognised the letter head of a local branch of solicitors emblazoned across the top. I flicked through it. 'I was going to come and see you, but as you've come here, then...' John let the sentence die away to nothing.

I continued to flick over the pages.

'That's not enough,' I said, finally reaching the punchline figure.

'It's a fair offer.'

'That's not fair, John. It's only slightly more than I put into the business in the first place. That was when the company was tiny. Now, it's much bigger. My share is worth more than this.'

'It's more than fair, considering how you dropped us in it. It's a take it or leave it deal, Kev. A full and final offer.'

'Come on, John, be reasonable. I put my life into that business.'

'Take it or leave it.' He leaned forward with his arm extended. In his hand he held a gold pen. I recognised it as the one I bought him when we landed our first big contract. I wondered if he realised.

'John,' I whispered.

He moved to the edge of his seat, bringing the pen closer to me. I took it from his grasp, folded the relevant page over and signed. He gestured with his open hand that he wanted his pen back. I dropped it onto the carpet, stood up and let myself out.

I peered through the lounge window to see Miriam come hobbling into the lounge and hugging her husband. She wasn't carrying any cups. Apparently, there was never going to be coffee.

I sat in the car for ages, not knowing what to do. They drew the curtains as if to shut out what they had done. The clock on the dashboard ticked away the time. With every minute, a fuming knot of anger grew in my stomach. I slammed my hands against the steering wheel and yelled out. No words, just a primal scream of rage. The fury of the past few months bubbled over. I flipped out.

I hurled myself out of the car and down his drive, banging on the front door. John opened it with Miriam peering over his shoulder.

'You can't do this to me, John.' I barged past him.

'Now look here, Kev–' he protested. I wasn't listening.

'I put my heart and soul into that business and that offer is an insult. A fucking insult.'

'Watch your language and get out of my house.'

'I want a proper settlement. I want something that reflects the hard work I put into making the company a success.'

'Get out of my house!' he yelled. Miriam screeched in support. John made a grab for my arm. I shoved him back and he toppled up the stairs.

'I want my money, John,' I shouted.

'Kevin, stop, you've hurt him,' Miriam screeched.

'Where is it John? Where is the document I signed?' I lurched to the right into the lounge, scanning around. The document wasn't there. I bounded past John, up the stairs. Miriam saw her chance. She dashed to the other room to find the phone.

I was like a mad man pulling drawers out of cabinets and throwing paperwork onto the floor. John appeared in the doorway.

'Get out of my house!' he yelled and flung himself at me. I stepped to one side and he clattered to the floor. He lay there groaning.

Miriam came at me from nowhere, banging her tiny fists down onto my shoulder.

'Get away from him, get away,' she screamed.

I pushed her away and went downstairs. *Where the fuck has he hidden it?* I went into the kitchen and emptied pots, pans and cutlery onto the floor. Then, for the second time that week, the sound of sirens pierced the night.

Chapter 21

The one thing to say about prison time is the fact that there's nothing to do *but* think. The monotonous parade of activities means you don't have to waste valuable head-time working out everyday stuff, like…when's lunch? What time is dinner? What am I going to do today? All of that is taken care of. You wake in the morning and step aboard a conveyor that transports you through the day, ensuring you are deposited back into your bed at the end of it.

My lawyer had pleaded that if I was to receive a custodial sentence it should be at a local jail. I had two young children and a wife, and it made sense to keep the disruption to their family life at a minimum. I was duly sent down and bundled off to Wymott prison, a category C establishment with more drugs in it than a Boots pharmacy. It was as local as they could get. My wife never visited once. She chose instead to cement her view with the kids that Daddy was a bad thing, and at least now she didn't have to bother with the niceties of working out visitation rights. That ship had well and truly sailed.

I had three priorities while serving my time – to keep myself to myself, keep myself fit and keep on thinking. After all, I had a lot to think about. The fury that had engulfed me had no place in prison. Being angry in a place that already contained more than a thousand angry men would get me killed. I channelled that anger into something positive, something creative. Each night, I would run through the priority checklist in my head. Every night, it was a full house of three ticks.

My thoughts were a collection of plans; each one ran like a movie in my head as I plotted how they would be carried out.

Working through the intricacies of what would happen kept my brain occupied and it helped the time to pass quickly. Nothing could be left to chance, everything was scheduled down to the last detail. However, I had given myself a challenging constraint – I was not allowed to write anything down. Every detail had to be committed to memory. Keeping a permanent record would have been a rookie mistake.

But there was one piece missing. One gaping hole. In many ways, it was the most important part, but I kept telling myself not to worry – it would come, eventually. After all, I was not exactly short of time in which to work it out. But it bothered me that the most significant part was missing.

My cell mate's name was Irvine. The rest of the wing called him Berlin. He didn't seem to care. They called me Pablo Escobar because I refused to do drugs. Enduring prison humour was a deep joy.

Irvine was a black monster of a man from Birmingham. He was a bloke of few words and those he did manage to utter were mangled beyond recognition by a chronic speech impediment. Chatting with Irvine was like predictive text in reverse. I had to figure out what he was trying to say, because on most occasions, he never got to the end. I got pretty good at it but like the real predictive text, sometimes I got it very wrong.

Irvine had the same outlook to doing time as I did, except his priorities were different. His priorities were lifting weights, lifting more weights, lifting heavier weights. He didn't have to worry with the "keep himself to himself" priority, because no one went near him. His reluctance to speak was seen as a smouldering attitude of "fuck off or I'll rip your head from your neck", which people did without ever being told.

He occupied the bottom bunk, which was fine. At least that way I rested easy knowing that twenty-two stones of prime beef would not come crashing down on me in the night. In fact, Irvine was as meek a man as I have ever met, kind and generous. Which was completely at odds with the horror stories another inmate told me about my new best friend.

In a previous life, Irvine had been a gangland enforcer, capable of the most ferocious violence which could be inflicted at the flick of a switch. He had a close call when a punishment beating went too far, and the man died. Irvine had an alibi that held up, however the other guy alongside him dishing out the kicking hadn't fared as well and was banged up for nine years. Irvine saw the writing on the wall and left Birmingham to settle in Manchester. He worked security for pubs and clubs in the city centre and kept away from trouble. That was until a disastrous stop and search resulted in him throwing a police officer through a shop front window.

Irvine did try once to explain to me what had happened, but it took so long I forgot most of it by the time he reached the end of the story. I simply patted him on the shoulder when he was done and smiled in a sympathetic manner. It was like patting one of those American style fridges. His release date was two weeks after mine. We said we would stay in touch. Well…I said we should and he nodded.

I was banged-up for eleven months, two weeks and three days, and during all that time I shared a cell with Irvine. It suited me fine. He didn't speak, which means I didn't have to either. We ate together, trained together, showered together – in a manner of speaking – and lived together. In one way, we were like an intense married couple minus the requirement to converse. In another way, it was like having your big brother around for your first day at school. The combined result was no one bothered Irvine and no one bothered me. This comfort allowed me all the time I needed to plan what I was going to do when I got out.

That was until I had served two months, one week and one day. I was called to the warden's office to be told I was being placed on a work experience programme at a local farm. What I knew about farming I could write on a postage stamp, so it was a bit of a surprise. Irvine said it would be good for me to get out and do something different. At least I think that's what he said.

So, one wet Friday morning, I was marched into a converted transit van after breakfast and ferried to a farm, along with three other inmates and a guard. It was like going on a school trip but without the happy faces and packed lunch. We drove for around forty-five minutes and pulled off the road, through a set of iron gates into a farmstead.

A man came out to meet us and chatted to the prison officer through the side window of the van. Once they had finished their chat the officer turned around in his seat, throwing his arm across the back.

'Now, listen up,' he bellowed. 'Working on this farm is a privilege and as such, it can be taken away from you at any time. You shovel shit from the time you get here to the time you climb back into the van. Is that clear?'

We looked at each other, not sure how to respond.

'I said is that clear?' he repeated.

'Yes, sir,' we said in unison.

'What do you do here?'

'Shovel shit.'

The guard turned, slid from his seat, and seconds later the back doors flung open, and we piled out into the damp cold of the morning. The sky seemed to bear down on us with the clouds scraping at the slate tiles on the roofs. The place stunk of the product we were going to shovel.

Over to the left was a cavernous barn, big enough to hide an ocean liner with five smaller outbuildings dotted around it. We were ushered across the muddy expanse into the barn. The stench was eye-watering and a shrieking, squealing sound pierced my ears. Pigs, fucking hundreds of them.

I looked out beyond the confines of the barn to see a whole city of pigs stretched out across acre upon acre of land. They were milling around their houses made from galvanised corrugated sheeting, each house looking like a mini air raid shelter. The expression "happy as a pig in shit" played over in my head. These pigs were very happy and there was a lot of shit.

We were briefed by the man who had come out to meet us. I assumed he was the owner or at least the head guy around here. He spoke with a soft west country accent which was quite at odds with his northern surroundings. He looked the part with his Burberry flat cap, green overalls and Wellington boots.

We changed into much the same gear, minus the hat, and followed him to a newer building. It had a red roof and white walls with no windows.

'This is where the money is made. We process the pigs in here,' he announced as we walked inside.

It was there that I learned a new skill – in fact, I learned three. From that moment on, I didn't have to worry about the gap in my plans. It had finally been filled.

Chapter 22

The Market Garden site now resembled the worst village fete in history with two white forensic tents shrouding the entrances to the freight containers. Powerful LED lamps gave the place a theatrical look, casting hard shadows across the ground while making the tents look like giant magic lanterns. Thankfully, it had stopped raining, but the mud was ankle deep.

Kray watched as they lowered the body down from the hook in the roof, laying it onto plastic sheeting. A dip test of the dark sludge in the ten-litre paint pot had confirmed that the contents were blood. The condition of the body confirmed it most likely belonged to Nigel Chapman.

High resolution cameras snapped away at the corpse but Kray already knew what the photographs would show. The victim's eye balls would be crazed with burst blood vessels, there would be two burn marks one on each temple along with scalded skin hanging off the bones, and Chapman's big toe would be missing.

The other forensic team were meticulously working their way around the Jag. They had obviously drawn the longer straws on their way to the crime scene.

Kray watched the proceedings with the rhyme *This little piggy went to market* echoing in her head. Her thoughts were interrupted by Tavener standing next to her.

'What is it?' he asked.

'This is going to get a whole lot worse.'

'It looks pretty fucking bad already.'

'This is just the start.'

'Yeah, you were right. You said there was another body.'

'No, I mean, there is more of this to come.'

'I don't understand.'

'*This little piggy went to market* – Chapman was killed in the location of his pet project which he named Market Garden. *This little piggy stayed at home* – Graham was killed in the same way at his home.'

'*This little piggy had roast beef,*' Tavener joined in.

'*This little piggy had none.*'

'*And this little piggy…*' Tavener didn't complete the rhyme, the gravity of what he was saying grinding him to a halt. 'Do you think–'

'There's going to be three more murders. Whoever is doing this is following the rhyme.'

'Fuck.'

'The faster we bring the two cases together, the faster we can join the dots to identify who's doing this.'

'I've informed Brownlow and told him to get his guys in first thing tomorrow to a joint briefing.'

'Good, did he say anything of interest?'

'Umm…' Tavener recalled the conversation in his head. 'Nope.'

'Sounds about right.' Kray tore her gaze away from the body on the ground. 'Get Walsh down to the station, I want you to interview him. I think he knows more than he's telling us.'

'What do you mean?'

'I'm not sure but when we were with him in the offices, he was on edge. I couldn't put my finger on it but I reckon he's hiding something.'

'Maybe seeing his boss hanging upside down with his flesh ripped off might loosen his tongue.'

'Yeah, that's what I thought. I need to prepare a press statement for Quade, they are all over us wanting a comment about the killings. Though why she can't sort it out is beyond me.'

'She *is* your best buddy now.' Kray gave Tavener a sideways glance. 'I'm gone,' he said, and slid off in the direction of Walsh who was waiting in the car.

Her phone rang. She groped around in her jacket pocket.

'Kray,' she answered. The voice on the other end spoke in slow measured tones. When they had finished, she disconnected the call without uttering another word. She stared into the tent to see the CSI team cutting the cable ties away from Chapman's wrists. She closed her eyes for a second and allowed an inner scream to resonate around her body.

Kray made her way to her car parked in the entrance to the site. Tavener was in the driving seat explaining to Walsh that he was needed down at the station. Walsh was in the throes of protesting when Kray arrived next to Tavener. She ducked her head inside the car.

'Mr Walsh, we have more questions for you but for now, we'll take you back to your office and will be in touch with you tomorrow.'

Tavener frowned and stepped out, standing next to his boss. 'But I thought you said—' he whispered.

The look on Kray's face stopped him mid-sentence.

'They've found another body.'

Chapter 23

What the hell is wrong with me tonight? I look at the clock – fifteen minutes past midnight. I'm lucky to be working a split-shift tomorrow which means a later start. The extra sleep will do me good. My headache has subsided, and now that I'm laying down, my legs feel back to normal.

I turn over in bed to face the wall. It was my favourite position in prison. With the wall inches from my face I didn't have to look at our thirty-two square feet of prime real-estate. I couldn't see the wash basin or the toilet in the corner, neither could I see the heavy metal door with the spyhole carved into the top. Or the small desk and the chair. The physical reminders of my incarceration where out of sight. All that filled my field of view was white paint. I could have been anywhere.

I stare at the wall in my flat and try to imagine myself somewhere else, but it's no use. I can't shift the recollections of prison. I close my eyes, my mind drifts, and I'm back there, re-living the whole chapter again.

One day, Irvine appeared in the cell carrying a newspaper. It was folded under his arm. He took it out and held it in front of me. My first though was, *I didn't know you could read.*

'Y-y-you sh-should rea-read the…' By that point, I had got the gist of what Irvine was saying and took the paper from his hand.

'What am I looking at?'

'P-p-pa-page t-t…'

'Two, ten, twelve?' Irvine raised his hand and I flipped over to page twelve. My wife's face stared out of the two-page spread. The banner headline read: *Living with Abuse* and underneath was the sub-title, *One Woman's Struggle.*

'Tha-tha-that's y-y-'

'Yes, that's my wife,' I added, my brain not able to take in what my eyes were telling it.

'N-n-no, i-it's you.' Irvine's thick black finger pointed to the second paragraph. There in black and white was printed the name Kevin Palmer.

'What the fuck is this?' I stood and marched around the confines of the cell holding the paper out in front of me, which meant I couldn't read the bloody thing, but my body needed to respond to the fight of flight response coursing through it. In the absence of being able to fight with Sadie, it chose flight. I stomped around swearing and cursing, eventually sitting down on my bed to read the damned thing properly.

As I processed the words on the page, the same question spun round and round in my head: *What the fuck is this?*

The article told the story of a man who was abusive to his wife, both mentally and physically. Who would not allow her to go out on her own, so strong was his jealously-driven rage. It told of a woman trying to protect her young children from a drunk who squandered their money on booze and whores, while she scrimped and saved every penny to put food on the table. It depicted a man who had let his livelihood go to rack and ruin, choosing instead to pursue three-day alcoholic benders instead of work. And worst of all – that man it depicted was me.

I hurried out of the cell to book an emergency call home.

I spent my allotted three minutes talking to the answer phone, either Sadie wasn't there or she wasn't picking up. I called twice on the house phone and twice on her mobile, leaving the same message each time. The summary of which was straight forward: *What the fuck are you doing?*

Over the next few days I sank into a bleak pit of despair. I spent the time cooped up in my cell pouring over the article until I could recite it in my sleep. Which, of course, I did, causing me to be sleep deprived on top of everything else. I punctuated my day with frequent emergency calls home, speaking to her voicemail so many times before eventually giving up.

The journalist's name was Teresa Franklin. She wrote a shock-column for the *Blackpool Telegraph*, a weekly rag with red-top aspirations way above its circulation of twenty-one thousand. I ventured out of my cell in search of any back copies I could lay my hands on. I wanted to learn more about Teresa-fucking-Franklin. I found six copies.

From her photograph, I would say she was early thirties with thick rimmed glasses and had her hair cropped into a pixie cut. Her articles were all two-page spreads, and on every one, I found a head and shoulder shot of her in the top corner, posing with a stern look. Two of the photos showed her sporting a different hair colour – one was red and the other was blue. Every article was prefixed with an introductory paragraph saying how Teresa Franklin was a woman who was going to shake things up with punchy local news and untold stories that were guaranteed to shock.

I tried to contact her by calling the paper but got bounced around and ended up back where I started. I tried to reach the editor to vent my opinion about the defamatory article only to be told he would ring me back. Day after day, it was the same. My blood boiled.

Irvine was a rock. I ranted at the man and he sat there and took every bit of venom I spat at him. If I couldn't rave at my wife and couldn't rant at Teresa-fucking-Franklin, then at least I had Irvine to yell at.

'I-it's o-okay, you kn-kn-kn–'

'I know,' I said to him, placing my hand on his massive arm. 'I know.'

One rainy afternoon, I chose not to call the newspaper. Instead, I sat in my cell penning a complaint letter. It was three pages long. I wrote it out twice, sending one copy to the editor and one to Franklin. I knew it would be read by the prison stasi and redacted accordingly, but I didn't care. The article was a pack of lies and I wanted a full retraction.

A week later, and with still no word from my loving wife, I waited for the newspaper to be delivered to the recreation area. There it was at the top of the pile – the *Blackpool Telegraph*.

I scanned through the pages. There, on page twelve, was their response. On the left-hand page was extracts from my redacted letter, beneath it were suggestions as to what the blacked-out words might be. On the opposite page was an article penned by Teresa-fucking-Franklin with the heading – *Even Prison Doesn't Halt the Abuse*. The sub heading read: *Now, It's My Turn*. I threw the paper onto the floor and sunk my head into my hands.

What the hell is happening?

I later read the article with both fists clenched. My letter had presented her with the ideal opportunity to replay the previous piece using excerpts to justify her claims, or more accurately, the claims of my wife. Teresa-fucking-Franklin was not only a vindictive, lying bitch, she was also lazy.

I stopped calling my wife. I stopped calling the newspaper. In fact, I stopped doing anything. Irvine would tap me on the shoulder when it was gym time.

'C-c-c'mon m-man.' He said. 'I-it w-will do y–'

'You go on,' I would say. 'I'm not in the mood.'

He asked me that every day for a week. Then, on the eighth day, everything fell into place. I received a large padded envelope, thick with documents. I tipped the wad of papers onto my bed, reading the first page in detail. I speed-read the rest, I had plenty of time to pour over the details later. I got up, changed into shorts and trainers and went to the gym.

On the bed was a fat wad of misery, otherwise known as divorce papers. I dealt with it in the only way I knew how. I formulated another plan. That made three.

Chapter 24

Kray pulled half a bottle of wine from the door of the fridge and emptied the whole lot into a fishbowl of a glass. She shuffled into the lounge and collapsed on the sofa. The clock on the mantelpiece told her it was one-forty-five in the morning.

She glugged at the wine like a runner drinks water. It felt good. It washed away the taste of death that had lodged itself at the back of her throat.

She had arrived at Franklin's house to be met by a wall of uniformed officers, all of them busying themselves securing the crime scene and holding back the prying eyes of nosey neighbours. Franklin's boss, a man by the name of Gerald Hopwood, was sat half-in and half-out of a squad car. His arse was in the car, but his body was bent forward at the waist, trying not to vomit onto his shoes for the third time that evening. Now, every time he wretched, nothing came out.

Kray had questioned him and found that he had been expecting Franklin to email him an article that she had written in time for it to go to print. She had failed to meet the deadline, so Hopwood had called both her mobile and house phone but had got no response. He was furious. He had made it clear how important it was to hit the publishing window, and she'd missed it.

Having called until his fingers hurt, he had jumped into his car and drove to her house with the intention of giving her a royal bollocking. The house lights were on, and her car was parked in the drive, but she had failed to answer the door. He opened her letter box to shout for her to let him in. It was then that he saw her naked body hanging upside down at the bottom of the stairs.

Her translucent face stared back at him through ruptured eyes with a gingham tea towel rammed into her mouth. That was his first vomit of the evening.

Kray chugged back more wine and stared into the middle distance, feeling like she'd been run over by a bus. To top it all, in the middle of checking out the body, Quade had called demanding to know why the press statement was not on her desk or waiting in her inbox. Kray responded with a 'I'm busy right now ma'am,' and hung up. She ignored the next three calls.

Kray had called Quade back at one-thirty am and woke her up. Quade stopped dead in her tracks when she heard what she had to say.

Kray brought the conversation to a close by saying, 'So, you might want to re-think what that press release is going to say, ma'am.' Kray took the silence at the other end of the line as tacit agreement. Her last action of the day was to make a call to the mortuary, and she was done.

Kray slurped the last of the wine and curled up on the sofa, dragging a blanket over her. Within minutes, she was sound asleep.

The radio alarm went off upstairs announcing the six am news. Kray stretched her arms and legs and rolled off the sofa. She padded into the kitchen, flicked on the kettle and headed for the shower. It was going to be a long day.

The traffic was light on her drive into work, and she was drawing down her second cigarette of the morning, sitting in the smoking shelter outside the station when Brownlow appeared.

'You found a connection, then?' he asked.

'Yes, Colin, we did, but more importantly we found Chapman's body.' Kray flicked the cigarette butt in his direction. It bounced off the ground and landed on his shoe.

'Look, Roz, I was angry and frustrated yesterday, I didn't mean—'

'Save it for the briefing, Colin, then you can explain to everyone why *you* found fuck all. Oh, and I've invited Quade. Should be fun.'

Brownlow looked like he'd shit his pants.

Upstairs, officers had started to congregate for the seven-thirty prayers. They took their seats holding coffees and notepads. This was high profile stuff and no one wanted to be late.

Kray joined them with a 'Good morning everyone,' and was pleasantly surprised with the positive reaction. Then, she realised ACC Quade had walked in behind her.

'Morning,' Quade said, waddling to the front of the room. Kray stood next to her.

'Morning, ma'am.'

'Roz. You okay this morning?'

'Didn't get much sleep last night, but other than that, yeah, I'm okay.'

'This is big.'

'Yes, ma'am, all the more reason to get it right.'

'DCI Jackson always gave the killer a nickname. Have you thought of one for this case?'

'No, ma'am, I haven't. With all due respect, I think it's the role of the gutter press to put labels onto vicious killers. It's our role to catch them. Just a thought.'

'Yes, you're right, of course.' Quade dropped the topic.

Brownlow sloped in and took a seat at the back of the room. Quade clocked him.

'I think we have a full house, so let's make a start,' Kray called out. 'Colin, if you could kick us off.'

Oops, there he goes again, shitting his pants.

Kray took her seat and, for the next ten minutes, proceeded to laugh her tits off – on the inside, of course.

Brownlow shuffled and fidgeted out front, trying to make one and a half days of shoddy policing sound like a weeks' work. His briefing contained nothing that could not have been uncovered by a rookie recruit using a laptop, an internet connection and a phone. Quade sat with her *unimpressed* look smeared across her face.

Brownlow didn't so much bring his briefing to a conclusion, rather he ground it to a halt. He kind of ran out of words. Kray was loving the awkwardness.

'Okay, let's open it up for questions,' Quade said, keen to maintain momentum. Officers and detectives bombarded Brownlow with a series of predictable questions, the majority to which Brownlow offered a stock response: 'We haven't got that far in the investigation.' It was plain to everyone in the room that DI Brownlow hadn't got very far at all. Brownlow looked over at Kray. It was her turn next.

Kray remained in her seat, sipping her lukewarm coffee. She had no intention of rescuing the little shit. *That will teach you to walk away from me.* She watched him drown. Eventually, the entertainment came to an end with Quade now wearing her *seriously fucked off* face, and Kray took the front.

She talked them through each of the murders, focussing on the ritual. She went on to explain the children's rhyme and how that had led her to finding the second body.

'If the killer is going to follow through the same pattern, then it is safe to assume that he has two more victims lined up.'

A hand shot up in the audience, a burly man with a cropped-top haircut. 'Could it be a co-incidence, Roz? I mean, I understand how the verses in the rhyme can be interpreted to describe the victims but we could be making connections that aren't there.'

'We could, I agree. I've put a call into the mortuary to get some early post-mortem results.' Kray's briefing was thorough with few questions at the end. Kray eased into more practical matters, forming the group into teams and allocating tasking orders for the day.

'There will be something that connects the victims. Go find it,' was her closing remark.

The briefing broke up and people began chatting in their teams. Brownlow looked like he had lost his way to the gent's toilet, flitting from one group to another trying to avoid the piercing gaze of ACC Quade. Eventually, Quade could take the charade no longer and called him over, marching him outside. Brownlow didn't come back.

There was a rap on the door and the face of Dr Chris Millican appeared. Kray wandered over.

'This is a surprise. Are you lost?' she asked.

He cracked a smile and ran his fingers through his fringe. 'No, I thought I'd deliver the info you asked for personally.'

He was wearing the same waistcoat and tight suit trouser combo that had caught her attention a few days previously. Kray kept her gaze firmly focused above the waistline.

'Bloody hell, you must be a busy guy if you do this for all your customers.' Kray ushered him across the hallway into her office and immediately regretted it. 'Please excuse the mess. Things are a bit hectic at the moment.'

Millican looked around at the neat piles of paper and clear desk. 'You're joking, right? It looks like no one works here.'

'What do you have for me?'

'The results you wanted.'

He handed over a sheet of paper. Kray scanned it quickly before casting her eyes to the ceiling.

'Bad news?' he asked.

'It is bad, but I was fully expecting it. Thanks for this.' She held the printout in the air. 'I have to get back in there.'

'Before you go,' Millican said, again sweeping his hand across his fringe. 'I wondered if you liked wine?'

'Do I like wine? I sometimes think it's the only thing that keeps me going.'

He shuffled on the spot, looking down at his feet.

'Only I wondered if you fancied having a glass of wine with me after work one day?' Kray looked into his smiling eyes, the words drying up in her mouth. 'I know a quiet little place not far from here that has the best wine cellar around.'

Kray regained control of her voice. 'Umm, I don't know what to say. I mean…' She spun the wedding ring around on her finger.

'I took the liberty of asking a couple of questions, so I know about your husband and what happened. I hope you don't mind?' He gave her that smile again, the one that reminded her so much of Joe.

'No, no, I don't mind. It's just that…your timing could be better.'

'Look, I understand, I just thought that if you fancied a wind-down drink at the end of the day… They do a sensational Chablis.'

Kray fiddled with her wedding ring. 'I need to get back to the briefing.'

'Okay.' Millican had his hand on the doorframe, already on his way out. 'If you do fancy trying that Chablis, you know where I am.'

'Thanks.' Kray held up the test results paper again and watched his pert bottom disappear down the corridor.

'See you!' he turned and called over his shoulder.

He caught me looking again! What the fuck is wrong with me?

Kray had to collect herself before going back into the incident room. That had taken her completely off balance. She was flattered and embarrassed in equal measure.

Her head was whirring - *It would make a nice change to do something different after work. And besides it's only… Get a fucking grip, woman, you got work to do!*

Kray stormed back into the incident room.

'Listen up, everyone, can I have your attention?' The noise in the room subsided as Kray made her way to the front. 'I have the results from the lab. They have analysed the stomach contents of last night's victim, Teresa Franklin, and she ate something shortly before she was killed. It had not had time to break down in her stomach.'

The room fell deathly silent.

'Do we win a prize if we guess what it was?' asked one of the team.

'The lab confirmed…it was roast beef.'

Chapter 25

I wake with a jolt. My nose is inches from the wall, and for a split second, I am back in prison and the events of the past week have been a dream. Then, I glance up and see the lampshade hanging from the ceiling. We didn't have lamp shades in jail. I breathe easy.

It's Thursday, I quite like Thursdays.

I roll over and glance at the clock. *Shit, look at the time!* It never occurred to me to set an alarm, I'm always awake around seven am. It's gone nine o'clock, and I'm working the ten-to-two shift today. I feel sluggish, despite just having the sleep of the dead. I have a pain lodged behind my eyes and my joints creak.

I hurry out of bed and straighten the quilt, tucking it under my pillows. A quick shower and an even quicker coffee and I'm down the stairs and out the front of the shop. My car is waiting, and the seats are cold as I get in and start the engine. The roads are pretty empty. It's too early in the day for the throngs of ogling tourists.

When I drive out of town, it begins to rain. My head is foggy but there is a flicker of after-glow from the thrill of yesterday. Watching that bitch bleed out was a lovely moment. I managed not to over-do it with the electricity this time which made it all the more enjoyable. She was conscious enough to understand what was happening. Her eyes caught sight of the blood pouring, then the pain kicked in when she realised it was coming from her neck. She didn't last long after that.

Shit, my tablets! I snap out of my thoughts when I remember that in my haste this morning I'd forgotten my pills. I spend the rest of the journey berating myself for my stupidity.

The car park is almost full as I pull up and run across the tarmac to get out of the rain. I go through my usual routine of clocking in and changing into my work gear. I deposit my latest treasure in a safe place and set off through the boning hall. The band-saws have not yet screamed into action and my ears are grateful for the relative silence.

At the back of the factory, I push through a metal door into my workspace and check the temperature on the tank. It reads sixty degrees Celsius. Perfect. I check the PH value of the liquor. That says eleven. Spot on. My work stations are ready to start the day, now all I'm missing is Cloe.

I can hear my customers arriving at goods-in and the clank of the trailer doors opening. Cloe bustles into the room, all hot and flustered. In a factory where everyone is either white or male, she is a novelty. The only black woman in the place, though maybe novelty is not the correct way to describe her. She is the female equivalent of Irvine, except maybe less attractive, and like Irvine she will probably say less than half a dozen words for the next seven hours of our shift.

She gives me a good morning wave of her hand and I wave back. That's the morning greeting out of the way.

I hear the conveyor start up, won't be long now. Cloe moves into position, ready to accept our first guest. The door in the wall opens up and the first pig swings in. Cloe takes hold of a front trotter and guides it over to the twelve feet long stainless-steel tank. I open up the hinged lid that runs along its length and a burst of steam rises up to the roof. The hog drops down and Cloe tugs at the front leg so the body of the pig lands length ways into the tank. I unhook its back leg from the chain and close the lid, pressing the green button on the control panel on the wall.

The whole contraption lurches into life. The rubber paddles running inside the full length of the tank spin round and round, rotating the pig in the hot water. I can time six minutes in my head to the second; I don't need to hear the buzzer to tell me time is up. After the allotted time, the machine stops and I lift the lid.

Another plume of steam clogs the air. Cloe wheels a metal table up to the mouth of the tank and presses a button. Eight levers lift the pig out of the water. I grab one leg, and Cloe grabs another, and we slide the animal out onto the trolley. It's like trying to keep a bar of wet soap on a wet metal coaster. The hog slips and slides on the polished surface. I close the lid on the tank.

The pig is hot and steaming and covered in a white scum, which is a mixture of hair and skin from the tank. Cloe washes it off with a cold-water hose. While she is doing that, I take a hooked blade and remove the toe nails from the hooves. Then, we both set to work with our knives, scraping fast because the next one will be with us any minute. We scrape the blades across the surface removing the last remnants of loose skin and hair. The flesh beneath is creamy white. It never ceases to amaze me how much it resembles human skin. The difference is, when I do it, human skin comes away under the pressure of my knife.

We flip the pig over and clean the other side. Then, I stick hooks through the tendons of the back legs and a second chain conveyor lifts the pig clear of the table and through a gap in the wall to the bunging and evisceration stage. I'm glad I don't work there. I'm a little squeamish about that kind of thing.

At noon, we take a break in the canteen. It serves hot food at all times of the day, needless to say, one of the options on the menu is always pork. It's cheap, and the food is good quality, but I always choose a sandwich or a bowl of soup. I will be eating a full Chinese takeaway again tonight, and if I'm not careful, I will be the size of a house.

I sit on my own before Cloe joins me. She nods and tucks into plate of food big enough to feed two people. I'm sure this is her main meal of the day. She doesn't say anything and neither do I. it's just like being back in prison.

The activity of the morning has helped to shake off my black mood and my headache has passed, though my hands keep going numb. I finish my sandwich and watch as Cloe carves her way through her meal. Memories come flooding back. I try to fight them off but they are too strong.

I give in, and with nothing better to do, I sink into another daydream.

My pathological hatred of the *Telegraph* and Teresa-fucking-Franklin, with her fluorescent coloured hair and pantomime glasses, continued unabated. I counted down the days until the next issue landed on the desk in the recreational area. I would pounce on it. tearing through the pages to reach page twelve. Her head and shoulders by-line picture glared at me from the top corner of the article.

Once the newspaper was discarded, I would cut out her column and keep them in my cell. Other inmates thought I had the hots for her. Nothing could be further from the truth. I wanted to fuck her, alright, but not in that way.

It was Thursday morning and I was waiting for the delivery to arrive. It was late and my anxiety was going through the roof. Had the bitch written another pack of lies about me or was it the turn of some other poor unfortunate to be in her firing line? Postman Pat arrived with his trolley.

'Here you go,' he said, being well used to me snatching it out of his hand.

I flicked through until I found her face goading me to do something to stop her. The page was headlined: *Local Businessman Takes 10 Pieces of Silver* and underneath was written: *Local Tradesmen cast onto the Scrapheap*. To my astonishment, the face of my ex-partner, John Graham, stared out at me from the page.

I scanned the article and it failed to sink in. I read it again and the cogs began to whir. I re-read it and my blood boiled over.

The article reported how Graham had sold the business to Brixton Construction, but, more than that, he had sold the plot of land that the business had occupied to one of those low-cost supermarkets. The article berated him for driving his loyal workforce out of a job. It quoted numerous tales of woe from the workers, each one saying how they would not be able to keep a roof over their head now they were out of work. Graham tried to defend himself, bleating on about how he had kept the workforce on as long as he could and had delayed accepting the offer from the supermarket. Oh, the social tragedy of it all.

The slant put on the story by the sensationalist Franklin was "fat cat boss sells out and to hell with the consequences". She tore Graham to shreds. But I couldn't have cared less about that; my attention was transfixed by a date in the article. The date they had made Graham the offer.

'He knew,' I said to myself. 'The fucker knew all along.'

The bastard knew three weeks before he forced me into signing the documents selling my share of the business for a pittance. He knew about the deal way before I went to see him. The fucker sold me out.

The paper carried a photograph of Graham standing at the gates of a huge house, probably taken when the journalist arrived at his new home, door-stepping him for a comment. He had obviously grown out of his three-bed semi. Under the picture the caption read: *This is what not caring looks like.*

The fucker stitched me up. Now, I had someone else to hate.

Plan number four was hatching in my brain.

While I was developing my new plan, Irvine was developing a problem of his own, and his name was prison officer Cyril Jenks. A fat, BO-ridden, shit-bag of a man nearing retirement who had taken a dislike to Irvine. Cyril was a classic school yard bully who doled out his barbed asides to those who were unable to retaliate.

Once Jenks had discovered Irvine's speech impediment, he rode him whenever he had the chance.

'Hey, Irvine, how are you today?' Jenks would say. Irvine did not want to engage and would try to avoid him. 'Don't walk off, Irvine, when I'm being friendly. I said, how are you?'

'O-o-o–'

'Come on, Irvine, spit it out, man. How are you?'

'I-I'm f-f–'

'Come on, Irvine, I've not got all day.'

'I-I–'

'For Christ's sake, Irvine, I give up. I try to be nice and you throw it back in my face.' Jenks would walk off shaking his head and laughing. Every time I saw the two of them together, I held my breath. *Any minute now, Jenks is going to be flying off the landing into the suicide net.* A number of times I had wandered over to rescue Irvine but Jenks continued regardless, completely ignoring my presence.

One day, Irvine burst into the cell behaving like the incredible hulk. He slammed his fists down onto the top bunk and the whole frame bounced off the floor.

'Wow, wow!' I tried to stop him destroying the furniture. It was like wrestling with a grizzly bear.

'T-t-that f-f-fucking Je-Je-' I managed to calm him down and sat him on the bottom bunk.

'Steady, Irvine, don't let him win. This is what he wants. He's winding you up.'

'I-I'm g-g-gonna fu …' He didn't bother with the rest of the words; it was pretty obvious what he was going to do to Jenks. His whole body shook with rage.

I reached across, took a toothbrush from the sink and knelt down in front of him.

'You trust me don't you, Irvine?' I said to him.

'Y-y-ye …' He nodded.

I held the toothbrush sideways and brought it slowly towards Irvine's face. He flinched away from me.

'It's okay, Irvine, trust me.' I moved it near his mouth. 'Bite down onto the toothbrush.' I said. Irvine's eyes said it all. He tilted his head forward and took it between his front teeth. I let go.

'W-what the f-fuck are you doing?' he asked, and almost fell off the bed.

My father had told me long ago about the trick with the toothbrush, though, in his case, it was a lollypop stick. He too had a dreadful speech impediment when he was a youngster and couldn't string two words together. He sang in a church choir and never stammered when he sang. The choir master got him to bite on the lolly stick one day, and the stammer went away. He said it had something to do with occupying the brain with doing something else. Whatever the science, it worked and in time, the problem went away.

From then on, every day, Irvine and I practiced speech exercises. I had seen the film *The Kings Speech* and researched different techniques using books we ordered from the library. We focused on breathing, rehearsed reading out loud in front of the mirror, I even got Irvine to practice singing while speaking and of course we carried out the toothbrush trick daily. We tried to identify which letters caused Irvine the most trouble so we could develop coping strategies to avoid them. This was less successful because it soon transpired he had trouble with all twenty-six.

Over time, he improved. We got our first real breakthrough when one day, Irvine stubbed his toe against the bed.

'Fuck!' he yelled, holding onto his throbbing foot. He cried when he realised what had just happened. "Fuck" became one of Irvine's favourite warm-up words.

He continued to be a target, as far as Jenks was concerned, and still got flustered when faced with the sadistic bastard, but at least now I was less concerned Irvine would hurl Jenks over the rail. Every day we would practise, and every day, Irvine would slap his massive hand on my shoulder and say, 'I-I owe you b-big time.'

And every day, I believed him.

Chapter 26

Kray had watched as the evidence boards filled up. Brownlow had been given the task of pulling together the information from the Nigel Chapman investigation, which, due to his bone idleness, had not taken long. However, the team who were now assigned to digging around into Chapman's life were being kept very busy. He was a flamboyant character who led an equally flamboyant lifestyle, and the social media material alone spilled onto a second board.

The profiles of Graham and Franklin were growing by the minute as new material was uncovered.

'She is a nasty piece of work,' said a young detective called Janice Parks as she read through the newspaper articles written by Franklin. 'A one woman wrecking ball. Any one of these people would have good reason to see her dead.'

Kray returned to her office with a dreadful sinking feeling to confront her ever expanding in-tray. *What the hell does half this have to do with law enforcement?*

Before she had chance to make a start, Tavener appeared at the door. 'Fancy a run out?'

'Anything to get me away from this lot. What is it?'

'John Graham had a business partner and the relationship turned sour when John bought him out of his share in the company. The partner assaulted Graham at his home and did a spell in prison. He was released from jail and lives here in town. I think he would be a good place to start.'

'What's his name?'

'Kevin Palmer.'

Tavener rapped his knuckles against the wood.

'Softly, softly with this, remember?' Kray whispered. Tavener nodded – message received. Palmer opened his front door. Kray stood in the doorway with her warrant card in her hand.

'Mr Palmer? I'm Acting DCI Kray. This is DC Tavener, can we come in? We have a couple of questions for you.'

Palmer looked down at Kray's card and then up into the face of the towering figure standing behind her. He took the wallet from her hand and examined it.

It's about time.

'Do you have a warrant, Acting DCI Kray?' The comment took her by surprise. Palmer paused for dramatic effect. 'Only kidding. Please come in, I've been expecting you.'

Tavener flashed a quizzical glance at Kray as they stepped inside.

Palmer gestured to the sofa and switched off the TV. 'Please take a seat. How can I help?' He sat in the armchair opposite, leaning forward resting his elbows on his knees. 'Who let you in downstairs?'

'Sorry?' asked Kray.

'Who let you in?'

'Oh, it was a woman, I didn't catch her name.'

'Chinese or English?'

'She was Chinese.'

'That will be Sunshine, Joseph's mum, she's lovely but her English isn't great.'

'Sunshine?' asked Tavener.

'Yes, when the family came to Britain, they chose what they wanted to be called. She liked the sound of the word sunshine, so adopted that as her English name. It's a common practice amongst the Chinese community. I know a lady called Purple and another called Rainbow.'

'That's all very interesting, Mr Palmer.' Kray had obviously heard enough cultural integration stories for one day. 'Why have you been expecting us?'

'It doesn't take a genius. I read the newspapers, Rosalind, or is it Roz?' Kray ignored the question. 'Anyway, I understand that John Graham was found murdered at his home. I was his business partner, so it makes sense that sooner or later you would come knocking.'

'When was the last time you saw him?'

'Oh, that would be the fateful evening when he swindled me out of my share of the business. I don't recall the precise date. It was a long time ago. But it will be in your records, I'm sure.'

'Is that the evening you assaulted Mr Graham?'

'That depends.'

'On what?'

'On who's side of the story you believe. He maintained that I hit him and pushed him to the floor. I told the court that the silly sod tripped over his own feet and ended up on the carpet. So, I suppose, who you believe is up to you.'

'But it was the night when you were arrested.'

'Yes, it was.'

'What was your relationship like before?'

'When we were working together, it was good. We argued over the direction the business should take, I wanted us to expand into bigger contracts but John was dead against it. But other than that, we got on well.'

'That was until he bought your share of the company.'

'I saw red when I realised he was taking advantage of my situation. Not sure I was particularly rational at the time, there was a lot of other stuff kicking off in my life.'

Kray looked across at Tavener. 'Where were you on the night of Monday sixteenth of October?' he asked.

'Mmm, not sure. Do you mind?' Palmer got up and walked into the bedroom. He came back with a thin diary in his hand. 'I use this to keep track of my shifts at work. I work for Sandringham Products and they have a weird shift rota. I have a memory like a sieve these days.' He flicked over the pages. 'Here we go, I worked earlies that day so got back here around three p.m. I normally have a sleep for an hour or two when I get back – not sure what I did after that but in the evening, I would have been here. I stay in at the start of the week, save a bit of cash that way.'

'Were you with anyone? Can anybody vouch for your whereabouts?'

'I was here on my own, watching TV.'

'So, there is no one who can confirm you were here.'

'I would have spoken to Joseph or his wife. They run the takeaway downstairs and I treat it as my very own built-in restaurant. I would have ordered chicken chow mein at around six o'clock. I always have chicken chow mein on a Monday and I stick around for a chat while they prepare it. They are a lovely family and boy do they cook a mean Chinese meal.'

'We will talk to Joseph, that's helpful.' Kray stepped in. 'But that will only account for you being in the flat at around six pm.'

'Yes, that's right, but the question you need to ask Joseph is… did he see me leave after that time?'

'Why would I ask him that?'

'Because there is one way into the building and one way out, and that takes you right through the front of the shop. If I had left that evening, he would have seen me.'

Kray flashed a glance at Tavener. She spun her wedding ring round and round on her finger. 'There must be a back entrance?'

'There is, but to access that you need to go through the kitchens at the rear, and you can only access that from the front of the shop. The same way you two got in. So, you see, if I had left, they would have seen me. Ask them, I'm sure they will be able to confirm that I was here all night.'

'What time do they close?'

'They have a late licence which allows them to stay open until two am, but more often than not, there is still a queue outside the door at that time of night.'

'Do you mind if we take a look around?'

'Do you have a warrant?' Kray looked at Palmer. The joke wasn't funny the first time. 'Of course, if you excuse the mess, help yourselves.'

Kray and Tavener got up and headed for the bedroom. It was smaller than the lounge with a single bed in one corner and a wardrobe in the other. A four-drawer cabinet completed the complement of furniture. The walls were white and a couple of cheap pictures broke up the boredom. There was no window.

The bathroom was off to the left. It consisted of a toilet, a sink and a shower. There was no bath, mainly because there was no room. A mirror fronted cabinet hung on the wall. A narrow, frosted glass window about a foot wide and two feet high was set into the back wall. Kray checked it out; the window was a solid piece of double glazing and didn't open.

They walked back into the lounge to find Palmer standing at the kitchenette filling a kettle.

'Do you want tea or coffee? I was going to make myself a hot drink.'

'No thank you.'

'Do you have any further questions?' Palmer asked.

'Not at this stage. We will be in touch.'

Palmer showed them out onto the landing and watched them go downstairs. He returned to the kitchen area and poured the boiling water on top of the coffee grains, giving it a stir.

'That went rather well, I think,' he whispered to himself.

Outside, Kray and Tavener sat in their car.

'Cocky little shit,' said Tavener.

'No. No, it wasn't cockiness. It was more like a quiet confidence.'

'Seemed fucking cocky to me. I'll go talk to Joseph, see what he says about the night Graham died.'

Kray had drifted off, staring into the middle distance. The scar on her cheek began to tingle as she gawked out of the windscreen.

'Roz, Roz!' Tavener broke her train of thought. 'I said—'

'Yes, go chat to him, but I'm sure he will confirm Palmer's story.'

'How can you be so sure?'

'I'm not, but Palmer is.'

Chapter 27

Kray dropped Tavener off at the station. The conversation with Palmer had set alarm bells ringing; the scars running across her body told her something wasn't right. There were too many things about this case that were sending her off the scale.

She headed to the industrial estate on the outskirts of town and pulled into a visitor's parking space at the front of a chrome and plate glass office block. She stepped out and walked the twenty feet to reception, the automatic doors whooshing open to welcome her.

The same glamorous receptionist greeted her with a 'Good afternoon, how can I help?' Her name badge read Dina Birchwood. Kray marvelled at her perfect makeup and perfect hair, recalling what she had looked like in the hallway mirror when she had left for work that morning. *God only knows what I must look like now, cos it wasn't good then.*

'My name is DI Kray. I need to speak with David Walsh.' She opened her wallet to reveal her warrant card, forgetting she was now acting DCI.

Dina nodded and picked up the phone. 'I have a DI Kray here in reception, David, she wants to speak with you.' Kray could hear the tinny voice protesting on the other end. The corner of Dina's mouth curled down and she cupped her hand over the phone. 'I'm afraid Mr Walsh is tied up at the moment. He's asking if it would be okay if he gives you a call when he's free?'

Kray leaned over the desk and took the phone from Dina's manicured fingers.

'We can do this down the station if you would prefer, Mr Walsh?' She heard a sharp intake of breath at the other end.

'No, no, I will come down.' Walsh blurted out.

'Now would be good.' The line went dead. Kray handed the receiver back to Dina whose mouth had now returned to its beautifully symmetrical self.

'If you would like to take a seat?'

'No, I'm fine right here.'

Dina pushed papers around to occupy herself. 'Terrible news about Nigel,' she said eventually.

'Did you know him?'

'A little. I said good morning to him and sometimes filled in when Debbie wasn't in.'

'Is she away from work a lot?'

'She pretty much comes and goes as he pleased, but then, she was…well, you know.'

'No, I don't know, but I can guess. How long had they been an item?'

'On and off about a year, I guess.'

'More on than off, or is it …?'

'Let's just say they were not exclusive.'

Not exclusive? Since when did that become an actual thing?

The lift doors behind reception dinged open and out bustled David Walsh. He came over and shook Kray's hand.

'Sorry about that. We are all at sixes and sevens this morning.'

'I can appreciate this is a difficult time. Is there somewhere we can talk?'

'Yes, sure.' Walsh waved his arm, pointing to a small glass-fronted office to the right of reception. 'Please take a seat,' he said, pulling a chair away from the small round table for Kray to sit in and pushing the door shut. He took the seat opposite, spinning his cufflinks round and round.

'How are you feeling?' asked Kray.

'Not good, if I'm honest. I've never seen anything like that before. I crunch numbers and make deals for a living not...' his words tailed off to nothing.

'It is a shock. I can assure you we have every available person working on this.'

Walsh didn't look the least bit re-assured. 'You wanted to ask me some questions?'

'Yes, when we spoke yesterday, I got the distinct impression you weren't telling me the full story. You were holding something back.'

Walsh's cufflinks were a blur. 'I don't know what you mean.' He looked into his lap.

'What is it you're not telling me, Mr Walsh?'

An hour and a half later, Kray pushed open the door to the incident room to be met by a wall of sound. The only person lacking any sort of positivity was DI Brownlow, who was sitting at a desktop terminal staring out of the window.

Officers were standing at the boards, deep in discussion, while others were talking on the phone. Tavener was looking over the shoulder of DC Janice Parks, staring at a computer screen.

'Gotcha!' he called out, hurrying over to the printer. Two pieces of paper spooled out into his waiting hand. He noticed Kray and waved them in the air.

'Listen up, everyone. Janice has found a link between John Graham and Teresa Franklin.' Parks took the printouts from his hand and pinned them to the notice board.

'Franklin writes a shock column for the *Telegraph*,' she said. 'This woman does not pull her punches and her articles are scathing. In February of this year, she wrote a piece about domestic abuse and followed that up with a second feature when the man named in the first article wrote to the paper disputing her claims. That man was Kevin Palmer, the same man who was in business with John Graham.'

She jabbed her finger at his name on the board. 'Palmer is on our system and has a history of violence. He was involved in a domestic dispute with his wife when she accused him of breaking into the family home, causing her to flee to a neighbour's house for safety. Shortly before that, he burned a woman by tipping coffee over her, though she didn't press charges. Then, he assaulted John Graham in a row over selling his share of the business for which he received a fifteen-month custodial sentence. While he is in jail, Franklin wrote the articles about him with the help of his wife Sadie. He has connections to both.'

'Good work,' Kray said, making her way to the front, standing next to Parks.

'We need to find something that connects Palmer to Chapman, and we'll be cooking on gas,' a tall man with a porn-star moustache said from the back of the room.

Kray cleared her throat. 'I've just had a meeting with David Walsh who is the Commercial Director for Brixton Construction the company owned by Nigel Chapman. He told me that Chapman had an affair with Sadie Palmer – Kevin Palmer's wife.' The room fell silent. 'The affair fizzled out, but it wrecked their marriage, and she filed for divorce while Palmer was serving time in prison. We have our connection. The same name crops up in all three.' Kray looked across at Tavener hunched over a desktop computer. 'We need to bring our friend in for a chat.'

'Roz…there's something else,' said Tavener.

'What?'

'When we spoke to Palmer earlier today, he said he worked for Sandringham Products.'

'Yes, I remember.'

'Sandringham Products is an abattoir. They slaughter pigs.'

Chapter 28

'For the purposes of the recording, I am Acting DCI Kray, also present is DC Tavener. You have not been arrested, Mr Palmer, however you are under caution – do you understand?'

'I do.' Palmer said.

'You have also waved your right to legal representation.'

'I don't a lawyer because I haven't done anything wrong.'

All three were sat in an interview room. Tavener was opposite Palmer with Kray to his left. Palmer sat calmly with his hands folded one on top of the other on the desk.

'We have questions to ask you relating to an ongoing investigation. Do you understand?' Kray continued.

'I understand,' Palmer replied. 'I didn't think you were very thorough this morning, so I've been expecting a return visit. Though, I was not prepared for it to be this formal.'

Kray ignored the comment. 'How do you know Nigel Chapman?' she asked.

'Wow! That's a blast from the past. I thought you were going to ask me about poor old John.'

'Can you answer the question, Kevin?' said Tavener.

'It's a short answer, Detective. We did business with him and he stole my wife. They had an affair and that was the end of my marriage. New Year's Eve to be precise, the night of the Chamber of Commerce dinner dance.'

'What happened?' Kray asked.

'He had the hots for her, she had the hots for him…do I need to draw you a diagram?'

'What did you do?'

'What could I do? I tried to patch things up between us but Sadie didn't want me in her life anymore. She threw me out, stopped me seeing the kids. Even when I heard they were no longer together, she didn't want to know me.'

'Did you confront them about the affair?'

'I did, but they just laughed.'

'That must have made you very angry.'

'It did, but there was nothing I could do about it. She held all the cards. She had the law on her side, the solicitor on her side, our friends on her side and even turned the kids against me. Why are you asking me about Chapman?'

'When was the last time you saw him?'

'I don't remember the date, but I do remember it was a week day. He'd just finished fucking my wife when I caught them in bed together.'

'What happened next?'

'That's when they laughed at me.'

'Where were you on Monday the ninth of October?'

'Christ, I have no idea. If I knew you wanted to talk dates I would have brought along my diary. Now, let me see…' Palmer struck a theatrical pose stroking his chin, deep in thought. 'If it was a Monday, then I was probably doing exactly the same as I did last Monday. I must have gone to work, got home, had a nap and then ate dinner in my flat watching TV. I told you this already. I have a set routine for the start of the week.'

'Would the owners of the takeaway be able to vouch for you?'

'I expect so. Did you talk to them about last Monday?'

Kray ignored the question. Frustratingly, when Tavener had questioned Joseph Woo, he had confirmed Palmer's story.

'How do you know Teresa Franklin?'

'Shit! What is this?'

'How do you know Teresa Franklin?' Kray repeated the question.

'I don't know her, but I know *of* her. She was the bitch reporter who wrote the articles about me in the *Telegraph* when I was inside. My darling wife told a pack of lies and that fucking woman printed it. I tried to lodge a formal complaint with the paper and she fucking wrote about that too.'

'You were angry towards her.'

'Angry! No, Acting DCI Kray, angry is not a strong enough word.'

'Did you want to harm her?'

'I'm not going to be so stupid as to answer yes to that question, now am I?'

Kray and Tavener exchanged glances.

'But you were angry?'

'It was more like…incandescent rage.'

'When was the last time you saw her?'

'I've never seen her. I only know what she looks like because she has her face plastered over her column in the paper. When I came out of prison the last thing I wanted to do was go back inside, so I thought it best to avoid her like the plague. Why are you dragging all this up? I thought you wanted to talk about John?'

'Where were you at six o'clock last night?'

'Now that one I do know. I was in bed asleep. I came home from work around four-thirty in the afternoon feeling absolutely knackered. I spoke to Joseph and his wife when I got in, pottered around the flat for a while, before heading off to bed. The takeaway was particularly noisy that evening and it woke me up at about seven-thirty. I went downstairs to get dinner and Anabel insisted I have it for free to say sorry. What is going on? Why are you—'

'Did you leave the flat at any time?' Kray interrupted.

Palmer said nothing. Kray spun her wedding ring around on her finger, watching his every movement.

'Something has happened to them, hasn't it?' Palmer said. 'You came around this morning asking about John, and I know he's dead. Now, you are asking me the same questions about Chapman and that bloody journalist woman. Are they dead too?'

'Did you leave the flat after you got back at four-thirty?'

'Fucking hell, someone has murdered them as well. And you think–'

'Did you leave the flat at all last night, Mr Palmer, answer the question.'

'No. No, I didn't leave the flat.' Palmer sat back in his chair and folded his arms across his chest. 'Well, I'll be damned.' He started to chuckle to himself. 'Graham, Chapman and Franklin all dead. My favourite people in the whole wide world – all dead.' He threw his head back and laughed. 'I tell you what, Acting DCI Kray, you certainly know how to give a guy a lift.'

'We are not saying that, Kevin.'

'You don't have to. It's written all over your face. And you think I did it? You think I killed them.' Palmer laughed and shook his head. 'Priceless, bloody priceless. Simply because I am an ex-con, the logical conclusion is it must be me. That is lazy police work, very lazy.'

Tavener shifted uncomfortably in his seat. Kray leaned forward. 'This is a serious matter.'

Palmer held his hands out in front of him, palms up with his wrists together. 'It looks to me, Acting DCI Kray, that you have me bang to rights. Slap on the cuffs and let's be done with all this nonsense.'

'Kevin, your behaviour is not helping.'

'Acting DCI Kray, you will appreciate that since my epic decline I no longer move in the same social circles as Nigel Chapman. I have not seen him since he was enjoying the afterglow having screwed my wife in our marital bed. So, I'm unable to help you identify the person who killed him. I am, however, absolutely thrilled with the news that someone has murdered the marriage-wrecking bastard. Equally, I have not reacquainted myself with John Graham since he forced me to sign away my share of the business for a pittance and I was jailed for an assault which I did not commit. But I'm delighted to hear that the thieving twat is dead. And as for that fuckwit of a journalist being dead as well, I will get drunk for a week celebrating that one.'

Kray leaned forward. 'Do you think you're funny?'

'No, but I'll tell you what is funny, Acting DCI Kray. I have the perfect motive for killing all three but we would not be sitting here having this "dancing around the handbags" discussion if you had a scrap of evidence. If you did, I would have been arrested by now and sitting in one of your cells waiting to be charged. You have my fingerprints and DNA on record. The fact that I am here tells me you have nothing. You have all the motives you could ever need but no evidence. Now *that* is funny, don't you think, Acting DCI Kray?'

Kray sat back, saying nothing.

Palmer shook his head, 'I'm right, aren't I? My name has cropped up three times in your lines of inquiry, throw into the mix a spell in prison and…hey presto! The easy answer is, it must be the ex-con. Can I encourage you to speak with Joseph and Anabel again, they will confirm that I was at home?'

'We will, Mr Palmer, we will.' Kray rose from the table and nodded to Tavener. 'Interview terminated at seventeen ten.'

'Oh, don't stop now. I was just beginning to enjoy myself.' Palmer said.

Kray and Tavener trooped out, closing the door behind them.

'I said he was a cocky little shit.' Tavener said.

'He's playing us.'

'What do we do next?'

'Get the team together we need to re-focus.'

'Can I have a coffee?' Palmer called out. Tavener scuttled off and Kray went back into the interview room.

'We have more questions and will need to hold you for a while longer.'

'That's fine, be my guest. But I will have to call work to let them know I won't be in. I need to speak to my supervisor or it will be marked down as an unauthorised absence. You said I was allowed one phone call.' Palmer pulled his mobile from his pocket.

'Yes, you are, but I will make the call. What's the number?'

'Can I get a coffee?'

'What's the number?'

Palmer read out a series of digits and Kray punched them into her phone.

'What's his name?' Kray paused as the phone rang at the other end.

'Vinny Burke.'

'Oh, hi, am I speaking to Vinny Burke? … Good … This is Acting DCI Kray, I need to inform you that Kevin Palmer won't be in work today. He is helping us with our inquires.' She paused, allowing the person on the other end to respond. 'Yes, that's correct,' she added. 'Thank you.'

'Everything okay?' asked Palmer.

'Yes. He's got a hell of a stammer, your boss.'

'Do I get a coffee now?'

Chapter 29

I've been cooped up in this bloody interview room for hours and the excitement of the day is wearing thin. Officers keep popping their heads in to check on me but they don't hang around. My initial adrenaline rush has crashed. I have to keep reminding myself that this is all part of the plan but I'm struggling to keep focussed. My head is woozy and I ache.

I imagine Kray and her team as they race against the clock.

I can picture her, somewhere in the building, barking out her tin-pot commands. 'I want everyone working on Kevin Palmer. I want forensics evidence that places him at the scene or anything which blows a hole in his alibis. Let's work all the angles, develop new lines of inquiry. We have to make this count. Remember, there are another two victims out there. We need to find them before he has a chance to finish what he started.' I imagine them running around like children trying to please the teacher.

The door opens and Tavener walks in holding a piece of paper.

'I have a warrant here to search your flat and your car. It would be easier if we had the keys – though, if we don't, that won't be a problem.'

They're so predictable. For a second, I toy with the idea of not co-operating, to break the boredom and have some fun, but the implicit threat of having my front door hanging off its hinges is enough to have me reaching into my pocket.

'The car keys are on the table in the lounge. It's a–'

'Silver Ford Fiesta. Yes, we know.' He takes the flat key from my hand and scurries off, closing the door.

'Any chance of more coffee?' I call after him. No response.

I sit and stare at the blank walls. It reminds me of my cell, that featureless rectangular box barely big enough to swing a cat let alone being big enough to house two grown men. Especially when one had grown a damned sight bigger than the other. The daydreams kick in once again, and I'm transported back there.

My time in jail was coming to the end; I had two weeks to go.

'K-keep your h-head down,' Irvine said, 'Don't m-mess up.'

It was sound advice, because I actually felt myself relaxing as I neared the finish line.

Then, one Thursday afternoon, my whole world imploded.

I remember having a conversation with a man who was wearing green corduroy trousers. He looked like an old geography teacher of mine but with worse fashion sense, if that's at all possible. His hair was swept over his head to hide his baldness and his specs were perched on the end of his nose. I was so busy thinking, *Who the hell wears green corduroys these days?* that I missed his punchline. He delivered it and watched for my reaction. He was visibly put out by my dead pan expression.

'Erm, sorry, can you say that again?' I had asked, as much to break the awkward silence as anything else. He repeated himself, placing an exaggerated pronunciation on the words he considered important. I found myself drifting back to his trousers. *I mean, who the fuck wears…*

Then, I caught it. The key word which lay at the end of the sentence following his laboured explanation.

'Sorry, say that again.' I had asked him to repeat himself. He huffed and shuffled around in his well-worn seat.

There were more key words. Words that I had missed previously but which now had a stark resonance. Words that formed like a pillar of ice inside my body. I couldn't move.

Try as I might, my mouth would not respond. The questions racing around in my head had no way out. They ricocheted off my skull causing my brain to freeze. He took my silence and gaping look as a sign that I had once again failed to grasp the significance of what he was telling me.

He began his speech once more, but I held my hand up, and he stopped.

'You understand?' he said flipping his pen around his fingers.

I nodded.

He reached into his desk drawer and pulled out a bundle of leaflets, peeled one off and pressed it into my dead hand.

'It's all in here.'

And that was it.

He opened the door, and I wandered out, wondering what the hell had just happened. I didn't make it further than one of the plastic chairs in the waiting room. I slumped down, staring into the middle distance. I have no idea how long I sat there.

All I could think about were my plans. Every time I broke my train of thought to look around, a new set of faces gawped back at me. The nursing staff ignored the fact that I was there. The place was too busy. My plans spun together in a whirl of imagined activity. At some point, I made it back to my cell. I laid on my bed and stayed still for hours.

In the days that followed, the rage grew. It burned with a ferocity that I struggled to contain. Irvine wanted to know what the problem was, but I couldn't tell him. I couldn't seem to get my mouth to form the words.

The plans loomed dark. All those hours spent working out the intricate details. Each one played in my head like it was on fast forward, as one ended so another began – over and over.

Then, they stopped. My predicament came into sharp focus – it was obvious what I had to do. I now had five plans. One plan for each verse.

In that case, I may as well do it.

I told Irvine about my news and about my plans.

He listened, his mouth slightly ajar the whole time, before saying, 'I-I owe you b-big time.'

Chapter 30

Kray sat in her car at the head of the cul-de-sac, drumming her fingers against the steering wheel. An hour earlier, she had pulled the team together and re-focussed their activities into three priorities – find holes in Palmer's alibi, find forensic evidence to place him at the scene and identify anyone else potentially at risk. Two names leapt onto the board immediately; Sadie Palmer, or Raynor as she was known since getting divorced, and Vanessa Wilding, the solicitor Palmer had burned by tipping coffee into her lap.

They had to be the next victims. No one else fitted the profile. They were the two people to complete the rhyme, Kray was sure of it. They needed to speak to them fast.

Kray chose to handle Sadie Raynor herself.

The interview with Palmer continued to spin around in her head. There was something about it that sent her intuition into orbit. Here was a man who was being questioned about a murder. During the questioning, he works out that he is also being implicated in two other killings. The natural reaction would be to panic and fly into a rage of protestations and denial. Instead, he welcomes the assumption that they are dead and calmly tells Kray she has no evidence. He even takes the piss out of the police, goading her to react. No, there was something about Palmer that screamed fake.

Kray saw the white Volvo estate in her rear-view mirror as it drew into the close. It glided past and parked on the drive. The back doors flew open and a boy and girl, aged around ten and twelve, shot out of the car, swinging their school bags in their wake. Kray wondered which London fashion house catwalk Sadie

Raynor had just stepped off on her way back from the school gates. Her perfectly styled Marilyn Monroe hair appeared first from the car followed by a pair of white trousers that fitted where they touched, a red low-cut top and a pair of high heels completed the look. The heels were tall enough to make Kray appear of normal height.

She walked over and introduced herself. 'Hi, Sadie Raynor? I'm Acting DCI Roz Kray. We spoke on the phone.'

'Oh hi,' she replied with a downturn in her voice. 'Look, as I told you, I haven't seen Kevin in…I don't know how long, so I don't see how I can help.' She strode away towards the three-bed detached house.

'It's important I speak to you, Sadie.'

'Well, okay, if you must. Come inside where we can talk.' She stuck her key in the lock and the kids rushed past. 'Excuse the mess!' she called over her shoulder.

Kray entered the hallway and could hear the kids clomping around upstairs. She went into the lounge. *What mess?* Kray thought, looking at the show-home condition of the room. *This makes my place look untidy.*

'Take a seat,' said Raynor.

Kray did as she was told and sank into a floral-patterned armchair.

'It's always a rush to pick up Tom and Bea from school.' Raynor perched herself on the edge of the sofa.

'Have you come straight from work?'

'No, the gym. Well, it's more of a club, really.'

'Really?'

'You said you wanted to talk to me about Kevin,' she huffed.

'Yes. When was the last time you saw him?'

'I reckon that was at his sentencing hearing. Don't recall the date. I was sitting in the gallery and watched him being sent down. I've not had contact with him since.'

'But your divorce went through when he was in prison. Did you speak to him then?'

'No, the solicitor dealt with all that.'

'And when he was released did he try to get in touch?'

'No, never heard a thing. In fact, I didn't know he was out until someone told me. Please excuse me being blunt but what is this about?'

Kray leaned forward. 'We are questioning your ex-husband about three serious crimes. In each case, the crime was committed against a person who he had every reason to hold a grudge against.'

'Who, Kevin?'

'Yes, Kevin.'

'You're not suggesting Kevin had anything to do with the murder of John Graham, are you? I heard about it on the news.'

'I'm not in a position to confirm or deny that, Sadie.'

Sadie rocked back into the cushions on the settee and laughed out loud. 'You can't be serious? Kevin doesn't have the balls to do anything like that! Christ, Kevin doesn't have the balls to do anything much – and I should know.'

'We are following several lines of inquiry at this stage.'

'But come on, I mean, Kevin Palmer! He's a bloody joke, not a murderer.'

'He does have a history of violence. You once fled your home to get away from him.'

'Roz, I don't want you to waste your time, so I'll let you into a little secret. My ex-husband didn't have the balls to do anything when he found me in bed with another man. The worst he did was kick a door. He's a loser, always has been and always will be.'

'But he was violent towards you?'

'Come on, Roz, you must have met him? If Kevin bloody Palmer raised a hand to me I'd kick his arse all around the house.'

'But you told the police he broke in, you said you feared for your safety.'

'I wanted him out of my life, he was holding us back. I ran to my neighbour's house so I could call the police. I saw an opportunity to build up a picture that I could use later on in the divorce courts. How the hell do you think I have all this?' She waved her hand to indicate the house.

'He was never violent?'

'Not that I know of. He was a sad excuse for a man who denied us the quality of life that we aspired to with his small-minded job and his small-minded ideas. He was a pussy – and I don't mean of the feline variety neither.'

'But what about the newspaper article?'

Sadie rolled back again and belly laughed. 'It was a crock of shit. I approached the woman who wrote the newspaper column with an idea for the piece, and she did the rest. I got paid for it as well. He was in no position to fight back. He wrote her a letter bleating about the injustice of it all, and she tore him to shreds.'

'It was all false.'

'I wouldn't say it was false. He did technically break in, and he did a bit of shouting. Let's just say, I told the papers what they wanted to hear. Kevin had held us back for years. I kept telling him to expand the business, win bigger contracts, think big. But would he do it? Would he hell. We scratted around with second-hand cars, in a house that needed renovating and went to Spain for a week in the summer. That's not me, that's not us. He was a director in the business, for Christ's sake.'

'So you–'

'Took matters into my own hands, that's what I did. We've done up the house, got nice things and a better life. I hate him for what he did to me, how he kept me down for all those years… Now, you seem like a nice woman, so I'm only telling you so you don't go disappearing up dead ends. But if you repeat any of this, I'll deny it.'

What a fucking charmer.

'We believe there is a possible risk to you and your kids,' Kray said.

'Not from Kevin there isn't.'

'I want you to take the threat seriously, Sadie.'

'Why would I do that? I don't take *Kevin* seriously. He's nothing. He's a nobody. I'm not sure what it is you're investigating, love, but you're barking up the wrong tree with him. Look, I'm only telling you all this stuff so you don't waste your time.'

A blue Mercedes pulled onto the drive.

Sadie got up. 'Now, if you don't mind, I'm off out tonight.'

Kray stood up and watched as a young smartly dressed man with slicked back hair and a designer-stubble chin got out. Sadie slinked her way to the front door and opened it wide.

'Hello, hun,' she said as he slid his arm around her waist, kissing her on the mouth.

'Hey, I got off early. Thought we could–' Kray appeared in the hallway. The man stopped. 'Hey, I'm Henry.' He flashed a set of glinting white teeth that matched the colour of his upturned collar.

'Hooray,' said Kray. Henry continued to smile, missing the joke completely. Kray pulled a card from her inside pocket and handed it to Sadie. 'If you see, or hear, anything out of the ordinary, please get in touch. Anytime, day or night.'

'What is this, hun?' Henry said, slipping his hand from her hip and onto her arse.

Sadie ignored him, picking the card from Kray's hand. 'The next time you see my ex-husband, tell him I wish him all the worst.'

Kray squeezed past the couple still in their embrace on the doorstep. She walked back to her car, truly believing that Sadie Raynor meant every word.

Chapter 31

Across town, an unremarkable looking woman is driving home after a hard day at work. Well, if you call hanging around all day drinking coffee hard work, then it certainly was a tough day. This was the third case this week where the victim had failed to show up at court. It is the malaise of the judicial system; people don't turn up, paperwork doesn't turn up, court rooms suddenly become unavailable – it's a bloody shambles.

She presses the button on the fob which she keeps in the centre console, and the up and over garage door lifts open. She is head over heels in love with her latest gift to herself. It is a week old now, and it still manages to bring a smile to her face every time she pulls onto her drive.

The door hits the limit switches and the whirring motor stops. She pulls the SUV into the garage and waits for the parking sensors to tell her she is far enough in. She kills the engine and steps out, no getting piss-wet through for her, now she has her new toy installed. The back tail-gate rises up and she leans in to retrieve her leather briefcase.

She hears the crackle a split second before the terminals jab between her shoulder blades. Her back arches like a crooked ballerina and her mouth gapes open, but nothing comes out. She slumps forward and is bundled into the back with a rag forced into her mouth, held in place with floor tape. It was a slick and practised move. Another crackle and she jerks around with the metal pins digging into the nape of her neck. Her feet and hands are bound together and a hood pulled over her head. The spasming of her limbs makes the job way more difficult than it should be.

Two mobile phones clatter to the concrete as they are discarded onto the garage floor. The tail gate is closed, and the SUV backs out from the confines of the garage, the motor kicks in, and the door closes.

Soon, the lights of the town disappear into the rear-view mirror and the darkness of the countryside wraps around the vehicle. It keeps exactly to the speed limit, passing the sign for Inglewhite, then takes a sharp left onto a narrow lane. By now, there is a commotion coming from the boot of the SUV. The big tyres make light work of the uneven road surface as the derelict farm house comes into view. The muffled yells intensify. The vehicle disappears from view into a large barn, and the driver steps out, pulling the wooden doors shut.

The tail gate lifts up and the screams hit a crescendo, but only until the surge of electricity shuts down her brain once more. She's pulled from the boot and carried across the barn, down a set of stone steps to a small damp room. The brick walls are covered in mould and the place is empty of the wood and coal that it used to store. She is dumped on the floor.

The man fills a plastic cup with water from a bottle and unwraps a folded square of paper containing a ground powder, tipping their contents into the cup. He swishes it around and waits. The woman comes around and starts groaning. He sits her upright, lifting her hood to expose her mouth. He removes the tape and pulls the cloth free of her mouth.

'Drink,' he says, offering the cup up to her lips.

She shakes her head.

'D-drink,' he repeats the order.

She shakes her head once more.

The man presses the button and the stun gun crackles, sending arcs of blue and white light dancing across the brickwork. The woman jumps at the sound.

'No, no, no, please,' she says, leaning her head forward to touch the rim. He tilts the cup and she drains the contents. 'Don't hurt me,' she pleads. 'I have money I can–'

The man rams the cloth back into her mouth and applies the tape. The hood is pulled back in place. She gags against the rag. He sits at the entrance to the underground coal house.

He can see her breathing heavily, trying to control the panic. He sits and waits.

After twenty minutes, her head drops and she keels over onto her side. He drapes a blanket around her body, ducks his head beneath the door way and leaves, locking the door behind him.

Chapter 32

Kray crashed through the door to the incident room which was full of excited chatter. 'Right, people, what do we have?' she said, not waiting for them to notice she was there. 'Who's first?'

'Roz, we checked out Palmer's flat.' It was Detective Janice Parks. 'Had a spot of difficulty getting past the Chinese woman downstairs but…anyway. We went through the place and there is definitely no other way out of that flat other than to walk through the front door and down the stairs. You have to pass into the front of the shop to exit the building by either the front or back door. It's like Palmer said – one way in, one way out.'

'Okay, that's not what we wanted. Who's next?'

'Sorry, Roz, if I could finish,' Parks continued. 'While we were there, we spoke to Anabel and Joseph Woo. They only have good things to say about Palmer. They know about him having been in jail but want to be part of his rehabilitation back into society. They confirmed that Palmer chats to the customers and always sticks around while his meal is being cooked. Anabel also confirmed that she had given him the meal for free on Monday night to say sorry for the noise. If he had left that flat on either last Monday, or the Monday before that, they would have seen him. Sorry, Roz.'

'Okay, thank you, Janice. Have we identified anyone other than Sadie Raynor and Vanessa Wilding who might be at risk?'

'No, nobody. They fit the profile and are top of our list of potential next victims,' said Tavener.

Kray glanced over at Brownlow who glared back. She ignored him. 'Anything new from forensics?'

'Nothing,' said a tall woman in a smart suit. 'We've re-checked the samples and gone through the inventory but it hasn't yielded any new information. We also traced the suppliers for the type of hoist used to suspend the victims and they are the most common model on the market. They are on sale all over the place as well as on eBay.'

Kray sighed. 'Okay, thank you, everyone.' She closed off the update and sidled over to Tavener. 'I fancy another go at Palmer but this time, we turn up the heat.'

'I'm all for that, Roz.'

Fifteen minutes later, Kray and Tavener walked in to find Palmer sat with his head resting on his forearms on the desk. He raised his head when he heard them enter. Three empty plastic cups were stacked in front of him.

'At last!' he said, shaking his head. 'I thought you'd forgotten about me.'

'No, Mr Palmer, you are very much in our thoughts, I can assure you,' replied Kray, pulling a chair out from the table and taking a seat. Tavener followed suit. He pressed the button on the tape machine.

'Interview resumed nineteen twenty-five, present are Mr Kevin Palmer, Acting DCI Kray and DC Tavener. Mr Palmer I have to remind you, you are still under caution and you have waived the right to have legal representation. Is that still the case?'

'Yes, it is.'

'This is for you.' Roz handed him a coffee. He took it from her with his left hand. Kray glanced sideways at Tavener.

'Kevin–' she said.

'Have you checked my alibis out? Have you checked with forensics?'

'Kevin, I want you to take a look at these photographs.' Kray was not going to be knocked off her line of questioning. Tavener opened a document-sized envelope and fished out a picture. It showed a naked man, suspended upside down in a hallway. The carpet below him was stained dark with blood. Tavener laid the photo in front of Palmer.

He brought out another showing another naked man hanging upside down in what looked like a metal-walled room. The third photograph showed a woman hanging in the same position at the bottom of her stairs.

'Do you recognise the victims?'

Palmer stared open-mouthed at the carnage in front of him.

'Shit a brick,' he said, scanning the detail. 'That's John.' He pushed his chair away from the table. 'That's fucking John Graham.' He examined the other two. 'My God, that's Nigel Chapman and Teresa Franklin, I recognise her hair. So, I was right?'

'You have a motive to kill each one these victims. You also have the skills.'

'Skills? What do you mean?'

'You work in an abattoir where you slaughter pigs.'

'So?'

'In each case, the victim was given an electric shock by attaching electrodes to their temples, they were bled dry by severing the major blood vessels in the neck and were scalded with boiling water and their skin was scrubbed raw. Does that sound like a familiar process to you, Kevin?'

Palmer said nothing, staring at the pictures.

'Does that sound like a familiar process to you, Mr Palmer?' Kray asked again.

'Yes, it's the process we go through when the pigs come into the factory.'

'And you do all three processes, that's correct isn't it, Kevin?'

'Yes, I rotate around all three jobs.'

'Let's recap, shall we? This is Nigel Chapman, who had an affair with your wife which led to the breakdown of your marriage; this is John Graham, who, in your words, swindled you out of your share of the business, and Teresa Franklin, who wrote a devastating article about you in the local paper. Anyone would want to wreak revenge on these people but not everyone has the skills you possess. Are you telling me that you didn't do this?'

'It was two articles.'

'What?'

'The journalist woman wrote two articles about me.'

Tavener lost his rag, stabbing his finger into the first photo. 'Are you telling us this is not your handiwork?'

'Nope. It is not my handiwork.' Palmer sat back and folded his arms across his chest.

'I'm finding that increasingly difficult to believe,' Tavener snarled.

'Kevin, you can see how this looks?' said Kray. 'What are we supposed to think?'

'If I am to believe what I watch on TV, your job is to find evidence, not make things up. Have you spoken to my wife?'

'Yes.'

'Bloody hell, no wonder you're in a bad mood. She can sour milk from twenty yards. What did she say?'

'I am not prepared to disclose that,' said Kray.

'If you've spoken to her, then you must have come away with the sense that she is a woman out to destroy me. Can't you see that?'

The scar on Kray's cheek came to life. Tingling and itching. She ignored it and ploughed on.

'What do you feel when you look at these pictures?' Tavener asked.

'I know this could get me into trouble, but the honest answer is – a sense of gratitude towards the bastard whose done this.'

Tavener shoved himself away from the table and stood up.

'For the purposes of the tape, the big Scots guy has stood up and looks mad as hell,' Palmer said. 'You need evidence, Acting DCI Kray, not a list of fanciful motives and a job description from an abattoir. From what I can see, you don't have jack shit.'

There was a knock on the door and Detective Parks stuck her head around the door. 'Sorry to disturb you but I need to speak with you, Roz.'

'Can't it wait?'

'No, ma'am, it can't.'

'Interview terminated, nineteen forty.' Kray gathered up the photographs and left the room with Tavener in hot pursuit.

Kray confronted Tavener. 'You need to cool off, go get a coffee.' She turned to Parks. 'What is it?'

'I tried to contact Vanessa Wilding, I couldn't get hold of her. I contacted her work but they said the office was closed for the night, so I went to her home. She wasn't there either. I called her mobile phone again and could hear it ringing from inside the garage. I forced the lock. The vehicle was gone and I found two phones on the garage floor. One is her personal mobile and the other she uses for work. I got into the house through the interior garage door and searched the property from top to bottom.'

'And?'

'The place is empty.'

'She's been taken.'

Chapter 33

The station had descended into melt down. A CSI team was despatched to Wilding's house and the details of her vehicle were circulated to the Traffic Division. A quick check of the Automatic Number Plate Recognition data base held at the National Traffic Operations Centre confirmed that Vanessa Wilding's SUV had not used any of the motorway networks in the surrounding area. A piece of information which made Kray say 'fuck' far more times than was necessary.

Her phone rang. It was ACC Quade. She closed her eyes and said *that* word again.

Kray made her way up the internal staircase to the top floor and strode past the bank of secretaries to Quade's office. She was squashed behind her desk and did not look happy.

'All I'm hearing is bad news,' Quade said, not bothering to welcome her visitor.

'It's tough, ma'am. We have a number of lines of inquiry and we are questioning a suspect.'

'So, I understand. His name is Kevin Palmer.'

'Yes ma'am.' Kray knew what was coming.

'This is Kevin Palmer, for which we have absolutely no evidence that puts him at any of the crime scenes. The same Kevin Palmer that has corroborated alibis for two of the murders. The same Kevin Palmer that we are still burning valuable police time by interviewing. That one?'

'Yes, ma'am, it's that Kevin Palmer.'

'And to cap it all, we now have another potential victim who looks like she's been snatched from her home, while Kevin Palmer is sitting downstairs drinking our coffee.'

'Kevin Palmer has a copper-bottomed motive to want to see every one of these victims harmed. Something will turn up. He's acting way too cool. It's him, ma'am, I'm telling you.'

'How the hell does he snatch another victim while he's enjoying our hospitality?'

'He must have somebody helping him.'

'Or maybe it's not him. Maybe the fact that we have no evidence is telling us something. We can't be blinded by motive alone. Is there any evidence to suggest he worked with an accomplice with the murders?'

'No, ma'am.'

'I think you are fixating on this suspect and that is preventing you looking wide enough. Bloody hell, Roz, it looks like we might have another victim to find.'

'But, ma'am, it's him. I know it is.'

'That's not enough, Roz. The chief is breathing down my neck on this one. He's worried and so am I. The CPS will never let us charge Palmer on what we have. We have a press blackout now in force but we can't hold that position for much longer. The more time we waste on Palmer, the less likely it is that we catch the sick bastard who's doing this.'

'I can hold him for twenty-four hours without charge, thirty-six, if you authorise an extension. That will give us time—'

'To do what, Roz? To find another naked body hanging upside down. I want you to spend that time trying to prevent it, not trying to pin this on Palmer.'

'But, ma'am...'

'We don't have a case against him and we need to target our resources into finding the real killer. Let it drop, Roz, and find Wilding.'

'Do what?' Tavener said a little too loudly. People in the incident room turned to listen.

Kray took him by the elbow and led him out into the corridor. 'Let him go.'

'But he's got every reason to want these people dead. It's just a matter of time before we dig up some evidence.'

'That's not how the ACC sees it. We have circumstantial at best. We have to cut him loose.'

'Shit! That makes no sense.'

'Come on, we're wasting time.'

Kray and Tavener headed off to the interview room where Palmer was being held. He was once more sitting with his head resting on the desk. He looked up when they entered the room.

'I'm getting hungry,' he said.

'We have no more questions, Kevin. You are free to leave.'

Palmer looked disappointed. 'Look, if I can get a sandwich, I'm more than happy to stay here helping you out.'

'No, that won't be necessary.'

'Are you sure?' Palmer stared at Kray and Tavener in turn. 'I mean, really sure?'

'DC Tavener will escort you from the station.' Kray stepped to one side, allowing Palmer access to the doorway.

'Well, if you say so.' Palmer got up and made his way out, stopping directly in front of Kray. 'Are you absolutely sure there is nothing else you want to ask me?'

'You can leave now.'

'Okay, be seeing you,' he called over his shoulder.

Kray was alone in the room. Her head was a shed. She knew the ACC was right, but she could not switch off the voice inside her mind telling her *it's him*. She sat at the desk and rewound the tape, pressing play. Something was bugging her about his testimony. She played and re-played the tape, spinning the ring round and round on her finger. Something wasn't right.

She pressed stop and hit the eject button. If there was any clue in his testimony, she couldn't find it.

Chapter 34

I slide into the driver's seat of the white van with the decorative lettering down the side and rummage around in the glove compartment. I pull out the cheap pay-as-you-go phone. It has one number programmed into the memory. I hit the keys and it rings at the other end.

'I'm on my way.' I disconnect the call not waiting for a response. The van eases out of the garage and I close the door behind it. Within no time I am heading away from town, sticking to the side-roads where I can.

An hour earlier, I had arrived home and left my car around the corner from the takeaway. I couldn't take the risk that the police might have put a tracking device on it, or maybe I've been watching too may TV cops shows. It seemed the entire Woo family was there to greet me.

'The police were here, they were asking questions about you and wanted to see the flat,' Anabel had blurted out as soon as I entered the front of the shop.

Joseph came from behind the counter. 'Are you alright? They said you were helping them with their inquiries. Scared mum half to death.'

'It's fine,' I assured him. 'Nothing to worry about. They thought I knew someone, but it turned out, I didn't. It's all a big misunderstanding.'

'But the flat, they wanted to see inside the flat. They had a warrant.'

'Yes, it turns out this guy that they thought I knew had stolen something and they wanted to be sure I wasn't hiding it. They found nothing. They have apologised and that's the end of the matter.' I had been impressed with how convincing I was at lying to my friend.

They had sat me at the back of the shop while they prepared dinner for me. Whatever I wanted, on the house. I thanked them, ordered crispy duck and pancakes and took the food up to my flat, exhausted. It was delicious. But I couldn't hang around. There was work to do.

I pass the sign for Inglewhite and turn sharp left. In the headlamps, the road hugs the van, almost appearing too narrow to let it pass. I pick the phone off the passenger seat and hit the same number as before.

'Two minutes out,' I say and hang up.

The farm looms out of the blackness, as does the big black man silhouetted against the brickwork. He swings open the left-hand door and I draw the van into the barn next to the SUV. He closes the door behind me.

I kill the engine and step out into the semi-darkness, a single camp light in the corner struggling to make a difference. I hold out my hand and it is grasped in a vice-like grip.

'Hi, Irvine,' I say.

'H-hi, Kev, g-good to see you.'

'Hey you been practicing?'

'E-every day, man.'

'How is she?'

'F-fast asleep.'

We walk to the back of the barn. Irvine picks up the camping light and illuminates the steps running down to the wooden door. I take the lamp from his hand and descend to the bottom, removing the metal tent peg holding the clasp in place and push it open. Sure enough, lying on her side, under a blanket, is Vanessa Wilding.

'Good work. Did you give her all the tablets?'

'Y-yes, all of them.'

'Let's get her into the house.'

Irvine steps forward and gathers the woman up into his arms like he's carrying a child. The blanket falls away and she stirs, groaning behind the gag. He moves past me and up the stairs. I follow him out. He carries her across the farmyard and into the house. It's in a bad state of repair with holes in the roof where we can see the sky and walls that look as though they could give way at any minute.

Through the side entrance and at the back of the property is what used to be the kitchen. It's relatively intact, with heavy wooden worktops and thick wooden beams set into the high ceiling. Irvine lays her on the floor.

'I'll be back in a minute,' I say to him as he stands over the moaning woman. I pace to the van and open up the back. It's full of the kit I need to do the job.

After ten minutes of walking back and forth, I assemble my gear in the kitchen. Wilding begins to come out of her drug-induced slumber, her body moving and stretching.

I look at Irvine. 'You can go now.'

'Y-you sure?'

'Wait for me in the van.'

He nods and walks away, leaving me in the company of the lovely Ms Wilding. I pull on a white paper boiler suit, gloves and over shoes and set to work. I loop the carabiner through the eye bolt in the hoist and stand on the petrol generator to reach the hook in the beam. The thick rope loops around her ankles and runs through the pulleys. I yank on the free end, and her feet lift from the ground. I tug more on the rope. She rises higher with every pull.

The pillowcase slips off her head as she comes clear off the floor. Her eyes are flickering. The hem of her dress falls down, exposing her upper thighs. I yank the pull-chord and the generator kicks into life, it was supposed to be silent running, but only if you're a deaf person. The last time I'd used it was in the shipping container. It might be a little on the noisy side, but it does the job.

I plug a couple of arc lamps into the sockets and the place floods with bright white light. The room looks worse under the harsh glare, but it's made Vanessa Wilding look a whole lot better. Her eyes flick open and she blinks.

She notices me, or, I suppose, an inverted image of me, and jerks around at the end of the rope. I pull the hunting knife from the bag and set to work on her clothing. First, the waist band of her skirt gives way as the blade slices through. I kneel down in front of her and grasp her shoulder to prevent her spinning, cutting every button from her blouse, exposing her bra. Her eyes almost burst from their sockets. Irvine's gag is doing a much better job than the ones I had tried. Her muffled screams don't make it outside the confines of the kitchen.

I push a finger through her tights and tear them from her legs. She spins on the end of the rope like a bobbin. I cut away her underwear, the edge of the knife scoring her skin.

'Sorry,' I say, as blood oozed to the surface.

I sit on the floor in front of her. She stares at me through wet eyes, tears rolling down her forehead.

'Do you remember me?' I ask. 'I suppose it is a little presumptuous of me to think you would, given the number of relationships and homes you must have wrecked in your time. Maybe a little flicker of recognition?'

She looked up into my face. Not a thing.

'You kept me from seeing my kids. I bought tickets to the zoo and you showed up without them. My wife had filled your head with all sorts of poisonous nonsense and you were only too pleased to dole out the misery. Time and time again you kept me from them. Do you remember the coffee?' I can see the cogs whirring, then the penny drops.

She nods her head and gargles a few words from behind the gag.

'If that was you apologising, then I'm afraid it's too late for that.' I stand up and take a good look at her white naked body. She has a good figure, all womanly curves and soft to the touch.

I unplug one of the arc lamps and replace it with the plug on the end of my box of tricks. The red LED comes on. She sees the electrodes dangling down from the box and goes crazy, thrashing around, jerking and spinning. I steady her with one hand and stick the pads in place with the other. I flick the toggle switch and the green lamp lights up.

She goes rigid when the rotary switch moves off the backstop. Her wide eyes stare at me. Pleading.

My adrenaline stops pumping. I remember all the pain and suffering this woman has brought to my door. Ice runs through my veins.

I move the pointer up to one.

Let's see if we can make those pretty eyes burst.

Chapter 35

I finish loading the last of the gear into the van. Irvine is crammed into the front seat patiently waiting. I strip off the paper boiler suit, gloves and over shoes and ball them together, dropping them into the rusting brazier set against the far wall. I take out the zip-lock bag and walk down the steps to the disused wood store, then I return and empty the remaining contents onto the pile of clothes. A splash of lighter fluid and the whole lot goes up in flames.

I lift the red container out of the van and open up the SUV. Petrol vapours rasp at the back of my throat as I dowse the interior. I save the last few fluid ounces for the glossy paintwork. I open the door to the barn and jump in beside Irvine.

'Y-you ready?' he asks.

'Yup, all done.' I take a flip-top lighter from the coin holder in the dashboard and strike the thumb wheel. After three attempts the spark ignites the wick with a blue and orange flame. I hold it between my fingers, watching the flame grow, hungrily devouring the lighter fluid. Getting stronger, growing by the second. I look at Irvine and smile, he smiles back.

I toss the lighter through my open window into the SUV. There is a second of silence, then a massive whoosh, as a ball of fire engulfs the vehicle. I shift into reverse, back out of the barn and drive away, watching in my rear-view mirror as the place takes on the look of an early bonfire night celebration.

We cruise along the country lanes in silence. Endorphins course through in my brain, making me want to dance and sing at the top of my voice. I resist the temptation and concentrate on driving safely. After twenty minutes, we reach a pub, a real old-style place set way out in the countryside with its mock-Tudor front and lead-lined windows. Shame it has a sign on it saying 'For Sale'. I pull into the car park and drive around the back, killing the engine.

'This is it,' I say.

'I'll g-get off.' Irvine offers me his hand. I put my child-like hand into his and he squeezes it. He reaches into his pocket and hands me a mobile phone.

'I-I destroyed the other one,' he said. 'T-the one marked with the r-red tape. J-just like you said.'

I take the phone and lob it into the glove compartment.

'Good.' I slap my hand against his massive shoulder. 'Maybe see you in a Manchester pub one day.'

'M-maybe, or m-maybe, I won't let you in.'

'Thank you for today. I owe you big time.'

'N-no, I owe you.' Irvine tugs the handle and slides out, then bobs his head back into the van. 'W-why did you t-torch her car?' he asked.

'How else were they going to find her?'

He nods and with a swing of his massive arm, bangs the door shut. Two lights flash amber against the darkness followed by the pale glow of an interior light as he squeezes his frame behind the wheel. He pulls away without looking back. I wonder if I would ever see my friend again but somehow, I doubt it.

Chapter 36

The naked body of Vanessa Wilding hung upside down from the oak beam set into the ceiling. The flesh was ripped from her bones and her dead eyes were cherry red. Her hair was matted with blood on one side where the arterial flow had dribbled down at the end. A ten-litre plastic bucket, that at one time had contained vinyl mat emulsion, was now filled with blood. The forth toe on her right foot was missing.

A passing motorist had made a 999 call to the fire brigade when he saw the flames from the road.

'Bloody joy riders,' was the overriding opinion of the firefighters after they'd extinguished the flames. They passed the vehicle details on to the police in the usual way and a sharp-eyed constable working in the control room had made a call to CID. Thirty minutes later, Kray was standing in the kitchen of the run-down farmhouse.

She looked at the body with both her fists clenched and tears in her eyes. Inside her head, a voice was screaming:

This little piggy went to market,
This little piggy stayed at home,
This little piggy …

Powerful lights gave the suspended corpse an iridescent glow.

'This one is different to the others,' Mitch said, snapping Kray away from the screaming in her head.

'In what way?'

'There is much more tissue damage.'

'Did the killer use more force? Or a different tool?'

'Can't be sure, but it looks like it was more of a frenzied attack. There are incisions caused by the blade which we have not seen before.'

'Maybe the killer got carried away.'

Kray couldn't bear to look at the body anymore and walked out.

'Roz, over here!' Tavener was at the entrance to the barn. Kray wandered over trying to avoid the worst of the puddles.

'What is it?' She entered the building. To the right was the torched remains of the SUV. The inside of the vehicle was charcoal black and the windows had blown out with the intense heat. The acrid smell of melted plastic still hung in the air. Remarkably, the structure of the barn had remained intact, and only one half of the roof had gone up in flames. Black smoke hung in the rafters like rain clouds.

'Fortunately for us, the brigade didn't drown everything in water. Apparently by the time they got here, the fire was dying down. We found this.'

Tavener took a pen from his pocket and poked the scorched material at the bottom of the brazier. 'This looks fresh.'

'What is it?'

'It looks like the burned remains of paper overalls and gloves, that kind of thing. It looks like there are more than one set. Also…' Tavener walked towards the back of the barn, beckoning for Kray to follow. 'I think whoever took Wilding held her in here.' He clicked the torch on his phone and shone the beam down the set of steps. He nudged open the door.

'There's a blanket. Now, that could be a tramp sleeping rough, but my guess is, when we test it, we'll find Vanessa Wilding's DNA all over it,' he said.

'Why would you do that?'

'What?'

'Why would the killer want to hold his victim here when she was murdered in the house?

'And why hold her at all?'

'This one feels different to the others.'

'I agree.'

'Get forensics to focus on the burned clothes and this blanket. This might be the breakthrough we've been waiting for.' Kray walked away.

'Where are you going?'

'To have an argument with a certain ACC.'

The traffic grew heavier the closer Kray got to town. She cursed the tourists under her breath as she hit yet another jam. Her mind was buzzing with what she had seen at the farm. The prospect of forensics finding evidence linking Palmer to the murders excited her. At last, something that might bust this case wide open and implicate the lying bastard. Mitch had been right when he said the body looked different to the others, her skin was hanging off in shreds with deep gouge marks cut down to the bone.

Kray had to convince Quade that Palmer was the prime suspect. *After all, how many more coincidences before she sits up and takes notice?* They let Palmer walk and hours later they find the next body. And the worse part of it all – her name was on the board. They knew she was going to be next.

Kray parked up and launched herself up the stairs, taking them two at a time. At the top, she had to stop to draw breath. Having a fight with Quade was going to be a whole heap more difficult if she couldn't speak.

I need to give up the cigs.

The ACPO suite was quiet, the secretarial staff having long since gone home for the night. Kray knocked at Quade's door. She could hear voices coming from inside.

'Come,' her voice boomed out.

Kray opened the door to find ACC Quade sat at her conference table drinking coffee with a man dressed in faded jeans and an open neck shirt. He was mid-forties with short dark hair and a tanned face.

'Roz, I thought you were out at the farm.'

What is this, an episode of Emmerdale?

'Yes, ma'am. I was at the murder scene, but I need to talk to you.'

'I need to talk to you as well. I was going to wait until the morning, but as you are here now… Would you like a coffee?'

The man in the open neck shirt was smiling at her. It was unnerving.

'What? No, ma'am, thank you.' Kray glanced at the man. 'If I might have a word with you in private?'

'Oh, sorry, Roz. This is DI Dan Bagley from GMP.'

'Hi,' he said. Roz nodded back.

Greater Manchester Police? What the hell is he doing here?

'Please, Roz, sit down.' Quade took another sip from her cup.

'Ma'am, I have something to discuss with you urgently. It concerns the latest victim.'

'And does it also concern Kevin Palmer?'

'Yes it does, ma'am, but I need to have that discussion with you privately.'

'That's why I wanted to speak to you and that's why I have asked Dan to join us.'

'I'm sorry, ma'am, I don't follow you.' Kray frowned and looked at Bagley.

'I was concerned after our last conversation, Roz.'

'Concerned about what?'

'Concerned that you had tunnel vision with this case.'

'That's not true. Kevin Palmer was, or is, our prime suspect. It's right and proper that we target our resources on him.'

'When you say prime suspect, you mean *only* suspect.'

'We are pursuing numerous lines of inquiry and Palmer just happens to fit into every one. We found a brazier containing burned clothing at the latest crime scene. I'm sure it will give us the forensic evidence we've been missing.'

'My concern is you have a bee in your bonnet about Palmer and cannot see the wider picture–'

'A bee in my bonnet?'

'And that is why I have asked DI Bagley to join the investigation. He brings a wealth of experience and will be an asset to the team. You will still be SRO on the case, of course, but Dan will help to bring a fresh pair of eyes.'

'Don't you have murders of your own you should be solving in Manchester?'

'Mary asked me if I could help out.'

Mary, who the fuck calls her Mary?

'Had a lot of experience of tracking down serial killers have you, Dan?' Bagley looked down into his coffee. 'No, I thought not. Look, I have nothing against you, and I'm sure you're a big hit with the guys and girls over in GMP, but we don't need your help. We know what we're doing here. We don't need this, ma'am.'

The silence in the room was painful. It was crunch time.

'Look, Roz,' Quade said, 'you haven't been back at work long. You had a spell on sick leave following a horrendous case where you became a target for the killer. You were attacked and injured. I truly admire the way in which you've got back in the saddle, but you need help with this one. You've got a one-track mind where Palmer is concerned and it's blinding you to other possibilities.'

Kray spun the ring round and round her finger. A necessary diversion to stop her punching Quade in her fat face. She said nothing.

'I've briefed Dan and he has some ideas that I want you to hear.'

Kray looked at him but said nothing.

'Let me start by asking you a question,' Bagley said, eager to get off the mark. 'Who is most likely to be the next victim?'

'It's written on the board in the incident room, so you already know the answer to that,' Kray snapped, still spinning the ring.

'Sadie Raynor, she is the natural choice, if we follow your train of thought. But that doesn't fit.'

'How come?' Kray asked.

'Because the killer follows the sequence of events in Palmer's life. Along the lines of the children's rhyme. Great piece of deduction on that, by the way, seeing that whoever is doing this is following the verses in the nursery rhyme.'

Patronising fuck.

Bagley continued, 'But if we follow the chain of events, Sadie Raynor would have been one of the first to be killed. She had the affair with Chapman, he was the first victim. It makes sense that she would have been killed around the same time.'

'Yes, I suppose so, but maybe he's leaving the best 'til last.'

'Maybe. But whoever is doing this does seem to be following a strict pattern and leaving Sadie alive goes against the flow.'

'That is a valid thought.' Kray had to concede.

'Let's look at another part of the case – the lack of evidence. Correct me if I'm wrong, but there is nothing that puts Palmer at any of the crime scenes, plus he has an alibi for two of the murders.'

'That's true but we haven't had time to question him over this latest killing.'

'Okay, let's stick to what we know. The other thing that is clear is he has every reason to want these people dead.'

'Agreed, his motives for carrying out the killings are strong.'

'Not only are they strong, but they are well known, they are in the public domain.'

'Err, yes, I suppose so.' Kray wasn't sure where this was heading.

'And Palmer uses the same techniques to murder the victims that he employs when he goes to work. Isn't there something inherently crazy about that? If you were going to kill someone, would you choose a method that's so close to home? It makes no sense.'

'It's what he knows and it fits with the rhyme.'

'But who in their right mind would do that? It's like Palmer is hanging a bloody big sign above his head saying, "I'm over here, come and get me".'

Kray said nothing.

'What is your opinion of Sadie Raynor?' Bagley said, breaking his silence.

'What sort of question is that? I thought we were dealing with hard facts here, not opinions.'

'What's your opinion, Roz?' Quade chipped in.

'I spoke with her at her home and my overwhelming impression was she is a woman on a mission. A mission to give herself the lifestyle that was denied to her by Palmer. She openly admitted to me that she lied about him being violent and about how she flaunted her infidelity in his face. She resents him for holding her back and has done everything in her power to destroy him. She considers him a laughing stock.'

'I've read the file notes and she seems to me to be a nasty piece of work.'

'Yes, I would say so.' The last comment of Sadie Raynor resounded in Kray's head.

Bagley looked across at Quade as if seeking permission. Kray could feel the punchline coming.

'I think, Roz, you've been looking at this investigation through the wrong end of the telescope.'

'What? What the hell does that mean?' Kray was well and truly lost.

'Sadie Raynor isn't the next victim. She's trying to frame Kevin Palmer.'

Chapter 37

I'm exhausted. I know I should be riding the crest of a permanent high, but I'm not. My body aches and I have a splitting headache, a clear sign that my inability to keep to a strict medication routine has taken its toll.

I'm sitting on the bathroom floor, the cold of the tiles penetrate the thin cotton material of my pyjama bottoms. I take the kitchen knife and prise away the wooden fascia at the bottom of the shower tray, exposing the plumbing beneath. I lay on my side and work my arm into the gap, feeling around. My fingers touch the plastic bag and I drag it free.

I slide the tab across, releasing the zip lock and pour the contents onto the floor. Boxes and plastic containers scatter around me and I line them up in order. I pick up each one in turn and pop the pills from the blister packs, counting out enough for the coming week. Then, I transfer them into the other boxes – one is marked Paracetamol, the other marked Ibuprofen and the last one has Cold and Flu written across it.

I gather up the boxes and containers, replace them into the bag and shove them back into the recess under the shower. The wooden fascia snaps back into place. I pick the boxes from the floor and place them into the mirror-fronted medicine cabinet mounted on the wall.

I catch my reflection as I close the door. I'm looking drained, washed out. Dark circles have appeared around my eyes and my skin is blotchy. I pop two tablets into my mouth and wash them down with a handful of tap water.

I pad out of the bathroom into the lounge. A tray of half eaten chilli beef and boiled rice is sitting on the worktop. I can't be bothered to clear it away. I head into the bedroom and curl up under the duvet, facing the wall. All the pieces are now in play, and all I have to do is wait, though, I have to say, that detective woman does seem to be a little slow on the uptake.

The body of Vanessa Wilding crams my thoughts. I can see her swinging back and forth as I drag the blade across her flesh. With each stroke the anger inside me burst to the surface.

I lost control.

I thought about my kids and how this fucking woman had denied me access to them. I thought about my wife spreading her poison and this woman lapping it up, eager to deliver the bad news. The more I thought, the harder I scrubbed. We were trained in work not to damage the skin of the pig. I can't say I took that into consideration when dispatching darling Vanessa.

It was great to see Irvine. I had forgotten how much I missed him. He was looking good and practicing his speech exercises was obviously paying off. If only we could have spent more time together, but given the circumstances that was not a bright idea.

My eyes close, and I drift off. My alarm will soon wake me for my early shift.

It was a very different story for Kray. It didn't look like sleep was going to visit her anytime soon. She was lying in bed, staring at the green glow of the digits on the clock. Even a long soak in the bath and two-thirds of a bottle of wine had not worked its usual magic. The events of the day were churning round and round with the same thought careering through her brain. *We knew who the next vic would be and still didn't save her.*

The only thing that broke her train of thought was that bloody interview with Palmer. Every time she thought about it, her scars pricked and tingled. She had listened to the tape so many times she could repeat it word for word, yet she could not put her finger on what was bugging her. But one thing she knew for sure – something wasn't right.

Eventually in the small hours of the morning she drifted into a fitful sleep, Palmer's words flying around her dreams like helium balloons in a storm.

My alarm goes off, I feel like shit. The fuzzy head of last night has been replaced with a sharp pain behind my eyes, and my body tells me I have the early on-set of flu – which I know I don't.

I drag myself out of bed and into the lounge. The smell of stale food greets me from the half-eaten carton sat on the table; it makes me gag. I pick up the bin from the kitchen, and with a sweep of my hand, I dispose of the plastic container. Doing it last night would have been a better option. I flick the kettle on to boil and head for the bathroom.

The room is cold and the morning air blasts at my face. I need to do something about that before it gets much worse. I stare at my reflection in the mirror and open the door to get my tablets. The less I see of my vacant expression, the better. A scoop of water washes down more tablets. Now, I need to eat.

The wind cuts through my coat as I walk to my car. The sun is not yet awake, and the onset of winter seems ever closer. The heater in my car struggles to de-mist the windscreen. If I'm not careful, I'm going to be late.

I pull into the car park and switch off the engine. My head feels like it is going to split in two, more tablets hit the back of my throat. It is way too early to take them but what the hell?

The factory is a wall of sound as I make my way to goods-in. The screeching, grinding and clanking penetrates my ears. I can't make out if it is a genuinely louder today or whether it's down to an increase in my sensitivity. Maybe a little of both.

'Where have you been, Palmer?' shouts Vinny Burke.

'Oh, err, sorry I was taken into the police station to help them with their inquiries. I tried to call but could get no signal.'

'You know the rules. You are supposed to contact your supervisor if you're sick.'

'But I wasn't sick. I was helping the police.'

'Yeah, fucking likely story. Still pissed, more like.'

'I don't drink.'

'No! What the fuck is wrong with you, Palmer? Never trust a man who doesn't drink, that's what my old man used to say.'

'I was helping–'

'Consider this a first warning.'

'You can't do that, there are procedures–'

'Fuck the procedures. You dropped us in the shit yesterday. Fucking short-handed all day, we were.'

'I was with the police, I've told you.'

'What, again! You need to be more careful. What is fucking wrong with you, Palmer?'

Yes, what indeed. What indeed.

Chapter 38

The clock on the dashboard read nine-fifteen am. Kray was parked in the cul-de-sac, waiting for Sadie Raynor to return from the school run. She had called ahead and left a voicemail. Bagley sat beside her dressed in a suit and tie and smelling of Boss aftershave.

Kray had caught the scent as soon as she had got into the car. It was her husband's favourite, mainly because it was her favourite. As she drove, she fought hard to stop her mind drifting back to happier times. It was one more reason to dislike Bagley and she didn't need another.

The seven-thirty am briefing had been short and sweet. Kray had introduced Bagley and said that he had a different line of inquiry to share with the team. Then she had sat down and handed him the floor. 'Over to you, Dan. It's all yours.'

She had felt a warm buzz of sadistic satisfaction thinking she was throwing him under the bus in front of the others. To her frustration, he took it in his stride and delivered a polished performance, setting out a compelling argument for changing the course of the investigation. He was also very delicate when suggesting that they had been looking in the wrong place for all this time.

Once they had disbanded, Tavener made a beeline for Kray. 'I don't get this. I thought Palmer was our man?'

'Yeah, well, Quade stopped the music, and now, we all have to find a different chair.'

Bagley had decided another chat with Raynor was in order and he wanted to be running point. He stared out of the side window of the car.

'This is not a power grab, Roz. I'm not looking to step on your toes,' he said.

'Then, why do both my feet hurt?'

'It was amazing what you did to bring down Strickland. You are a CID legend, did you know that?'

'No, I didn't know, but then I don't get to Manchester much.'

'Sometimes, we all need help.'

'Yeah, and sometimes, we don't.' Kray was saved from any further polite conversation by the sight of the Volvo pulling into the road. 'Here she is. Remind me again why we are not doing this down at the station?'

'I thought it might be better if we went softly-softly at first.'

'Yes, well, good luck with that, because there is nothing softly-softly about Sadie Raynor.'

They watched as Raynor stopped on her drive and flung open the driver's door. A pair of shapely legs came into view, clothed in a short skirt, the sound of her high heels striking the driveway. Her Marilyn Monroe blonde bob caught in the breeze as she stepped out and her top clung to her chest.

'Put your tongue back in and let's go,' Kray said not waiting for an answer.

'Where has she been? I thought–'

'That's what passes for school-run gear these days.'

Bagley pursed his lips.

'Ms Raynor, I wonder if we might be able to have a word?' Kray called over.

'I got your message but was too busy to call back. Look, if this is about Kevin again, I'm not interested. I have more important things to do than worry about that tosser.' She pushed her key into the lock and bustled her way into the house, leaving the front door open for them to follow.

'I see what you mean,' said Bagley as they both trooped in behind her. Raynor plonked herself down on the sofa, wrestling with the hem of her skirt.

'Okay, what is it this time?' she said. It was more of a challenge than a question.

'This is DI Dan Bagley,' Kray said. 'We want to ask you a few questions to eliminate you from our inquiries.'

'Fire away.' She continued to tug at her skirt.

'Where were you between the hours of four pm and eight pm yesterday?' Bagley wasted no time, jumping straight in.

'Yesterday? What do you mean yesterday? I thought this was about poor old John and how I needed protecting from my loser ex-husband. Err, well, I got back from picking up the kids, that's when I spoke to you, and then…' It was painful to watch the cogs turn in her brain. 'Oh, yeah, Henry came over and we went to his place.'

'What time was that?' asked Bagley.

'I made the kids a quick tea, and then we shot off about five o'clock.'

'You took the children with you?' asked Kray.

'No, they stayed here with the babysitter. Henry pays for all that child care stuff.'

'Where did you go after that?' said Bagley.

'Nowhere. We got there around five-thirty and spent the evening at his place.'

'What did you do?' said Bagley.

'Well, we didn't play Scrabble, if you get my drift.'

'Did you stop over?' said Kray.

'No, I got back around eleven o'clock.'

'Was there anyone else there who could verify this?'

'No, I'm not into threesomes.'

'We will need Henry's address and details from you,' said Bagley.

Sadie nodded. 'Okay.'

'Where were you on Monday sixteenth of October at around eight pm?' Bagley was keen to move on.

'How the hell would I know?'

'Do you keep a diary or write things on a calendar?' Kray asked, knowing full well what the answer was going to be.

'Do I look like a secretary to you?'

Bagley was unsure how to answer without giving away a personal preference, so he shut up.

'How about the Monday before, that would be the ninth of October?' Kray had another go.

'You're having a laugh,' Sadie said. 'Does this really work? I mean, when you ask people about random dates, and they tell you where they were and what they were doing?'

'Yes, once they've had time to think.'

'Well, I'm telling you now you're wasting your time with me. I can't remember what I did yesterday let alone bloody weeks ago. Oh, no, wait a minute, I can definitely tell you what I did yesterday.' It was obvious to Kray and Bagley that whatever she and Henry had got up to after they had deserted the kids, it was worthy of a place in Raynor's memory bank.

'Sadie, it is important that we can eliminate you from our inquiries. For us to do that you need to tell us where you were.' Kray was trying to keep the frustration out of her voice.

'Well, I don't see how I can, and anyway, I have things to do today.' She got off the sofa, adjusting her skirt. 'So, if you don't mind, I have to get a move on.'

Bagley flashed a look at Kray, who cocked her head to one side and raised her eyebrows.

'No, Ms Raynor, we can't do that,' he said. 'We need to know where you were on those dates.'

'And I told you I'm busy. Now, if you don't mind, I will show you both out.'

'Ms Raynor, you can either answer our questions here or down at the station. It's up to you.'

'Down at the station? Now you *are* having a laugh. I'm a busy woman – things to do, people to see. Now, if you don't mind …' She strutted across the lounge, into the hallway and opened the front door.

Bagley followed and stood in the hall. 'This is serious, Ms Raynor. We need you to answer our questions.'

'And I told you, I don't know.'

'You are leaving me no choice but to continue this discussion down the station with you under caution.'

'You what? You've been watching too much television, Detective. There is no way I'm going down the cop-shop to help you lot any further. We're done here.'

Chapter 39

S adie Raynor sat in the police interview room sporting a face like a smacked arse. She had shouted and bawled at Kray and Bagley when they had taken a firm line and insisted she join them at the station. The only thing that calmed her down was the threat of being arrested, a threat that Kray had sincerely hoped they would be able to carry out. She eventually climbed into the back of Kray's car and was quiet for the entire journey.

The interview, however, had not gone well. Sadie could not recall her whereabouts on the dates in question preferring instead to provide them with a list of possible options all of which needed to be checked out. She might have been at the club, or at Henry's place, or having her nails done. There was a lot of times when she could have been at Henry's place – spending time with Henry seemed to feature strongly in her daily routine.

She was not best pleased when Kray announced that they would need to corroborate her story, which would take some time due to the scattergun nature of her testimony.

'How long is that going to take?' she had asked, the prospect of an afternoon in the company of Henry evaporating before her eyes.

'Don't know. It'll depend upon how quickly we can speak to people.'

'But what do I do about my arrangements for the day?'

'You need to make a call,' was all Kray offered.

The day dragged on, filled with the arduous task of tracking down the people Raynor had mentioned in her interview. Kray got a phone call from forensics and seized the opportunity to head off to the lab. She also took the opportunity not to tell Bagley, a small piece of rebellion that made her smile.

Kray dressed herself in the long white coat, hairnet and overshoes that she picked up from the visitor's locker. The protocol about cross contamination of evidence had to be rigorously applied.

She pushed open the door onto a brightly lit room filled with clinical benches and expensive looking apparatus. A young woman was stood looking through a microscope the size of a shopping trolley.

'Oh, hi Roz.' Her name tag read Charlie Fuller.

'Hey, Charlie, thanks for the call.'

'Yes, I thought you would want to see this.' She pushed back her chair and wandered to the back of the room. There, laid out on a long work bench, were the contents of the brazier from the farm. 'What we have here are the burned remains of four white paper boiler suits, pairs of over shoes and latex gloves.'

'Christ, this must have taken you ages?'

'Yeah, we've been working on it for hours, separating out the fragments and trying to piece them together. Some of the matching articles were completely destroyed in the fire. For instance, we have part of a left-hand glove here, but no corresponding right glove.'

'Have you tested them?'

'We have, but so far, we've come up with nothing.'

'That makes one set for each murder. There must be some traces of DNA?'

'So far, nothing.' Fuller pointed to the second and third coverall in the line. 'I've taken samples from these and sent them for analysis.'

'Are you telling me that we have all this and nothing concrete to go on?'

'Not exactly. We ran a tox screen on Vanessa Wilding's blood and found a high concentration of Diazepam.'

'So, she was drugged before she was killed.'

'Yes, she was.'

'That would tie in with holding her in the coal house. She must have been out cold.'

'That would fit. But this is what I wanted you to see... We found these in the bin.' Fuller held up a Petri dish.

'What is it?'

'Hair follicles. We found them in the brazier and on the floor surrounding it. We also found two strands of what looks like the same hair in the coal house.'

Kray's heart rate spiked.

'Have you matched them to Palmer?'

'They didn't come from him.'

'What?'

'Sorry, Roz, this is definitely not from Kevin Palmer. Take a look.' She beckoned Roz over to the microscope and gestured for her to take a look. Kray peered into the lenses.

At first, she could not get into the right position. Then, her brain unscrambled the biopic image. There on the slide was a single strand of blond hair.

Chapter 40

The forensics lab had become a crowded place all of a sudden. Charlie Fuller was getting edgy. Her fear of evidence contamination was growing by the second.

'I don't fucking believe this.' Kray said under her breath.

Bagley was looking through the eyepiece of the microscope. He straightened up. On the outside he looked all serious and professional, when on the inside, he was grinning like a Cheshire Cat. An hour earlier, he had been pissed off that Kray had not told him about the call from forensics. But when he found out the reason for the call, he had struggled to keep the smug look off his face.

'When can we expect to get the DNA results back?' he asked.

'If we push hard it, could be twenty-four hours,' replied Fuller.

'Can't we get a faster turnaround than that?' Kray said 'This is urgent.'

'So is every other sample waiting to be tested. A one-day turnaround is the fastest I've known.' Fuller shrugged her shoulders.

While Bagley was trying hard to hide his euphoria down in the forensics lab, Sadie Raynor was sitting in the interview room, not a happy woman. She had been forced into providing a sample of her most treasured possession – her hair.

'Why the hell do I need to do that?' she had yelled at Kray. 'Do you have any idea how much this cost?' Kray had considered the question carefully, then thought it was obvious to everyone in the interview room that she didn't.

'Charlie, can you prepare us a slide with the hair found at the crime scene and one of the strands taken from Sadie Raynor?' asked Kray.

'You do know that's an unscientific comparison, don't you?' Fuller responded. 'It would never stand up as hard evidence.'

'Yeah, but in the absence of being able to do anything else, it will have to do. And besides, I want to see for myself.'

'Okay, give me a few minutes. I'll need to select a sample with minimum damage.' Fuller scurried off to the back of the lab.

'I'm not gloating,' Bagley said, obviously gloating.

'I understand your logic, Dan, and if I were in your shoes I would be reaching the same conclusion, but this feels all wrong. Sadie Raynor might be a callous bitch, but she's no killer. What does she gain from framing her ex-husband? Nothing, except another twist of the knife, and I think she's twisted that enough already.'

'I'm simply looking objectively at the evidence and there is nothing that puts him at the scene. Quite the opposite. He has corroborated alibis. We can't ignore that.'

'I know, I get the logic. But my intuition tells me this isn't right.'

'And my intuition tells me it makes no sense for Palmer to hang a sign around his neck with "I killed them" written on it.'

Fuller called them over. 'This is what you wanted to see.' She stepped away from the microscope. 'The top one is taken from Raynor the bottom sample comes from the farm.'

Kray peered first. She backed away seconds later, sucking air through her teeth.

'They look identical,' she said.

It was Bagley's turn. The samples were the same colour and thickness, they even had the same kink in them. They looked identical to him too.

'What about the other crime scenes?' he asked, pulling himself away.

'We rechecked, and in the cases of John Graham and Nigel Chapman, there were similar hair follicles found at the scene. They have been sent off for DNA analysis as well.'

'What about Teresa Franklin, the journalist?' asked Kray.

'We didn't find any at the house, however, we have despatched a team over there now to take another sweep.'

This was getting worse by the minute for Kray. Tavener appeared in the doorway. 'Well?' he asked.

'We'll have to wait for the DNA results, but under the microscope, they look the same.' Kray answered, walking over to him. The two of them huddled together in a corner.

'Shit, the case is building against her,' Tavener said in hushed tones.

'It is, but I don't like it.'

'What does Bagley think?'

'He's like a dog with two dicks. This is substantiating his theory.'

'It's falling into place too easily.'

Bagley's phone rang. 'Hello,' he said, answering the call. 'Okay I'll come and pick it up.'

'What was that?' Kray called over.

'Well, in the spirit of making progress, I took the liberty of getting a warrant to search Raynor's house.'

'You didn't say anything to me,' Kray said.

'No, I didn't. You coming?'

Bagley strode out of the lab.

'Shall I come too?' asked Tavener.

'No, I need you here babysitting Raynor.'

'But you are going to need people–'

'I need you here.' It was Kray's last word on the subject. She hurried off after Bagley, who had disappeared through a set of double doors.

Tavener watched her go, shaking his head.

Kray pushed open the front door and they walked inside. The house was much quieter without the constant chatter of Sadie Raynor to fill it.

She and Bagley were accompanied by two other officers, all of them wearing blue gloves. One of the officers looked like he was fresh out of school and the other had the appearance of somebody who should be well way past retirement.

'What are we looking for?' asked the young one.

'Anything that might be connected with the murders,' Bagley said, realising he'd stated the bloody obvious. 'Roz, you and me take the upstairs, and you two can make a start down here.'

Kray and Bagley swept each of the three bedrooms, the bathroom and en-suite.

What the hell does one woman want with so much underwear? Kray opened yet another drawer full of lace. Bagley found a long pole with a hook on the end and opened up the loft hatch. He disappeared up the ladder into the roof space. Kray could hear him clomping around above her head.

He re-appeared, ten minutes later. 'Nothing up here.'

'Nothing here either,' Kray said, coming out of the bathroom.

They made their way downstairs to join the others. The lounge floor was covered in cushions, and the settee and armchairs were upended. The older guy was on his hands and knees, examining the hessian backing. He looked up when Kray appeared in the doorway and shook his head.

Kray wandered through into the dining room with a set of French doors that opened up onto the patio. She pushed down the handle and the door inched outwards.

'How did you know about that?' Bagley asked her.

'Something Palmer said in his statement when he supposedly broke into the home and attacked Sadie. He said—'

'Ma'am I found something.' The younger chap was on his hands and knees in the hallway.

'What is it?' Bagley asked.

'It's a key.'

Kray marched across to where he was and knelt beside him. 'What sort of key?'

'I don't know. Take a look.' He gestured for her to look beneath the occasional table sitting against the wall.

Kray ducked her head down and looked up. There, taped to the underside of the table, was a small chrome-plated key. She reached up and unstuck it, holding it between her fingers. A key-ring hung down with a plastic tag attached. There was writing scribbled on it. Kray handed it to Bagley.

'What the hell does 17 P O R mean?'

Chapter 41

The incident room was buzzing. The news about Sadie Raynor and the hair found at the crime scene had galvanised them into a frenzy of activity. They beavered away, delving into every corner of her life – social media, financial information and phone records all contributed to building up a picture of her whereabouts.

Kray and Bagley walked in with the key found at her house wrapped up in an evidence bag.

'Okay, listen up, people,' Kray announced. 'We have a new lead. This key was taped to the underside of a table in Raynor's house. It has a tag with 17 P O R written on it. The key has the letters HEN stamped on it, along with a ten-digit number. We need to find out what it opens?'

Bagley pinned two blown up photographs of the key and the tag onto the board.

'17 POR sounds like a location but there's no postcode that I know of that starts with POR,' said one of the team.

'It looks like the type of key used in a filing cabinet, or a locker or a desk drawer,' said another.

'It's none of those,' Tavener said, standing by the board. 'This is a garage door key. HEN stands for Henderson. They make garage door locks and the ten-digit number is the series identifier for the key. We are looking for a garage.'

The place went quiet.

'Bloody brilliant!' Bagley exclaimed. 'Raynor's house doesn't have a garage. The tag could be short-hand for an address. Get trawling the internet to find garages for rent and see if we get a hit.'

The whole room seized upon the new information. Kray walked over to Tavener who was still looking at the board.

'How the hell did you know that?' she asked.

'My uncle worked for the council replacing locks, I used to help him when I was young. Never thought doing an apprenticeship in garage door mending would come in handy.'

'That's amazing.'

'Isn't it just?' Tavener walked off and sat behind a desktop computer.

Kray returned to her office. The mail tray was spilling over, setting her teeth on edge. She switched on her laptop and her email inbox looked the same.

'Bloody hell,' she said as the unread email count hit nine hundred and fifty. She clicked on the first one with a red high importance flag next to it. There was a rap on the door. It was Bagley.

'Hey, have you got a minute?'

'No,' Kray said, not lifting her head from the screen. He came in anyway.

'It's about DI Brownlow.'

'What about him?'

'I've noticed him skulking about, pretending to do stuff, when actually he's doing jack shit.'

'Yup, that's Colin Brownlow for you.'

'So, I told him he should pick up the slack in other areas of the department. I'm sure there are lots of things he could be doing while we manage this case. I told him to–'

'You said what?' Kray had her head up now, giving Bagley the laser treatment.

'He wasn't adding value to the investigation. I figured he still has his nose out of joint.'

'Who the fuck are you to tell him anything?'

'I told him to–'

'I run this department, which means I get to decide who does what. Not some fucking tourist from GMP.'

'I'm sorry if I've over stepped the mark, Roz, I was only thinking—'

'Thinking what exactly? Thinking this woman doesn't know what she's doing, so I better do it for her? Is that what you were thinking?'

'No, not at all.'

'Well, it fucking looks that way to me. We have a chain of command here and your name appears nowhere on it. Keep your nose out of running my department, is that clear?'

'Yes, it is, but—'

'Is that clear?'

'Yes, I'm sorry. I thought that—'

'Well, don't.'

'Do we have a problem here?' It was ACC Quade. 'I thought I was coming down here to hear good news.'

Kray shut up and stared at the desk.

'We do,' Bagley jumped in, 'have good news that is. We found a garage door key hidden at the home of Sadie Raynor and we're in the process of tracking down where it might have come from.'

'And what was all this about?' Quade waved her hand between Kray and Bagley.

'It was nothing, ma'am, a misunderstanding, that's all,' Kray replied, glaring at Bagley.

'Do I need to *help* you two work together?'

'Not from me, ma'am,' Kray said, shaking her head.

'No, everything is fine,' Bagley followed suit.

The room was filled with a stony silence.

Tavener appeared at the door. 'I think we got something.'

Kray seized the opportunity. 'I'm right behind you.' She got up from her desk but had to allow Quade to shuffle out of the way before she could get out of her office.

'What is it?' Kray said when she entered the incident room.

'Lockup-Rentals is the name of a firm with a ton of locations all across Blackpool and the surrounding area.' Tavener spun the computer screen around to face Kray. 'They got one in Great

Marton about twenty-minute drive from here. I brought it up on Google maps – it's located on Preston Old Road.'

The same stony silence that had invaded Kray's office was now permeating the inside of Kray's car. Or it would have done, if it weren't for Bagley giving the owner of Lockup-Rentals a hard time on the phone.

'Mr Andrews, you don't seem to grasp the importance of the situation. We are on route to your premises, and when we get there I want to see you waiting for us, otherwise, I'm going to drive to your offices and take you there myself.' The voice on the other end protested. 'I don't care if you have the Queen coming round, you need to meet us at your garages or…' The line went dead. 'Fuck it, he's gone.'

'We need him to unlock the garage for us or we'll have to wait to serve a warrant.'

Bagley stared out front, saying nothing.

Quade had made a point of wagging her finger at Kray as they left the station, as if to say, "I got my eye on you". So, she was on her best behaviour – for now, at least. Before they had left for Marton, Kray had gone over to congratulate Tavener on his quick thinking only to have him grunt at her. He hadn't bothered to ask if he could join her with the garage search. He presumed that her new Mancunian playmate would be riding shotgun.

Kray and Bagley were travelling south, out of town. Preston Old Road was flanked on either side by shops and houses of every description – three bed semis, terraced houses, minimart shops, chippies, the full spectrum of Blackpool life could be found on this street.

After Bagley had finished his tirade, they travelled the rest of the way in silence.

All of a sudden, Bagley yelled, 'Stop! I think it was back there. We missed it. Andrews said it was next to a Tesco Express.'

Kray tutted under her breath and spun the car around in a junction. Fifty yards ahead, a man in his forties sporting a beany hat and dressed in a grey tracksuit and off-white trainers was standing on the side of the road outside the supermarket.

'Mr Andrews has come to welcome us?' Kray said as she drew up to the kerb.

'Are you the policeman I spoke to just now?' said the man in grey.

'Mr Andrews?' asked Bagley, leaning out of the passenger window. He flashed his warrant card.

'The garages are down here.' Andrews pointed to a lane passing between two houses, he gestured for them to follow him. Kray turned left and drove through a narrow entrance. The lane opened up onto a courtyard and stretched off to one side were two lines of white garage doors that faced each other. A swanky car was parked over to one side.

'Thank you for coming out,' Bagley said, without conveying an ounce of gratitude in his tone.

'You said you had a key from one of my lock-ups,' Andrews said.

'We do.' Kray offered up the evidence bag.

Andrews took it from her hand and examined it. 'Yup, this is one of mine. P O R – Preston Old Road.'

'Do you remember who rented it?'

'Hang on.' Andrews walked over to his car and came back clutching a sheaf of paper. 'This is the agreement. It was a woman. She paid in cash for three months.'

Bagley took the papers from his hand and flipped through them. 'Do you remember what she looked like?'

'I see a lot of people, I have a lot of garages. But I do recall this one, because most people pay by card. I remember checking the notes were genuine. You can't be too careful these days. She paid one hundred and eighty pounds for twelve weeks.'

'What did she look like?' he asked again.

'I don't know. She was average height with blonde hair. That's all I can remember.'

'How old was she?'

Andrews shook his head and shrugged. 'I couldn't tell. Oh, I've also brought this.' Andrews held up a key. 'I give my customers one key and keep the other for security reasons. You would be surprised every time the lease runs out and I don't hear from them again. I keep a spare key to clear out the garage when that happens.'

Kray took the key and compared it to the other. They were identical. She gave it back.

Andrews walked towards the one with the number seventeen stencilled on the front. The spare key slid into the lock and he turned the handle. The up and over door arched up.

To Andrews, the contents of his premises seemed innocent enough. It was neat and tidy with everything in order.

Bagley reached for his phone. 'I'll seal off the area,' he said over his shoulder, walking back to the entrance of the narrow lane. The person on the other end picked up. 'Yes, hi,' he said. 'Get a CSI team and a couple of uniforms down to the garages on Preston Old Road ASAP.'

Kray stared into the garage with her stomach in her mouth. She tore her gaze away from the items stacked in regimented order against the walls and scanned the paperwork. The taste of bile filled the back of her throat. The name scribbled at the bottom of the agreement read S. Raynor.

Chapter 42

I ghost through my shift at the factory. Burke continues to give me the evil eye whenever he can. I hate that man. His only saving grace is his monumental stupidity. Laughing at him behind his back is my only comfort.

I don't have as many customers today, for which I'm grateful. I'm back on "sticking" duties which is less physically challenging. Not sure I could cope with a heavy day.

I'm getting clumsy and I'm finding that judging distances is difficult. It took me four attempts to insert my key into my locker, the damned thing kept blurring and moving around. I went to the canteen for a coffee before starting work in an effort to give me a well needed boost and almost knocked it over when paying for it. The mug wobbled off balance before I caught it. The woman on the till gave me a sideways glance as if to say, *Heavy night, was it?*

I banged into furniture while getting ready this morning and hit my head on the bedside table when I bent down to get my slippers. And then, there are the fucking headaches. The searing pain that washes against the back of my eyes.

I screwed up my meds and I'm paying for it.

'It's a strict regime,' I remember she had said as she handed them over. 'The best thing to do is build them into your daily routine. That way you don't have to think so much and if you're not at your best, you have a better chance of keeping to the schedule.'

Fat chance of that when the police are breathing down my neck. But I shouldn't complain. After all, I am the architect of my own pain.

I shove the bloodless carcass through the rubber curtain separating my workstation from the one next door and my next customer arrives behind me, her back-leg circling in the air. I turn her away from me to stop her swinging. As I bend over, the whole room begins to spin. The sound of rushing water courses through my head. I steady myself by holding onto the pig as it traverses along the overhead track. I see my target and plunge the knife towards her neck, only I miss and the blade digs into the back of my hand. The chain mail glove does its job, and the point blunts against the stainless-steel mesh.

I stagger back trying to find my feet but I'm swimming in a sea of confusion. My back hits the wall and I lash out with both hands to arrest my fall. Every second that passes, the pig is travelling further along the conveyor. The clock is ticking. I reach over and strike the emergency stop button. An angry synthetic alarm screams that something is wrong, a yellow flashing beacon lights above me.

My legs give way and I slide down the wall onto my haunches. My head feels like it is going to crack wide open. All the while, the pig is hanging by its back leg, the sudden stop makes her swing to and fro, turning slowly.

I try to stand but my legs refuse to work. I drop the knife and press my hands to my head in an attempt to ease the searing pain behind my eyes.

Burke bursts through the door. 'What the fuck's going on?'

'I…I…I felt faint.' I'm look up into his snarling face.

'For fuck's sake!' He snatches the knife from the floor. The pig is convulsing on the end of the chain. Burke plunges the blade into its neck and a torrent of blood gushes into the drain. 'I am not taking this write-off on my shift.'

He storms out and into the room next door, still holding the knife. I can hear raised voices.

'I don't give a shit about that,' Burke yells. 'Do you have any idea how much one of these costs? Get out of the way,' the other voice protests, but Burke brushes it aside. 'Thanks for the advice. I'm fucking doing it.'

Moments later, he yanks open the door and is towering over me. 'Are you pissed again?'

'No, no, I felt faint. Sorry I had to stop the line.'

'You realise I will have to report this, don't you?'

'Yes, I'm sorry.'

'If anyone asks, you stuck the pig and then felt faint. You got that?'

'Yes, I got it.' I haul myself up onto my feet, the pain subsiding. He hands me my knife.

'How do you feel now?'

'Okay, I think.'

'Good. You may as well take an early break while we reset the process.'

'I'm sorry about that. Don't know what happened.'

'I know what happened. You fucked up again, Palmer, that's what happened.' He pulls on the red stop button and initiates the reset sequence. I stare at the pig dangling from the rail. 'Well, what are you waiting for? We are short-handed again today, so I want you back in fifteen minutes. Is that clear?'

I shuffle out of the room. I'm already popping pills like Smarties. It's time to take some more and try not to knock my coffee over.

Chapter 43

With a handful of mediocre exam results and a university education that only lasted three weeks, Sadie Raynor was never going to win a Nobel prize. But if there was an equivalent accolade for reading people, she would have a trophy cabinet stacked full of them. And what she could see in Tavener's face scared the shit out of her.

The more the clock ticked away, the more her blasé facade was crumbling around her well-turned ankles.

Her head was racing with the unknown. She knew about the murder of John Graham and the police had been clear that they wanted to know where she was on that date. But they had also asked her about other dates – *had there been other killings?*

When Tavener had asked her to provide a sample of her precious hair, she'd freaked out, demanding legal representation. Forty minutes later, she was joined by Hector Cunningham, a duty solicitor, who advised her that it would not look good if she refused to provide the required ten strands of hair.

'Fucking ten?' She had exploded. Cunningham shrugged his shoulders. Tavener left with the hair strands in an evidence pouch.

She had been at the station now for four hours. A neighbour was going to pick up the kids from school if she wasn't back in time, and the way this was going, that seemed highly likely. Tavener appeared in the interview room with another coffee.

'Here,' he said, placing the corrugated paper cup in front of her. She looked up, the glamour was fading fast.

'How much longer?' she asked, picking up the drink, her hand trembling.

'I can't say.'

'Detective, you can see this is causing Ms Raynor considerable distress. Do you know how long you are going to detain my client?' Cunningham had a deep gruff voice out of keeping with his slight frame.

'I don't know, as soon as I do—'

The door opened and in walked Kray and Bagley. He looked like a dog with a newly acquired bone while Kray looked like she didn't want to be there.

'At last. Can I go now?' Raynor stood up.

'No, we have more questions for you,' Bagley said noticing the presence of Cunningham. He took the seat opposite Raynor and Kray perched herself next to him. Tavener walked out and closed the door – yet again feeling that three was a crowd.

Bagley pressed the button on the tape machine and introduced the people around the table. He stated that Raynor was not under arrest, neither had she been charged with an offence. Her whole demeanour relaxed when she heard these words only to go into melt down when he placed her under caution. It was obvious that Bagley was taking the lead.

'What? What do you mean "could be used in evidence against me"? I've not done anything!' She looked at her solicitor, imploring him to wave his magic wand and make the whole thing disappear. Cunningham sat and stared at his notebook.

'I am going to show you a series of photographs, Sadie, and it is vital that you answer our questions,' Bagley said.

'I've answered your bloody questions.'

Bagley laid out the pictures of the murder victims on the table. Raynor's thoughts must have bounced off a couple of satellites before landing back in her head. She gazed at the images impassively for what seemed like an age, then leapt back from the table.

'Jesus Christ!' she yelled.

'Please, Sadie. Sit down.'

'Fucking hell! What is this?'

'Sadie, I need you to sit down,' he repeated. Raynor returned to her seat with both hands clasped over her mouth. Her eyes as wide as saucers. She scanned the parade of carnage laid out in front of her.

'Oh my God, that's John!' She was on her feet again. 'Fuck, and that's Nigel.' She walked around the interview room with her face buried in her hands. 'Jesus Christ, he's dead? Nigel is dead?'

'Sadie, I must ask you to sit.' Bagley raised his voice but she was too far gone to hear him.

Kray watched the woman dissolve in front of her. With every anguished cry, Kray died a little inside.

'Who…what…' Raynor continued on her walkabout.

Cunningham stepped up and put his hand on her shoulder. 'Sadie, you need to take a seat.' He led her back to the table.

She sat there with tears running down her face. Her hands shaking.

'Would you like some water?' Kray asked.

'No,' Sadie said, picking up the coffee and spilling it over her hand. 'Oh my God, I know them too!' she screamed, dropping the drink. 'That's…that's—'

'Sadie, you need to calm down.' Bagley was struggling to prevent the interview descending into chaos.

Raynor had her hands on the photographs, twisting them one way then the next.

'This is Vanessa, and this is—' She clamped her hand to her mouth just as the vomit filled her throat. But it was too late.

Sadie threw her head between her legs and spewed on the floor. The three others sprang from the table to avoid the splash. Sadie's designer shoes didn't fare so well.

'Oh God…' Raynor coughed up the foul-smelling liquid.

'Shit.' Kray opened the door to the interview room. 'Let's get her cleaned up and reconvene.'

Bagley announced the interview was over and paused the recording.

An hour later all four were sitting in a different interview room, three doors down from the one that was now in quarantine.

Raynor was wearing a pair of flip-flops. The corridor stunk of puke.

Bagley repeated the protocol of resuming the interview and spread the photographs onto the table. Everyone except Raynor, was conscious of having to make a sharp exit should the situation call for it.

'I'm sorry,' she said. 'It was the shock. I know these people and they're dead. Murdered.'

'We appreciate this is distressing but we have to ask the questions, Sadie. You understand, don't you?' Bagley said, Raynor nodded.

'All the victims were killed in the same way, except for this one,' Kray pointed to the head and shoulders shot of Teresa Franklin. 'She was forced to eat beef before she was murdered.'

'Beef?' Raynor said, screwing up her tear-streaked face.

'Yes. Each of the murders followed a sequence. They followed the verses from the nursery rhyme *This Little Piggy*. What can you tell me about that?'

'What can I tell you? Nothing! Do you think I did this?' she shrieked.

'We checked out your whereabouts, Sadie, and it isn't good,' Bagley said. 'The night Vanessa Wilding was killed, you were with your boyfriend Henry. On the night that Teresa Franklin was murdered, you said you were either at the club or with Henry. The club have no recollection of you being there, but Henry says you were with him. On Monday the sixteenth, when John Graham was killed, you think you were with Henry – he says you were. And on the ninth of October, when Nigel Chapman was attacked you gave us a long list of places you might have been, and again, Henry says you were with him. In every case, you were with Henry, and in every case, no one else can corroborate your story. Do you see the problem?'

'No, no, I don't.' She snivelled and wiped away the snot with the back of her hand.

Bagley cleared away the photographs and laid a clear plastic bag on the table. 'Can you explain how hair matching yours was found at three of the murders?'

Raynor's eyes almost popped from her head. Her mouth moved but nothing came out. 'But ... but ... how can that ...' Raynor burbled.

'That is inconclusive until you have the DNA results,' Cunningham chipped in.

'You're right. We are awaiting the results. But it does look like your hair under a microscope.'

'That does not constitute scientific evidence, DI Bagley, and you know it,' Cunningham was not letting go.

'I realise that but I'm building up a picture. Sadie? Hair that visibly matches yours was found at three of the crime scenes – at John Graham's home, Vanessa Wilding's home and a shipping container where we found the body of Nigel Chapman. What do you have to say?'

Raynor stared at Bagley, then at the evidence bag on the table, then back to Bagley. 'I...I...I...don't know.' She stuttered. 'I have been to John's home, but...'

'How long ago was that?'

'I don't know, quite a while ago.'

'Have you ever been to this place?' Bagley produced another photograph of a derelict farm.

'No, I've never seen that place before.' She looked at her lawyer, shaking her head.

'This is where we found the body of Vanessa Wilding. We believe your hair was found there too.'

'But...but I've never been there.' Raynor got up from the table again, running her hands through her unkempt locks. 'You think that I did this?'

'Please, Sadie, take a seat.' Cunningham put his hand on her arm.

Bagley pulled out another evidence bag containing the key. 'What can you tell us about this?' he asked.

Raynor shook her head, once more seated at the table.

'We found this taped to the underside of the table in your hallway. Are you saying you know nothing about it?'

'What! In *my* hallway? I've never seen this before in my life.' Raynor picked up the bag, turning it over and over in her hands. 'How...'

'It is the key to this garage.' Bagley slapped another photo onto the table. 'And when we opened it up, we found these.' He dealt the blown-up photographs to her like he was dealing from a deck of cards. One showed a small red hand hoist with a chain running through the pulleys, in the corner was a neat stack of white disposable boiler suits in cellophane packets along with boxes of overshoes and latex gloves, a camping stove, a portable generator and cooking pots lay against one wall and an empty ten litre paint can was against the other.

Raynor's eyes were welling up with tears.

The last three pictures showed a pair of industrial wire cutters, a packet of black cable ties and a small black box with cables attached to either end.

'How do you explain these?'

'I can't. I've never seen these before.' Her voice cracked.

'Then, why was the garage key hidden in your home?'

'I don't know! I've never seen this before.'

'This is the rental agreement for the garage. Is that your signature Sadie?' Bagley placed the document on the table.

Raynor stared at it. 'No...no, what is this?'

Bagley laid the photograph of Vanessa Wilding in front of Raynor. 'This woman was killed at the farm, but before she was murdered, she was abducted and held in a room in the barn. We believe hair matching yours was found there too. Are you telling me you know nothing about this?'

Raynor shook her head, unable to speak. Tears ran down her face.

'I put it to you, Sadie, that you committed these murders in an attempt to frame your ex-husband.'

'Frame Kevin? Why the hell would I want to frame him?'

'Revenge. You said yourself how he held you back, how he blighted your life. You concocted a story which contributed to him being sent to jail. You also told my colleague that the newspaper article was a pack of lies.'

'But I wouldn't do this!'

'What happened to the money from the sale of the business?' asked Bagley, changing tack. The question threw her.

'What?' she asked.

'When your ex-husband sold his share of the business. What happened to the money?'

'I cannot see the relevance of this line of questioning,' Cunningham said.

'What happened to the money, Sadie?'

'I took it,' Sadie said.

'That's right, Sadie, you took it. Three days after that money was deposited into your husband's business account, you transferred it into your own.'

'I needed the cash for the kids and for the house,' she yelled.

'You took the money to furnish a lifestyle which you believed you deserved. A lifestyle that had been denied you by Kevin Palmer. You set out to destroy him, and now, you want to see him gone for good.'

'No. No, I didn't murder anyone.'

'You want to see Kevin Palmer locked up and you would do anything to make that happen.'

'No. No. I didn't do this. I swear on my kids' lives, I did not do this.'

'Are these the kids that you palm off with a babysitter while you screw around with your boyfriend? Who I'm sure also helps to fund your lifestyle and who is your only alibi.'

'That is quite enough detective inspector Bagley.' Cunningham interjected.

'This is crazy. I did not murder these people.' Sadie screamed, waving her hands around her head like she was swatting away flies.

'Then how do you explain the key and how do you explain the hair? You have made it clear that you want your ex-husband out of your lives for what he's done to you.'

'Yes, I mean, no, I mean, yes, I might have said that–'

'Detective inspector, this line of questioning–' Cunningham tried again.

'Sadie Raynor, I am arresting you on suspicion of murdering John Graham, Nigel Chapman, Teresa Franklin and Vanessa Wilding.'

Raynor jerked away from the table with her hand to her mouth as vomit sprayed through her fingers and onto the floor. Bagley's reactions weren't fast enough this time.

Chapter 44

If you put ten coppers in a pub, it's going to get noisy. Put ten coppers in a pub who believe they have just cracked a multiple homicide case, and you'd be forgiven for thinking a bus load of Millwall supporters had arrived. Quade was propping up the bar getting in her second round of the evening – enjoying the popularity, however fleeting.

Bagley was holding court with a gaggle of people hanging on his every word. He bent over at the waist and beckoned for them to lean in, he said something and they burst into gales of laughter.

Kray sat at a table on her own nursing a small Pino, hardly bringing herself to taste it. Tavener flopped into the seat beside her. 'Not celebrating?'

'No.'

'Look, Roz, I know how hard this must be, but the weight of evidence is overwhelming. You have to admit that.'

'Palmer did it,' Kray didn't look up from her drink, 'and he's put Sadie Raynor squarely in the frame.'

Tavener glugged at his beer. 'That's not how the CPS see things.'

'Maybe not.'

'The DNA test results will be the clincher when they come through tomorrow.'

'I have no fucking doubt they will be a one hundred-percent match.'

'Look, Roz, you can't–'

'If you're about to say, "You can't win them all", I'm gonna slap you.'

'Yeah, well, do you know what, Roz? There are times when you can't.' Tavener got to his feet and joined the others.

The lumbering bulk of Quade came into view. She dumped herself next to Kray.

'Cheers, Roz, great result.' She held up her glass and Kray chinked her drink against it with all the enthusiasm of getting a yeast infection.

'Cheers, ma'am.'

'Come on, Roz, we're off duty now. It's Mary.'

'Cheers, Mary.' Kray repeated the chink.

'I know this has been tough on you, what with coming back into work and this landing in your lap, but you've done a great job.'

'If I had done such a great job, I would not be looking at Dan Bagley right now.'

'He's is a good detective. It's my role to take the helicopter view, and from what I could see, you needed support.'

Helicopter view? It wouldn't get off the ground. Kray sighed and took a sip.

'I'm telling you there is something not right about this.' Kray spun the wedding ring round on her finger.

'Oh, not again, Roz. Let it drop.'

'I can't put my finger on it, but all my intuition says Sadie Raynor is not a killer. There is something wrong.'

'I agree, Roz, and do you know what it is?' Quade said leaning forward. 'What's wrong is you refusing to acknowledge the evidence against her.'

'I know how it looks, but it's Palmer, I'm sure of it.'

'Do you honestly believe Palmer set this whole thing up? He killed those people in such a way that he put himself in the frame for murder, when all the while, he had concocted the evidence in such a way to incriminate his ex-wife. Even you have to admit that's a long shot.'

'I know but you've watched the interview footage. You saw the way she reacted. How many times have you seen that?'

'Never.'

'And neither have I. That was not for show. That was shear panic and blind fear. Sadie Raynor is not a killer.'

'The evidence tells us that she is. And besides, there is no forensic evidence connecting Palmer to any of the murders, and he has rock solid alibis for three of them. You have to let this go, Roz. You backed a horse and got it wrong, it happens.'

Bagley pulled up the chair next to Kray.

Have I got a fucking sign hanging over my head saying, 'please come talk to the sad person'?

'Cheers, guys, a job well done.' He held up his glass. 'I've cleared it with GMP, so if it's all the same to you, I'd like to stick around to tie this one up tight.'

'Fine with me,' Quade said.

'Yup,' answered Kray.

A loud whoop went up as the door opened and three more police officers with smiles a mile wide joined them in the bar. There was much shaking hands and back slapping.

'Looks like I'm going to be in for a busy night,' Quade said, leveraging herself up from the chair. 'My round!' she called out, followed by another bout of whooping.

'You okay?' asked Bagley.

'Not really.'

Bagley swigged at his drink. 'Hey, on a different subject, are you going to go for it?'

'Go for what?'

'Jackson's job.'

'I don't know what you're talking about.'

'Jackson is coming back to work but not here. He's put in for a transfer to Merseyside and will drop down a rank. He's bound to get it, so that leaves his seat vacant.'

Kray screwed up her face. 'What are you talking about?'

'Mary told me. Jackson isn't coming back, so they are going to be interviewing for his job. I thought you'd be throwing your hat into the ring.'

'No, she didn't mention anything to me.'

'Oh, maybe she wants to tell you officially. She told me in passing. I have to say, I really fancy it. This is a great team and I could do with a change of scenery.'

Kray got up from the table, gathered up her coat and left.

The full beam headlights arced across the gravel of the empty car park as Kray swept past the gates. She didn't bother with the parking bay lines sprayed in white on the floor. Not many people visited graveyards after dark.

She got out and slammed the door, stomping up the grass verge, ignoring the path to the left. Wisps of grey cloud scudded across a clear night sky. The stars were coming out to play.

In the distance, Kray could see the twinkle of the illuminations along the promenade, and the Pleasure Beach appeared to throb against the darkness. A stream of red and white car lights moved slowly along the seafront like two opposing snakes. Beyond that was the oil-black of the Irish sea.

The view would have been one to catch Kray's attention, were it not for her being so angry that her hands hurt from gripping the steering wheel so tight. She marched over the grassy hill and down to the peaceful place of rest for so many. Or it would have been peaceful, had she not started yelling well before she reached her husband's headstone.

'The fat cow didn't tell *me* about a fucking job interview! Oh no, but she tells her Mancunian puppy dog.' Kray stopped at the one marked Joseph Kray. 'So, we all know how that's going to turn out. She's been keeping me sweet until she can replace me. Fucking bitch.'

Kray continued to stomp around, walking up and down in front of the black marble stone.

'And another thing, we're going to bang up an innocent woman. Don't get me wrong, she's no fucking angel, but she didn't kill those people. But the Mancunian puppy can't see it and there's nothing I can do. Oh, and to cap it all, I have Tavener acting like

I've eaten his last Rolo, so all in all, it's been a shitty day. And I know I've not asked how you are because I fucking know already – you're dead! Why are you not here to help me? Why am I facing this on my own?'

Kray stopped marching about and bent over putting her hands on her knees. Speaking without breathing was an exhausting thing to do.

'I know Palmer did it. Every time I think of him, these…' Kray pulled at her shirt exposing the scars on her right shoulder, 'go into overdrive. I know it was him, but I can't prove it, and tomorrow, the DNA will come back. Then, it will be all over for Sadie Raynor.'

Kray slumped down onto her haunches, her anger having left her. She leaned forward grasping the top of the stone and rocking back and forth.

'I'm not sure I'm cut out for this anymore. It cost you your life, nearly took mine and is now going to turn me into a fucking crazy woman.' She felt the cool breeze touch the back of her neck. 'Yeah, I know I was always crazy, so how would you know the difference.'

Kray rested her forehead against the cold stone. Tears welled in her eyes. 'I'm lost without you,' she whispered.

She heard a voice inside her head.

It was not her husband. It was Palmer. He was spouting off the same words that were recorded in that bloody interview – what the hell was it doing ruining such a moment? Palmer's words raced around inside her head. She tried to drown them out with Joe's voice, but it was no good. Palmer got louder and louder. The same interview that played over and over, keeping her awake at night and rousing her early in the morning. His words banging on and on.

Kray wanted to be with Joe. She wanted to hear his voice.

'Agghh!' She shoved herself away from the stone. 'This fucking job!' she yelled into the night air.

Then, she stopped. Palmer's words, repeating in a loop.

The scars on her body burned red hot against the chill of the night.

That was it. The voices stopped.

He's made his first mistake.

Chapter 45

Kray watched as the first splats of rain hit the windscreen. The orange light from the streetlamps washed the dashboard in a parchment yellow glow. Her long coat was wrapped around her legs to shield them from the cold leeching into the car. Despite having just four hours' sleep, her mind was sharp as a tack.

Normally, a visit to the graveside would be followed by consuming a bottle of wine and a chocolate bar while soaking under a foot of bubbles in the bath. But not last night. Kray had spent the rest of the evening trawling through online back copies of the *Telegraph*, seventy-two of them, to be precise. She went to bed sober and had eaten proper food, if a mince-meat and pasta something from the corner shop, warmed up in the microwave, could be considered proper.

She watched the front of Mr Woo's Takeaway and waited. The digits on the clock told her it was five-thirty am. The wedding ring spun round and round on her finger.

Kray saw a dark shadow appear against the glass in the shop door. The door swung inwards and a figure stepped out into the rain, pulling a hood over his head. The figure let the door close behind him and walked up the street towards Kray. She sank down in her seat. After twenty yards the man turned left, and Kray saw the indicator lights flash orange in the dark. The car pulled away. Palmer had left for work.

Kray looked at her watch. *Was it too early?*

She picked up her phone and dialled.

'Roz?' Tavener croaked.

'Yes, sorry about the early call. I need you to do something for me.'

'Are you okay?'

'Yes, I'm fine. I need you to go to the station and dig out the search warrant we used to gain entry into Palmers flat.'

'What? Why would you want that?'

'I don't have time to explain now. Can you do that for me?'

'Err, yeah, I suppose so.'

'Meet me at Palmer's place as soon as you have it.'

'But it's out of date. Why would you—'

'I'll explain everything when you get here. Can you do that for me?'

'Yes, I'll sort it.'

'Thanks. Oh, and Duncan? Can we keep this between ourselves for now?'

'Sure.'

The line went dead. Now all Kray had to do was try not to freeze while she waited.

The passenger door sprung open and Tavener slid into the front seat carrying two coffees in one hand. He gave one to Kray. A blast of cold air followed him into the car, something Kray could well do without. It was still dark and the rain had stopped, the wind had a bitter chill.

'Sorry it took so long. Quade and Bagley were sniffing around, and I figured you wanted this under the radar.' He handed over one of the drinks.

'Bloody hell, they were in early, obviously didn't drink enough last night. Thanks, I need this.' Kray cupped both hands around the cup and enjoyed the warmth penetrating into her hands.

'How long have you been here?'

'Feels like half my sodding life. I needed to be sure Palmer was out. He left for work around five-thirty.'

'You've been here since—'

'Don't, just...don't.'

'Do you want to tell me what this is all about?'

'Yeah, but before I do, I just wanted to say that I was a jerk in the pub last night. And I've probably been a jerk on numerous other occasions and not realised it. I know you only have my best interests at heart.'

'You were a jerk.'

'Yeah, well…'

'Was that an apology?'

'Don't push it.'

'Apology accepted.' Tavener raised his coffee cup and she bumped hers against it. 'Now, what is *this* all about?' He put his free hand into his jacket and brought out the search warrant.

'Do you remember when we brought Palmer in for interview?' she said, staring into the middle distance.

'Yes, I remember.'

'What he said has been churning around in my head. I've had this nagging feeling that something wasn't right. An inconsistency which I couldn't put my finger on, it's been driving me nuts.'

'And…'

'You spread the photographs of the victims in front of him and his very words were, "My God, that's Nigel Chapman and Teresa Franklin. I recognise her hair".'

Tavener shook his head. 'I don't recall what he said, but I do remember he recognised the bodies.'

'Teresa Franklin had bright yellow hair.'

'She did.'

'There is a head and shoulders shot of her at the top of every column she's written for the *Telegraph*. I trawled through them all last night. She has red hair, blue hair, silver with purple streaks, but never yellow. How could he say he recognised her hair when he told us he had not seen her after being released from prison?'

'Maybe he meant the cut, or the fact that it's a wacky colour.'

'Maybe or maybe not. I think he knew her hair was yellow because he'd seen her. He made a mistake.'

'Okay, but you've still not told me why we need *this*?' He held up the warrant.

'Because of this…' Kray pointed at a van pulling up outside the takeaway. A man jumped out and opened up the back. A small woman with grey hair got out of the passenger seat and opened up the shop. The man pulled boxes of vegetables from the back and carried them in.

'You wanted to be here when the veg was delivered?'

'No, I wanted to be here when Joseph Woo's mother opened up the takeaway to get ready for the day. Come on.'

They stepped from the car and headed towards the van. The man came outside and closed the back doors. He got in and drove away.

Kray pushed open the door to the takeaway. 'Hello,' Kray chanted. 'Hello, Mrs Woo.'

A face appeared from the back. 'No, sorry, we closed.'

'Mrs Woo, I am Acting DCI Kray.' She held out her warrant card. 'We met the other day.' The old woman's eyes flashed with recognition. 'This is my colleague Detective Tavener.'

'Yes, yes, I remember.' She came around the counter to meet them. 'My son is not here.'

'We don't want to talk to your son, Mrs Woo. We want to look at the flat upstairs. We have a search warrant.'

Tavener was cringing. *What the hell are you doing?*

Mrs Woo took the document. 'You want to see upstairs?'

'Yes, if we can, that would be very helpful.'

'Okay.' She gestured towards the stairs.

'We don't have a key, Mrs Woo. Do you keep a spare key here at the shop?'

'Yes, yes, we do.'

She turned and walked to the back. Kray glanced at Tavener, whose eyebrows could not get any higher.

Mrs Woo came back with a key in her hand. 'Give it back to me.'

'Thank you,' Kray took it and they went up the flight of stairs to the front door of the flat.

'I can't believe you just did that,' Tavener said under his breath.

'You can go now, if you like?' Kray paused with the key in the lock.

Tavener shook his head.

The front door opened and they filed into the lounge.

'What are we looking for?' he asked.

'A way out.'

Tavener tilted his head towards the open door.

'No, another way out. One that doesn't take you through the front of the shop. Palmer's alibis rely on the fact that this place has one way in and one way out. He has eye witnesses that put him at the property at the times of the murders. We need to prove otherwise.'

'And if we do, it will be totally inadmissible.'

'I'll worry about that later.'

The lounge and kitchenette had cream painted walls with cheap pictures and no windows. Kray started by looking into the cupboards and rapping her knuckles against the walls behind them. Tavener took the bedroom. The same paint had been applied to this room with a single bed in the corner and standalone wardrobes. There were no windows or skylights.

'Is there a hatch leading into the attic?' Kray asked.

'No, nothing. It looks solid.'

Kray was on her hands and knees, feeling around the perimeter of the room looking for anything loose.

Tavener emerged from the bedroom and went to the front door. 'I'll check he can't get onto the roof from the first-floor landing.'

Kray got to her feet and pushed open the bathroom door.

The room was cold compared to the rest of the flat. Kray rapped the walls with her knuckles and stamped her heel onto the floor. Everything was solid. She opened up the shower cubical and did the same with the tiled surfaces. She went back to the walls and tapped her way around the room. Nothing. She opened up the wall-mounted medicine cabinet and saw the boxes of tablets sitting on the shelf. The door clicked shut.

She stopped, holding onto the wash basin with both hands and stared at her reflection in the mirror.

'What the hell are you doing?' she said under her breath. 'You don't even know what you're looking for.' She dropped her chin onto her chest.

Kray became aware of a chill on the side of her face. It felt like a draft. She looked up, trying to locate the source. It was coming from the frosted glass window.

She held out her hand and could feel cold air blowing onto her fingertips. It was coming from the beading which ran around the inside of the double-glazing panel. She moved her hand around the glass. At the corner, it was blowing a gale.

Kray turned on the torch on her phone and shone the piercing light onto the window frame. Running along the beaded edges were tiny indentations and scratches. She went into the kitchen and came back with a knife. She then eased the tip of the blade between the beading and the frame. The plastic trim came away. She slid the blade down and the beading separated from the moulding exposing the double-glazed glass panel below.

A grenade went off in her head.

How could I have been so stupid?

Kray and Tavener scurried downstairs, thanked Mrs Woo and handed back the key. They walked along the street and hung a left. The backyards of the properties butted up against one another with a narrow alleyway running between them. They darted up the alley until they reached the back of the takeaway.

'Well, I couldn't do it,' said Tavener.

'No, but then, you're built like a brick shit house.'

'Thanks very much.'

'You know what I mean.'

'Palmer is, what? Five feet nine, twelve and a half stones. He could fit through there.'

Kray and Tavener were looking up at Palmer's bathroom window. Directly below it was a wall that ran along the length of the backyard, separating it from the yard next door.

Tavener put both hands on top of the wall and heaved himself up.

'There is a back door on either side and a window, but if you weren't looking up, you probably wouldn't see.'

'That's how he does it. He prises the beading away from the frame and the double-glazing panel comes out. He slips through the gap, drops down onto the wall and he's away.'

'After making sure he puts on a good performance downstairs in the takeaway so people know he's there. Bloody simple.'

'Bloody genius is what it is,' Kray said.

'We need to figure out a way for Bagley to find this. But now he has Raynor in custody, he's not going to be interested.'

'Not unless we make it interesting for him.'

Chapter 46

My head feels like it's about to explode. One minute, my vision is fuzzy, and then the next, I'm seeing two of everything. Not helped by the fact that my arms and legs keep going numb. I feel like shit.

I didn't bother to call in sick for work. It's not as though I'm going back there. I can picture Burke stomping around trying to cover my job, secretly relieved that a member of his team wasn't going to wind up sprawled on the floor with the line stopped. He's probably looking forward to me coming back so he can roast my arse and give me another warning. He's going to have to take out his sadistic frustration on someone else.

I've reached the conclusion that my deterioration isn't due to the mishap with my tablets. I'm getting worse by the hour and struggling to function. They said this might happen.

I collapsed into bed last night and everything went black. It was like somebody flicked a switch and I was out cold. When I woke this morning, I felt hungry which I thought was a good sign, and my every intention was to go to work as normal and complete my shift. But by the time I got out of the shower, the problems of the previous day came flooding back. When I left the house, I could hardly put one foot in front of the other. Every muscle in my body screamed at me to climb back into bed, but I feel time is running short, and I have things to take care of.

Nothing seems to help anymore. I've drank strong coffee, eaten a mountain of food from the fridge, but still have no energy. I lost track of the tablets as I popped them from their blister packs and into my mouth. I can barely keep my eyes open. And what the fuck is going on with these tremors that sweep through my body?

I gaze down at the scrunched-up pieces of paper scattered across the table. My thoughts refuse to behave. I cannot construct a sentence without it descending into gibberish. I have written about half a page which is coherent, but the rest is a fucking mess.

I had this great idea of making another video but every time I hit the red button, my mind freezes – I mumble and trip over my words. I've lost count of the number of times I've pressed play only to stop and delete the damned thing.

I put the pen down, wander into the lounge and collapse on the sofa, the soft cushions swallowing me up. I need to get my act together and sort out the final chapter. Up to now, everything has gone to plan, but the final piece of the jigsaw is proving difficult to manoeuvre into place. Maybe if I have a short nap I'll be refreshed when I wake. I need to get it done. The police have been slow off the mark but they are gaining ground fast. That Roz Kray is sharp and it's only a matter of time.

I wonder how my darling ex-wife is doing?

My eyes close and drift away.

Chapter 47

Kray and Tavener split up when they reached the station; he went to the canteen while she headed for her office. It was mid-morning.

The incident room sounded like the pub the night before.

'Having another party?' she asked a young detective.

'The DNA results came back on Raynor's hair. It's a dead match.'

Kray feigned a delighted smile and went off in search of Bagley. She knew exactly where she would find him.

Sure enough, he was sitting in Quade's office with a coffee in hand. Kray knocked on the door.

'Hey, Roz,' Quade said. 'Come in, we were just talking about you.'

I fucking bet you were.

'I heard the good news,' Kray said.

'Yes, everything pointed in that direction but it's good to get positive confirmation.' Bagley had his usual dog with two dicks look on his face. 'We were thinking of holding a press conference this afternoon.'

'Sounds like a good idea,' said Kray. 'Though, there is one piece of the jigsaw missing.'

'Oh, how so?' asked Quade.

'Sadie Raynor formulated a highly elaborate plan to frame her ex-husband and we have enough evidence to put her away for a long time. But...'

'What, what's missing,' asked Bagley.

'Well, several things, actually – the toes.' Quade and Bagley looked at each other. 'Raynor went to a lot of trouble to ensure the

215

murders were in line with the nursery rhyme. Even to the extent of forcing Teresa Franklin to eat beef. But we've never found the toes.'

'Maybe she discarded them, threw them away,' Bagley said.

'Maybe. But that doesn't fit the profile, does it? Serial killers like to keep trophies, and if she had the intent of framing Palmer, I would have expected her to plant them on him. They are a key piece of evidence that's missing.'

Bagley flashed a glance at Quade. 'That's right. We've been so absorbed in building the evidence case against her, we missed that.'

'Do you have any ideas?' asked Quade.

'I do, ma'am. I reckon she's planted them in Palmer's flat. We searched his place once and came up with nothing but I think we need to tear the place apart.'

Quade stroked her chin.

'I like it,' said Bagley. 'Get a team together.'

'Wow, wait a minute,' Quade said. 'Palmer is the victim here. We can ill afford to be making matters worse by smashing his front door. Go pick him up from work. I'll sort the warrant.'

'Yes, ma'am.' Kray turned her back and walked away, grinning from ear to ear.

The team assembled in the incident room. Kray briefed them on what was going to happen. Bagley went to wait at the takeaway with the others, while Kray and Tavener headed off to the factory to pick up Palmer.

Kray and Tavener walked into the reception of Sandringham Products. It was light and airy with a half-moon desk set against one wall. Sitting behind it was a young man wearing glasses. He looked up and smiled.

'I'm Acting DCI Kray. We need to speak with one of your employees. His name is Kevin Palmer.' Kray flashed her warrant card.

The young man looked as if this was an everyday occurrence. 'I'll see if he's available.' He picked up the phone and scrolled through the pre-programed numbers. 'Oh, hi, this is Mat in reception. I have two police officers here who want to speak with Kevin Palmer.' The voice on the other end went into a long rambling speech. He cupped his hand over the mouthpiece. 'Kevin's not in work today. He was due on shift but hasn't showed. His supervisor is on his way. He wants to speak with you.'

Kray raised her eyebrows. Normally, they get told to bugger off.

Two minutes later, Vinny Burke burst through the doors at the back.

'I'm the shift supervisor,' he announced. 'This is the second time this week that Kevin has been a no-show and you guys are making my life a bloody misery. How many more times are you going to stop him coming to work?'

Kray read the name sewed into his white coat. 'Sorry to hear that, Mr Burke, but we thought he was on shift today, so if he hasn't turned in, it's not down to us.'

'Well, it would be good if when you do detain him, you give him the opportunity to call, at least that gives us a chance to plan around him not being here.'

Kray had her second bombshell moment of the day. She took her phone from her pocket and dialled a number.

'Do you have your works phone on you, Mr Burke?'

'Err, yes.' He took it from his pocket. His mobile remained silent while a continuous tone came from Kray's phone saying the number she had dialled was unobtainable. 'What are you doing?'

'Is that your usual work's mobile?'

'Yeah, I've had it ever since I was made supervisor. What is this about?'

'Nothing, Mr Burke, sorry to have troubled you this morning,' Kray said, before turning and walking off.

'If you see Kevin, tell him he's on another warning,' Burke called after her and Tavener.

'I'll be sure to do that.'

In the car, Tavener turned to Kray. 'Care to tell me what happened in there?'

'When we had Palmer in custody, he asked to make a call to his workplace to tell them he would not be on shift. He gave me the number and I made the call. I spoke to a man called Vinny Burke.'

'The man we just met. So?'

'The Vinny Burke I spoke to had a stammer, and the mobile I called was not the one in his pocket. Palmer played us. The call I made was the signal to abduct Vanessa Wilding. Fuck!'

Forty minutes later, Kray and Tavener were pushing open the door to Mr Woo's Takeaway for the second time that day. A few customers lined the walls waiting for their lunch, intrigued with the fact that the place was full of coppers. The warrant must have proved more difficult to obtain than hoped.

Bagley was talking to Joseph, who was getting pissed off with his shop being used as a meeting place for the police. Kray fought her way to the front, standing shoulder to shoulder with Bagley.

'I am DI Bagley and we have a warrant here to search the flat of Kevin Palmer.'

Joseph frowned, 'But my mother said—'

'Yes, we were here the other day,' Kray jumped in. 'We'd like to take another look, if that's okay. I think Kevin said you keep a key to the flat here?'

'Err, yes, that's fine.' Joseph beetled off into the back. The customers were delighted with the floor show. He returned and handed it over.

'Thank you.' They trooped up the stairs, Tavener and Kray hanging back.

'Where the fuck is Palmer? Do you think he's in the flat?' Tavener asked.

'Don't know. It will make things lively if he is.'

The sound of the door opening at the top of the stairs was followed by the sound of Bagley giving instructions. Palmer was not at home.

'Okay, we are looking for something small. Maybe a container or a bag,' said Bagley. 'We need to be thorough but try not to break anything.'

'I'll take the bathroom,' said Tavener.

'Right behind you,' added Bagley. Kray also followed them into the cramped room.

While the other officers were pulling drawers out and had the settee turned over, the three of them rooted around the bathroom. Kray sat beside the shower cubical and noticed the corner of the wood around the base standing proud of the seal. She picked at it with her fingernail. It was loose.

Kray took a pen from her pocket and worked the nib in between the joint and prised it away. The wooden surround came free. She flicked on the torch on her phone and shone the beam into the gap under the shower tray.

'Give me some room, guys,' she asked, lying on her side. A plastic bag was stuffed behind the plumbing, against the wall. She could just reach it, her fingertips clawing at the bag.

She was aware of the conversation going on above her between Tavener and Bagley.

'Check this out, Dan. There's tool marks around the beading on the window.'

Kray was only half listening.

She retrieved the bag, sat up and opened it up, tipping the boxes and jars onto the tiles. *What the hell are these?*

'Go get a knife from the kitchen,' Bagley said. Tavener did as he was told.

Kray got up and opened the medicine cabinet, checking out the boxes of Paracetamol and Cold and Flu remedies. They contained the same tablets as those stored under the shower.

Tavener returned and handed the knife over to Bagley who set to work.

'The beading has come away from the moulding,' he said.

Kray's head spun with a thousand possibilities.

This little piggy went to market,
This little piggy stayed and home,
This little piggy had roast beef,
This little piggy had none,
And this little piggy went…

The final line resonated in her head.

'Shit, the whole double-glazing panel comes out.' Tavener said as Bagley popped it from the moulding.

Kray ran the lines over and over.

And this little piggy went…

She put the tablets in the bag and bolted for the door.

'Fuck me,' Bagley said.

Kray glanced back to see Bagley with his head and shoulders through the gap in the wall where the window had once been.

Chapter 48

Kray drew her car onto the drive. Palmer's car was already there, pulled as far forward as it would go. She picked the plastic bag off the passenger seat and got out. The boot lid popped open and she reached in for her telescopic baton.

Kray walked around the back of the house to the garden to open the patio door. It was unlocked. She crept into the dining room and could see a bunch of screwed up papers and a mobile phone sitting on a three-legged tripod on the dining room table. The tripod was sitting on a pile of books.

Through the archway, Kray could see Palmer lying on the sofa. She flicked open the baton and went inside. His face was ashen. He looked like he'd aged fifteen years since their last encounter.

'Palmer,' she said. 'Palmer, wake up.' She reached down to feel his pulse. It was weak and erratic.

Kray pulled her phone from her pocket. 'Can I have an ambulance please to fifteen Maybourne Crescent. It's urgent.'

'No, no, don't do that,' Palmer woke up, his voice was thin and croaky. He struggled to sit up and slumped back into the cushions.

'You need a hospital.'

'No, Acting DCI Kray, I need two things. Firstly, I want to know how my wife is doing, and secondly, I need a stiff drink.'

'Sadie's not so good.'

'Pleased to hear it.' A satisfied smile spread across his face. 'I thought I had more time, but it would appear not.'

Kray tossed the bag of tablets onto the sofa next to Palmer. Cartons and plastic bottles spilled out onto the floor.

'How long did they give you?'

'Three to six months without treatment, nine to twelve months with a mix of chemo and radio.'

'And you chose the "without" option?'

Palmer nodded.

'How long have you had?' she asked.

'Five months.'

'Sometimes, when it happens, it happens fast.'

'So, they say.' Palmer pushed himself up against with his elbows. His body shook with the effort. 'Is this the end of the line? I somehow pictured it differently.'

'We have a team over at your flat. I suspect one of them is climbing out of the bathroom window and onto the top of the wall at this very moment. So, yes, this is the end of the line.'

There was a long pause.

'How did you figure it out?' Palmer broke the silence.

'I knew all along, even when the evidence was piling up against Sadie, I knew.'

'It's a shame, Roz. I wanted the fun to last a little longer but I guess I've had a good run. Presumably that bitch of an ex-wife of mine is in the cells awaiting a court date. I bet she shit herself when she was charged. Sadie always thought she could brass her way out of anything, but not this time.'

'Why did you do it?'

'That's easy. I'm surprised you have to ask. To make her suffer, the way she made me suffer. I wanted her life to fall apart. I wanted her to know how it feels when you lose everything. When every single thing that makes your life worthwhile crumbles to dust.'

'This was about revenge.'

'Oh yes, it was that alright. I would lie in my cell at night, fantasising about how I would kill them all, one by one, watching the life drain from their bodies. Then, leaving a trail of crumbs for you to follow. A trail of crumbs leading straight to my wife. Of course, I had to throw you off the scent first by putting myself in the frame, but…'

'Did you use the patio door to get in and plant the key?'

'Yes, it was the easiest way. Mind you, I had to come back four times to get the hair from her hairbrush. She kept locking the damned thing.'

'I remembered reading about the patio door in your statement to the police.'

'Very good, Roz. Well done.' Palmer hissed a laugh.

'Who rented the lockup for you?'

'I hired a hooker. You would never believe the look on her face when I told her what I wanted. She said she'd done some kinky shit in her time but never anything like that. She reckoned it was the easiest sixty quid she'd ever earned, and if I ever wanted to get my rocks off again by hiring more garages – she was the girl for the job.'

Palmer closed his eyes and drifted off. Kray walked over to the dining room table and unwrapped one of the scrunched-up pieces of paper. Palmer stirred again.

'Is this your confession?' Kray asked.

'Yeah, supposed to be. I kept screwing it up. How did you know I was going to confess?'

'Because your wife was never the fifth little piggy,' Kray paused. 'The fifth little piggy was you. That's how I realised where you were.'

'Bravo, well done again.'

'How does the final verse go? And this little piggy went wee, wee, wee all the way home. That's right, isn't it, Kevin? You ran all the way home – to your home.'

'I did.'

'The origin of the nursery rhyme is French. Everyone thinks that when they say 'wee' they are mimicking the noise a pig makes. But it's not, is it, Kevin…'

'Ha, no, it's not.' He shook his head, croaking out another thin laugh.

'It's *oui,* the French word for yes. The last little pig escapes and runs all the way home saying yes, because he's escaped being sold at the market.'

'My word, you have thought this through. I'm impressed.'

'It took me a while but I got there in the end. You ran all the way home to make your confession – you ran all the way home to say, "Yes".'

Kray held up the creased paper and read it out loud. 'Yes, I killed John Graham. Yes, I killed Nigel Chapman. Yes, I killed Vanessa Wilding, and yes, I killed Teresa Franklin. You didn't want your wife to go to jail, did you, Kevin?'

'I did, but only for a short while, only until it was my time. I wanted her to feel what it was like. To lose your liberty along with everything else – but I loved her, you see. I couldn't deprive the kids of their mother, however shit she might be. Despite everything she put me through, I loved her. She was my world...is my world. I wanted to teach her a lesson, that's all.'

'Who helped you abduct Vanessa Wilding?'

'No, no, no. That will go with me to my grave. Don't try looking, Roz, it won't help.'

'He had a stammer, I spoke to him.'

'I don't know anything about that.'

Kray took a seat opposite. 'What stage are you?' she asked.

'Stage four.'

'What is it?'

'Brain cancer. I have what's called glioblastomas. It's a bit of a mouthful, so they affectionately call it GBM4. It's aggressive and in a place where they can't operate. All I can do is manage the symptoms, hence all of these.' Palmer pointed at the drug haul scattered over the carpet. 'I take steroids that make me sick, followed by anti-sickness pills to keep them down, and painkillers which aren't working anymore.'

'It was a nice touch transferring your meds into the other boxes, so when we came around we wouldn't suspect anything.'

'I know. I was proud of myself with that one. I couldn't risk you finding out before I was ready and I knew you would be snooping around.'

'Were you diagnosed while in prison?'

'I'm afraid so, by a guy that looked like a geography teacher. I must admit, it did rather take the shine off getting out.'

Kray paused, then said, 'I got a question.'

'Really? You seem to have things all worked out.'

'Where are the toes?'

'Ah...now, that's a very good question. I was worried that, despite my taped confession, you guys would not have believed it. I'd built a water tight case against my wife and some police forces don't like to admit their mistakes. So, the toes were my backstop insurance, in the confession tape I was going to tell you where to look.'

'And where was that?'

'In my locker at work. They are in a glass jar, preserved in alcohol.'

'But she could have planted the jar.'

'Yes, she could have, but I was intending to send you guys two video clips. Go get my phone.'

Kray went into the dining room and lifted the mobile out of its tripod cradle.

'Please.' Palmer held out his hand. He fiddled with the buttons on the screen, his fingers trembling. Eventually, he handed it back. 'Press play.'

Kray hit the red button. It was Palmer talking into the camera.

'Hello to everyone in police land. By now, you will know that I killed those people and first made it look as though it was me, then made it look as though I was being framed by my wife. Smart, eh? You will have also received my confession tape in a separate email. That tape tells you where to find the toes of the murdered victims – *This little piggy went to market* – and all that. Well, just in case you don't believe the tape, I want you to see this.'

Palmer held a glass jar up to the camera with a clear liquid in it.

'As I am the fifth little pig, it is only right and proper for me to do the honourable thing.' He crossed one leg over the other and brought his foot up to the camera. The sole of his foot filled the screen. Then, a thin metal object protruded from between his little toe and the one next to it. A similar one appeared the other side. It was the jaws of a pair of wire cutters.

There was a crunch and the jaws snapped together. Palmer's high-pitched scream made the speaker buzz, and the video picture twisted and turned in the air. Suddenly, Palmer's face filled the screen holding the bloody pulp of his severed toe.

'This should convince you.' He plopped it into the jar will be with the toes cut from the victims. 'So, you see, in this way–'

Kray pressed stop. Palmer's shoulders were rocking back and forth. He was laughing, though it sounded more like air escaping from a tyre.

'You are fucking sick,' Kray said.

'No, Roz, I'm fucking clever. Are you going to arrest me now?'

'Yes.'

'Even though I hold the ultimate get out of jail free card?'

'You might recover enough to go back in jail.'

'I doubt it.'

The noise of sirens filled the close as the ambulance drew up, and the paramedics piled out and banged on the door. Kray let them in, spoke to them briefly and walked out for some fresh air. She watched through the bay window as they checked his tablets and engaged in measured, well-practiced conversation.

Within minutes, they had him strapped to a chair and hooked up to oxygen. Kray pulled her phone from her pocket to call Tavener.

'I got Palmer,' Kray said. 'How did it go with Bagley at the flat? Has he–' Kray listened for the next thirty seconds without uttering a single word. Then, she said, 'Okay,' and disconnected the call.

The front door opened, and Palmer emerged with the tubes and pipes dangling around him. The man and woman dressed in green scrubs guided him to the back doors of the waiting ambulance.

Kray sauntered over and put her hand on the back of the chair.

'I'm sorry. We have to get this man to a hospital now,' said the woman paramedic.

Kray leaned forward and whispered in Palmer's ear. His eyes bulged from his face.

'Noooo!' he shouted into the face mask. He started to cough. 'No, no, no. Nooooo!' They lifted him in the back of the ambulance and drove away, the blue lights doing their hurry-up dance.

Chapter 49

Kray stared at her bedroom ceiling, waiting for the alarm to go off. It wasn't necessary. She hadn't slept. That damned nursery rhyme had kept her awake all night.

The presenter announced the news headlines and she headed to the shower to prepare for, what she already knew, was going to be a shit day. When she slipped out of the house to her car, the morning was as black as her mood.

Her takeaway coffee was making little impact as she negotiated the traffic on her way to the station. She knew the jungle drums would have gone into overdrive and the team would be on their way in. She parked her car and sat in the smoking shelter, drawing on a much-needed cigarette. The drizzling rain pitter-pattered on the Perspex roof, counting down the time when she would have to face the inevitable.

Kray stubbed the fag out on the metal grid, shouldered her bag and marched across the concourse to the main entrance. She took the stairs one at a time – no need for urgency today – and shoved open the door to the incident room to find it already full with coppers. The atmosphere in the room wrapped her in a hundred wet carpets, smothering the breath from her body.

All faces turned in Kray's direction, each one etched with the same expression, "We know what happened, but we need to hear it from you". She made her way to the front. Tavener was sat at the back of the room. Kray couldn't look at him.

'Good morning everyone, thank you for coming in. I'll make this brief. At around four o'clock yesterday afternoon, Sadie Raynor killed herself in her cell. She used her blouse to fashion a ligature and hanged herself. When custody officers found her, she was already dead.'

A low murmuring rippled around the room. Tavener sat with his head bowed.

'We need to corroborate the testimony given by Kevin Palmer but all indications point to him being responsible for all four murders. He is currently in hospital suffering with an aggressive form of brain cancer. I will be in touch with the ward staff to find out when we can interview him. That's all.'

The room emptied, except for Tavener.

'We didn't save her.' He crossed to the evidence board and tapped the mugshot of Sadie Raynor. 'Her name is on this board and we failed to save her.'

'I know.' Kray put her hand on his shoulder. 'I don't believe she meant to kill herself, it was a last-ditch cry for help. Palmer got what he wanted, for Sadie to have a taste of what he had endured. The difference was, she couldn't endure it.'

'If we had uncovered the evidence at the flat earlier, she would still be alive.'

'Maybe. But one thing is for sure; you can either torture yourself playing "what if" scenarios or you can move on. This will eat you up if you let it.'

Tavener gazed at the photograph of Sadie Raynor. 'Where's Bagley?' he said.

'He's with Quade in a crisis meeting with the chief, both of them no doubt fighting to save their careers. The IPCC are on their way, along with an investigating officer from GMP, which is an interesting twist in the tail for Bagley. And all the while, Palmer is tucked up in a hospital bed, slipping away quietly in a haze of morphine.'

'What the hell are we doing, Roz?'

'Our best, Duncan, we're doing our best.'

'It doesn't feel like it.' He crossed the room and disappeared out the door.

Kray went to her office to drown in her inbox. She pulled her phone from her pocket, dialled a number and waited for the call to connect.

'Hi, are you free sometime this morning?'

There was a momentary pause while a certain Home Office pathologist, with a penchant for wearing tight trousers and a waistcoat, consulted his diary.

'Sure, fancy a coffee?'

Acknowledgements

I want to thank all those who have made this book possible – My family, Karen, Gemma, Holly and Maureen for their encouragement and endless patience. To my magnificent BetaReaders, Nicki, Jackie and Simon, who didn't hold back with their comments and feedback. I'm a lucky boy to have them in my corner.

I would also like to thank my wider circle of family and friends for their fantastic support and endless supply of helpful suggestions. Not all of which are suitable to repeat here.

16138565R00141

Printed in Great Britain
by Amazon